The Groupie

A HOCKEY ROM-COM

SOME GIRLS LIKE IT COLD

STEPHANIE QUEEN

D1607714

A Heartfelt Thank You

Sandy Lipinski started out as someone who read my books and enjoyed them, someone I enjoyed talking to on social media. I don't know how many years later it is, but I now count her as a friend, and more than that, she's an invaluable member of my team, a real contributor to my books.

She has been proof-reading my ARCs out of the kindness of her heart and doing an great job of it. (In fact, any mistakes you may find are all on me.)

To a wonderful woman who generously shares her talent and her wonderful sense of humor to make me smile and who bolsters my confidence in the goodness of the human race. 🤍

Praise for Stephanie Queen

Stephanie Queen is a USA Today Bestselling and International Digital Award Winning author.

Here's what reviewers have to say about her Hockey Romance:

"I'm a fan of Stephanie Queen and [The Puck Bunny] didn't disappoint. Quinn is a great character, with depth and a ton of baggage. Sara is caught up in a crush realized and trying to be independent. The banter is good and the other characters bring the whole story together"

— SIOUX M, REVIEWER

"Oh my I loved [The Puck Bunny]. I love Sara and her quirkiness and I loved reading how she grew into herself. I love Quinn for seeing her for her and being the gentleman. I love their chemistry. Love the story. I couldn't put it down."

— JESSICA, REVIEWER

Chapter One

ZAK

A slick magazine with my photo on the cover slides across the table landing in front of me. Fucking *Boston Magazine* Bachelor of the Year edition. One of the guys snickers, and the others take notice with loud whistles and hoots.

I toss the magazine aside.

"There have to be a hundred other bachelors in this city more deserving of that fucking award than I am. I don't get why they picked me." I speak to the table at large filled with various teammates from the Boston Brawlers hockey team. After winning our fourth straight game, we're out at our usual haunt, The Tea Party.

"Maybe it's your notoriously well-traveled dick that got you into the running," Finn says. The equally notorious goalie for our team has a lot of balls calling me out.

I flip him the finger. "Hey, didn't Delaney coerce you into a fake engagement to get you and your dick out of trouble?"

He flips me the finger back and squeezes his arm around his wife and former victim of Delaney's fake engagement plan. "Watch out, or it could happen to you, too."

I snort a laugh, and the others at our table laugh at my expense.

My teammates are clearly enjoying my recent award more than I am. Maybe that's because they're not the ones who need to stave off random marriage proposals from women they've never met.

Jonas is here with Mindy, his bride, an ex-puck bunny. Finnegan Reed always shows up, and even the old men, Rafe and O'Rourke, showed up tonight, along with another half dozen younger single guys. Sheila and her regular crew of groupies are here—and I use the term *groupies* fondly because they're actually super-nice super fans—and they're all gorgeous, friendly, and fun.

Sheila has the balls to slap another copy of the offending magazine in front of me.

"How about an autograph from the famous Bachelor of the Year for a friend?" She bats her eyelashes to mock me because that's how it is between us.

"Really? *Et tu*, Sheila?" I shove her magazine back to her. "This is crap. They should've picked that other guy, the runner-up, what's his name...?"

"No one is the pretty boy you are, Mr. B.O.Y. of Boston," Jonas says.

I flip him the finger. I hate the moniker Candice Montgomery, Boston Magazine's editor, christened me with in front of the entire team at her party last night and the way she paraded me around like chattel. I don't remember being so fucking irritated by a woman before in my life as I did in that moment. That's what a woman drooling, with fangs bared while she sharpens her knife, getting ready to eat you for dinner will do to a guy who normally worships at the altar of all females.

"You are a notorious flirt," Sheila says, nudging me in the ribs.

"It's the flirting with one particular woman that got me into trouble. I never should have... Never mind."

My phone pings, and I slip it from my jeans pocket to check it. A text from Candice. Shit.

"Let me guess," Finn says, eyeing my frown. "It's the magazine lady."

I nod and read it over.

> Candice: I'm still waiting to give your hockey stick a test run. Would you be interested in a late-night visit? My place or yours?

How do I respond to that without getting into trouble? No way do I want to get involved with this woman. She has *"serious relationship"* written all over her flirtations, but I have to figure out how to turn her down without causing any drama. This fucking magazine award of hers, *and her*, have turned my previously blissful life upside down. Things used to be so simple. I take a deep breath. Then I slip the phone back into my jeans pocket. Not dealing with her tonight.

But I can't afford to ignore her forever since she has juice in the media business, and the Brawlers' PR vice president, Delaney, warned me to play nice. I went to Delaney to ask for help in getting out of the whole Bachelor of the Year thing—especially the award night—but she was no help at all. To Delaney, I'm not a hockey player—I'm an opportunity for the Brawlers to gain positive publicity and raise awareness.

"You never should've taken Candice what's-her-name home for the night," Finn says.

"Candice Montgomery. Tell me something I don't know." I don't tell him that nothing ended up happening between us, thank fuck, due to the fact that she ended up borderline, fall-down drunk, and I don't do drunk women.

O'Rourke shakes his head. "I could see that train wreck coming. What were you thinking?"

"In my defense, I was buzzed, and she was hot, and it never occurred to me to do anything differently than I would normally do in that situation." That situation being an opportunity to take a hot lady home at the end of the night for a shot with my hockey stick. But I only do casual hook-ups, no dating, and that message somehow got lost in her excitement over the whole award thing. She's the kind of lady who believes the whole *Pride and Prejudice* thing—the universal truth that *a single man, in possession of a good fortune, must want a wife.*

I figure I'm at least a decade out from that universal truth coming into effect.

Yeah, I know all about Jane Austen and *Pride and Prejudice.* Good story. I have three sisters in Minnesota, where the winters are long, so when we weren't playing hockey, we did a lot of reading. My mom and sisters influenced some of my reading and also my deep appreciation for the female of the species. They're kind, generous, caring and soft especially compared to the rough competitive guys I've been playing hockey with all my life..

Except when they're in husband-hunting mode. That's what *Pride and Prejudice* taught me about women. Since I've been in the Bachelor of the Year spotlight, I feel like Darcy times a hundred, thanks to social media. I can't go out anywhere without being accosted—by that, I mean I'm the target of purposeful flirting, and the purpose is marriage or at least a serious relationship.

Maybe I should take all their numbers and get back to them in ten or fifteen years. But patience doesn't seem to be part of the deal when a female is husband-hunting. They all have clocks ticking. And they're all in competition, and I've seen what that can be like. I have the torn shirt to prove it.

"Bingo." Finn points at me. "Taking women home for the night can get tricky."

"As it turns out, she's not a believer in one-night-only," I mutter. "Now, I need to lay low and get off her radar—and everyone else's radar, for that matter."

"Sure, you do. I give you ten seconds."

"Seriously, I don't need the complication of ladies thinking I'm a bachelor ripe for the plucking, hovering around me to get a chance at me like I'm some kind of hockey-playing brass ring—the wedding kind."

"So that means if a girl doesn't want to marry you or doesn't know who you are, she's okay for flirting?" Sheila says.

I shrug. "I don't want to become a monk, but I need a clean slate of some kind, or I'll need to hire security."

She rolls her eyes.

"You love the attention," Jonas says. "Isn't this award a dream come true for a committed bachelor?"

"I was doing fine on my own, thank you very much. The kind of attention I'm getting now is the unwanted kind and a complication in my previously simple and perfect life."

In truth, my mother warned me this might happen. But I've been having too much fun for the past five years to notice any problems. The ladies I've met have, for the most part, been as fun-loving and free-wheeling as I am. I've never spent more than a handful of nights with any of them; most of the time, it's one-and-done.

Now that Candice put a target on my back as the most eligible bachelor in Boston, the *ultimate marriage material* to quote her article, I've been getting more attention—but from a different kind of lady. The marriage and family kind. Shit. That's way too hard to deal with. I don't like letting women down. It's not in my DNA.

"Good luck finding the lady who doesn't know who you are," Finn says. "Not in the places you travel. You'd have to change your entire strategy for hooking up." His grin is wide enough to make me want to punch him, but I nod because he's right. Shit.

I think about the sad truth and take a breath of resignation. "Exactly. I need to lie low for a while. Even if that means I become a temporary monk."

"There must be a woman or two left in this town who still doesn't know you from a tree trunk," Finn says. "Maybe someone's grandma." He laughs.

"Fuck you."

Sheila pats my back. "We'll find someone for you."

"No worries, kiddo. I can stand a rearrangement of my focus for a while. I'll ride this out with my dick in my pants and stay out of trouble." Last thing I need is Candice following through with her threat to do a follow-up article, or heaven forbid, to go through with her plan to team up with a charity and auction me off. Shit. I had to bribe her not to mention the auction to Delaney. The PR lady for the Brawlers could care less whether I want to be auctioned off or not.

I don't mention to the group that it's been a few weeks already since I've kissed a woman and made her blush. The lack of female company makes me twitchy, like something's seriously off, like I'm missing a few fingers or my balls.

Sheila pats my back again as I sign her fucking magazine. She sees right through me because we're old friends now, though we started our relationship in bed a few years ago. She's a fan—a self-described Boston Brawlers groupie and the Queen of the Tea Party, where her group of friends hangs out to watch games and stay to party with the players.

While I'm trying not to cry in my beer, I feel a draft and a zing of something run down my spine. I look up and see a woman walk into the bar. My mouth opens and goes instantly dry.

A woman?

I mean a fucking vision. If someone spied on my wet dreams and created the ultimate hot sexy lady for the sole purpose of tempting me into doing anything and everything she wants, this would be that woman.

She flicks long, lush dark hair over her shoulder and checks out the place with brilliant dark fringed eyes. And her body? It's the kind that would make Barbie dolls jealous. Last but not least, by anyone's score, she has a fucking sexy world-conquering attitude that I can see in the tilt of her chin, the glint in her eye, and the way she carries herself with perfectly squared shoulders. She has the kind of confidence a lot of women don't have when walking into a bar alone—make that no woman I've ever met.

That's who just walked in the fucking door. *Shit*. She's heading this way.

Keep your fucking butt in this seat, and do not flirt with her. Do not even look at her.

No more complications.

No fucking flirting.

Chapter 2

RYLEE

I limp into a bar in Boston by myself to see what my hometown has to offer a woman wanting to forget her mortality for a change. For tonight.

The place is old. It's dim enough to hide and small enough to be seen. Perfect. When I notice a group of women in a corner having a ball with a group of guys who are as hot as sin and out for trouble, I head straight for them.

I want a part of that trouble.

I introduce myself by sitting on the lap of the biggest, hottest guy here. And I mean big.

"I'm Rylee." I put out my hand to shake his. Grinning, he clears his throat and shifts. Then I feel exactly how big he and my tummy does acrobatics like I swallowed a circus performer.

We stare at each other, speechless, appreciating our *position*. He was hot from a distance, but up close—and I mean, within a dart of my tongue—he's stunning. Dark, playful eyes that shout *take me home* to my pussy stare back at me. If I try to speak, I might stutter.

"I'm Zak." His gravelly voice does things to my head, disconnecting my heretofore perfectly ample speech center, and all I can do is communicate with my eyes as sparks shoot through me.

Meanwhile, I hope to hell his dick lives up to the promise I'm sitting on.

"Well, you're a ballsy one. I'm Sheila," a woman says, smirking more than smiling as she walks up to us, standing close to Zak as if she has a right. Shit. She must be with him and I've intruded on her.

Even with the prize of this extraordinary treasure I'm sitting on I know I need to give him back. "Sorry for intruding." I make a move to jump off his lap, but he holds on.

"Not if you're interested in a threesome," she says.

If I had a drink, I'd be spitting it out. As it is, my mouth opens, and I'm once again speechless. My man Zak rumbles underneath me like an active volcano and chuckles. I nearly faint with how he nestles against the exact spot—Is he the distraction I was looking for?

"Don't say that unless you mean it," he says to Sheila, and I look between them. Sheila gives a sassy smile, and I regain my speech. Are they serious about a threesome? Oh, no. Apparently, I have lines I don't cross. Who knew?

"Hold on there." I attempt to hop off Zak's lap before there's any misunderstanding, and I suddenly feel like a chicken. Like one of those people I kid who aren't as adventurous as I am.

So what if I like to confine my adventures to non-orgy activities?

But Zak holds onto my shoulders, a light hold, and his smile softens to reassuring as if I'm a skittish pet. Maybe I am.

"No need to run," he says. "We're joking about the threesome. Been there, done that. Not worth repeating."

"Why not?" Sheila says. "Something go wrong?"

"What could go wrong when two ladies want one guy's attention?" He exaggerates a shudder and takes a sip of his beer.

She laughs, and I get the idea that these two know each other well. Very well.

But I shove that disturbing thought aside because I like the feel of his big hands heating me, caressing my shoulders and arms. It feels...good. More than sexy good...*good*.

"What went wrong, cowboy?" I say, picturing myself riding him.

"I had trouble, I kid you not, breaking up the fight. Those women had skills, and they were determined to draw blood. I was damn lucky it wasn't my blood they were after and vowed never again."

"Good call." I don't bother squelching my grin because I'm picturing him naked, trying to break up a catfight between two naked women, and immediately realize how difficult it must have been. Shit.

He whispers in my ear, "You're picturing that scenario, aren't you?"

"Hard not to."

"I'll give you something hard," he whispers.

"I'm getting that feeling."

Sheila rolls her eyes.

"You're not a hockey fan, are you, honey?" she says.

"No, why?" I look between Zak of the big boner and the slightly tipsy, slightly older Sheila.

"Just confirming. I'm outta here," she says.

"Don't go..." I say feeling like I need to make up for barging in. "Do you hang out at this place?"

"Sure. After every home game," she says.

"Game?" I give her a blank look. "Okay—how about if I buy you a drink—"

"We'll see." She stands and blows Zak a kiss, then rounds up her friends around the table to leave with her. I notice the guys at the end of the table grinning and gesturing in Zak's direction as Sheila talks to them.

"Guess it is about time to leave," Zak says, turning me on his lap in a delicious move to face him. "Were you going to stay, or can I give you a ride somewhere?" His eyes have that glazed intensity that spells sexual arousal, and I feel mine answering back, along with all the juices in me.

"Yeah," I whisper. "How about to oblivion and back?" I haven't had a chance to have one drink. So I grab his half-full mug from the table and swig it down. I'm not exactly a chicken, but something about this guy's intensity calls for a boost to my courage. All I'm looking for is one night's distraction, but a frisson of nerves zips through me like a warning sign that he may be more than I can handle—and I don't mean physically, though he is a big guy.

"You're thirsty," he says. "My bad. I didn't even buy you a beer. We can stay for one more if you want—"

"Hey, Zak—you coming?" One of the other guys throws a jacket in his direction and flashes me a smile. He has one of the women tucked under his other arm.

Zak says to me under his breath. "That's my ride—or our ride." He raises a brow and one corner of his mouth in question.

"How about if I'm your ride instead?" I say.

A slow smile lazes over his face. "I like you, Rylee. You're my kind of bold. I'll take you up on that ride."

He helps me off his lap and takes his time standing, the bulge in his pants causing him obvious discomfort as his buddies snicker.

"I'm going with the lady. This is Rylee." He rattles off the names of three guys and the two women with them.

"Sorry we have to run," One of the guys says to me, "but we have—"

Zak cuts him off. "See you later."

He sweeps me into his arm, taking possession of me like we're together, and we follow the others. I try to keep my limp to a minimum. Other patrons shout good night and good luck and all kinds of things, and I'm wondering who these guys are because everyone knows them.

They must be regulars at this place, and I'm glad I stumbled into a friendly neighborhood bar in Boston because I wasn't sure there were any left. Figured they were all tourist joints or overrun by business suits. *The Tea Party* seems different.

"Let me buy you a drink first," he says, stopping at the last high top before we get to the door. "What'll you have?"

"Jack Daniels, straight up."

He blows out a whistle.

"Don't be shocked. I can handle it."

"I guess we'll find out."

We sit down though on separate bar stools. Too bad, because his lap was comfortable, and sitting on him was a lot like foreplay. But my ankle is throbbing, so I'll sit anywhere. The whiskey should help, though ice would work better. The super attentive server, wearing a name tag over her ample left breast that says Liz, comes rushing over as soon as Zak looks in her direction.

"Two Jack Daniels, straight up."

"Going for the heavy stuff tonight? I thought you only ordered whiskey when you—"

"Tonight is special," he says, cutting her off. The girl flicks a glance at me, and I smile. She doesn't. Shit, this guy's popular with the ladies, but I shouldn't be surprised because he's got a lot going for him in the looks and body department—especially one particular part of his anatomy.

The girl leaves, and he clears his throat.

"What's wrong with your ankle?" he asks.

"You noticed that? I thought I was doing well hiding my limp."

"I've seen a few ankle injuries and recognize the signs. I know how subtly favoring one side affects a person's gait."

"What are you, an orthopedics doctor or physical therapist?"

"Nothing like that. You from Boston?"

"Sure. Why wouldn't I be?"

"You would, but you've never been in here before." He sweeps an arm up toward the sign that says The Tea Party.

"How would you know? You a regular?"

"It's my second home."

"You would sleep on the bar if they let you?"

"Exactly."

"You a drunk?" I know he's not. He's far too fit and his eyes way too bright, but I'm not above teasing a guy.

He gives me his best panty-melter smile and puts one very large hand on my thigh. He squeezes, and I feel like I've been branded, the sting running through my bloodstream leaving a deliciously hot trail.

Liz, the server, returns with a smile and a tray holding two whiskey-filled shot glasses. She stumbles, crashing into Zak and spilling one of the glasses before I relieve her of the tray and put it down.

Zak stands, and it's like he turns from a giant into a mountain as he helps the girl regain her balance. She turns and scolds some guy on his way out the door for shoving her. I'd swear she fell on purpose.

"I'm so sorry, Zak. I'll go get you another shot right away."

I pick up the un-spilled glass and hand it to him.

"No problem. We can split this one."

He turns to me and lets go of the girl, sitting back down.

"Great idea." Pulling out his wallet, he hands her a fifty-dollar bill. "Have a good night, Liz. We'll be leaving after this."

Liz leaves reluctantly and without bothering to wipe up the spilled shot glass, but I'm not calling her back.

"Sorry about that," Zak says to me. He sips the whiskey and swallows like it's not his first or even hundredth time. Then, with two hands, he pulls me and my stool close to him like I'm as weightless as whipped cream. *Why am I thinking of whipped cream? Maybe because you want to squirt it all over his body and lick it off him.*

"It wasn't your fault." I'm concentrating on the fullness of his lips and wonder if he's a trumpet player. My insides tumble in that pleasant pre-sex warm-up way.

He slides his hands from the stool to my hips. The heat his hands generate picks up the branding process where he left off before the interruption.

"It sort of is my fault," he says.

His words are puzzling enough to distract me from his lips and stray thoughts of branding and kissing. "How do you figure?"

"She has a crush, and I should stay clear of her."

I nod. "That a common problem?"

"That, Rylee, is the kind of question that'll get a guy in trouble no matter how he answers it."

I shrug. "Call me unfair." I think I'm smiling at him because he's smiling back and it's doing all kinds of fun things to my belly, warming me up for more fun things to come.

He leans in, and my heart speeds up.

"Looking at you is unfair." His voice is low and raspy. "Your eyes are showstoppers. I bet you have guys stumbling all over you on the regular."

"All the time. I had to take out an extra insurance policy."

He laughs. He raises his hand and runs a finger gently over my eyelashes. The gesture is heart-stopping in its simple reverence, and the sensation sends goosebumps everywhere. My pussy swells up, and I want to wrap him in my legs this instant.

But I don't—of course not. That's not something I do. It's not even something I think of doing. This reaction to him isn't normal, or at least not how I normally act with men. Sure, I like men, but—not like this. I'm not boy-crazy. Never was. I have things to do in life. I have no plans to attach myself to a man. Ever. Life taught me to keep relationships to a minimum and to stand on my own. Independence is the most important thing. I have my family, Mama Cass and Suzie. That's plenty to take care of for an independent girl with ambition.

I pick up the whiskey and put the shot glass to my lips, and he watches. My insides are already sizzling, but I throw the whiskey down my throat for its medicinal value. I stand to test the ankle, and I don't feel a thing. But I'm not sure if it's staring at him or the whiskey that has me so distracted.

"Let's have some fun, cowboy."

"Your place or mine?"

No way can we go to my place. Mostly because I'm staying with Mama Cass, and going there is out of the question. "Your place."

He stands, but not without that tell-tale struggle, and my eyes go straight to the bulge in his jeans which might have grown larger. My thighs clench. He reaches out a hand and lifts my chin so my eyes meet his. "You game for a night of fun?"

"A night you'll never forget," I say while my heart thumps too fast, and I feel like I've swallowed a tennis ball.

"One night only." He says and stares, not moving, as if there's a question in his statement.

I shrug. "Of course."

Chapter 3

ZAK

The first thing I see when I open the door to my condo and we step inside the entryway is my roommate's jacket. It's strewn on a chair in the great room. "Shit." Fucking Nowicki came home early. That's what I get for taking in an underpaid rookie for the season.

"What's the matter?"

I turn my attention to Rylee. "Not a single blessed thing." I hope to God my roommate is asleep. But as I lower my mouth to kiss her perpetual smartass smile, I hear the bang of a door from down the hall. Fuck.

She jumps before my lips touch hers.

"Hey," Nowicki says, "I thought I heard someone come in." He's all too cheerful as he appears from the hallway striding into the great room.

I stifle a sigh and opt for polite and to the point. With any luck, Nowicki will find somewhere else to spend the night like he usually does.

"This is Rylee..." I don't know her last name, and despite my questioning look, she doesn't supply it. I smile, and my dream girl keeps getting better and better because there's nothing simpler than first names only. "And that," I gesture with my thumb, "is my clueless roommate Nowicki."

"I'm not clueless. It's always a pleasure to meet a gorgeous young lady."

When did he turn into a forty-year-old man with manners? He moves in, presumably to shake Rylee's hand, but I pull her in close to my side, and he wisely stops at a safe distance. Not that he was going to move in on her, but I want this interruption on my way to tasting how sweet she is to be as short as possible.

"Nice to meet you, Nowicki," she says. "Do you have a first name?"

"Ted."

Shit. Last thing I need is these two striking up a conversation. It won't be long before she finds out who I am. My gaze darts to the coffee table in the corner of the great room behind her. And there it is. The Boston Magazine with me bare-chested on the cover, and the headline reading "*Bachelor of the Year: how long will he last before he's snapped up?*"

I need to move that out of sight and fast. I definitely don't want her getting the idea I'm interested in being *snapped up*. I'm stoked that she isn't out to strike up a relationship with a ripe-for-the-plucking famous hockey player, that for all she knows, I could be a plumber, and we're here for the pure enjoyment only. No complications.

I'm relieved I found her because, with the Bachelor of the Year target on my back, I've been truly worried I'd be monking it for a while. The idea of catching a bachelor and curing him of his condition has all kinds of women chasing after me. They're not like the groupies at The Tea Party, who are only out for fun. Those ladies are great. They're into my two favorite things as much as I am. Hockey and sex. Maybe not as much as I am, but we have those things in common, and I like spending time with them and women like them.

But Rylee is perfect. She's a total knockout, and she's not a

Brawlers fan, so she clearly doesn't know I play hockey or who I am. I won't lie; the anonymity gives me an extra rush of excitement with a small side of trepidation. Not an unwelcome feeling.

I go to the coffee table to dispose of the magazine, but I turn, and she's there, following me into the room and looking around with curiosity, not in a hurry to get to my bedroom. She's one of those women who is in charge of themselves, who has something going on and knows what she wants. Plus, she's got a face and body that could stop traffic and an innate sexiness that surrounds her like a spider's web.

Count me in as caught in that web like a doomed fly.

"How about a drink?" Ted says, following us. She turns to him, and I motion behind her back, picking up the magazine and shaking my head *no* before tossing it under the couch.

"Sounds great. You got whiskey?" she asks.

Ted looks at me, confused.

"Only the best. Pappy Van Winkle," I say, wrapping an arm around her as I guide her to the dining room, where we have a bar set up. Not that I want to give her whiskey, but I needed to get her out of the great room, away from the radioactive magazine.

"Look at this place." She spreads her arms. "This table must be ten feet long." She runs a hand along the shiny, smooth surface.

"It's marble," I tell her, enjoying that she's impressed. "My designer would spear me through the heart with a hockey stick if she knew all we ever use it for is beer pong."

A wicked smile stretches across her face like a sexy devil has taken over her soul. "My favorite game. How about if we play—except with whiskey."

Nowicki lets out a whistle, staring at her like she's an alien. Maybe she is because I don't remember a woman ever volunteering to go up against me in beer pong.

Of course, Rylee doesn't know my reputation. She has no idea I'm the team champ—a fact that was covered in the Boston Magazine article. I exchange a *shut-up, or you're dead* glance with

Nowicki. My need to keep her in the dark about my hockey team status—or my beer-pong reputation—has ratcheted up substantially, along with my arousal.

"Are you sure?" I say. "I wouldn't want you to over-indulge—"

"You saying I can't hold my liquor, big guy?"

"I'm sure you can, but—"

"Besides, I only had half a beer and half a shot. I'm still thirsty. You're way ahead of me. All liquored up."

"Yeah, Zak. Maybe she needs a few shots before she—"

I cut Nowicki off before he finishes whatever his thought was because I can tell it isn't going to be flattering or discrete based on the glint in his eyes.

"All right, let's play, but house rules for a co-ed game of whiskey pong calls for the stripping bonus." I lift a brow in challenge, hoping she'll back down, but not too sure she will.

"You're on," she says, rubbing her hands together, and I get that spider web sensation again. "This should be fun. I can't wait to see you guys butt naked."

"Nowicki's not—"

This time Nowicki interrupts me, endangering his future roommate status. "I'm most definitely in for this game." He moves into the dining area to get the red cups and whiskey set up.

Fuck. The only way I'm going to get rid of him is to punch him or beat his ass in the game—hopefully, before Rylee gets wasted. *Hell.* No way am I letting that happen. Before she has more than two shots, I'll either throw the game or call it.

"Maybe you better put some more clothes on, Ted. Just sayin'." Rylee points toward his gym shorts, the only thing the guy is wearing.

"I second that motion," I say.

He laughs and returns to his room, presumably to put on a shirt.

"Sorry about my roommate. I thought he'd be asleep since he didn't come out with us tonight."

"No problem. I'm wide awake with jet lag. Besides..." She moves in close, and I jump at the chance to wrap my arms around her killer body, roaming my hands over the curve of her hips and ass. She tries to stand on tiptoe, but stumbles. I lean in so she can whisper in my ear. "I like to build anticipation." Her words churn up my testosterone as if it needs any churning, but I notice she's leaning into me, tilting to one side.

"Your ankle is bothering you, isn't it?" I help her to a chair, and she lets go of me reluctantly to sit. "Let me check it out."

"No big deal. I only twisted it."

"It's slightly swollen. I'll get you an ice pack." I don't wait for her answer because I know what to do for ankles, and I know she needs to keep off it and keep it iced, or it'll get worse. It looks like there's a possible avulsion fracture based on the slight bruising.

Opening the freezer of our giant refrigerator, I take one of the many ice packs out and grab an ace bandage from one of the kitchen drawers. The large up-to-the-minute kitchen doubles as an infirmary and medical supply room, a side effect of playing a contact sport as a profession. As I return to her, Nowicki waltzes out into the open from the hallway dressed up like a clown with garments strewn all over him, including a pair of boxers on his head covered by a hat like it's a cotton plaid wig.

Rylee laughs, and I pull up a chair to sit opposite her.

"Whiskey pong is on hold while one of the contestants gets medical attention." I lift her leg gingerly and rest her ankle on my lap with the ice pack while I wrap an ace bandage around it to secure it in place.

"Fuck. What happened while I was gone?"

"An old skydiving injury," she says. Nowicki laughs, but I watch her face, and I'm not sure if she's serious, but I'm not sure she's joking either.

"You'll have to tell us the story," Nowicki says.

"Another time."

"Looks like strip whiskey pong is out for tonight and after I got all dressed up," he says mournfully.

"Looks like it," I confirm and warn him with my eyes to make himself scarce. I want to minimize his opportunity to blow my anonymity.

"I can still play," she says. "On one foot, maybe?" She laughs. "Although I have to admit that ice feels really good." Her eyes flash an invitation to find another way to make her feel even better, and I swear my entire body's temperature goes up ten degrees.

"No strip whiskey pong," I say with an arch of an eyebrow, "but I'm sure we can find another game to play where you're lying down."

"Okay, I'm outta here." Nowicki turns to leave, thank God, then he stops and points at me. "Don't forget we have—"

"Not a damn worry in the world." I cut him off before he mentions morning skate.

He shakes his head. "If you say so." He flashes a smile in Rylee's direction. "Nice to meet you. Take care of that ankle. Though it looks like you're in good hands." He walks back down the hall, and I hold my breath until I hear his door shut.

"So, you have good hands, then?" she whispers, leaning in, and I get a glimpse of healthy cleavage.

"Baby, before this night is over, you won't even know you have an ankle." I bend my head and whisper in her ear as I wrap my arms around her, helping her to a stand. My hands glide over her curves, and the firmness surprises me in the best way possible. "Jesus, you're in some kind of shape." I breathe the words into her mouth, my blood pumping hard as I focus on her plump lips.

When I capture her bottom lip between my teeth, the salty-sweet taste and the cushiony give of her flesh drive me and my dick to the next level of need. "Baby," I moan and then take her mouth in a kiss like I need her to live. She's breathless, and even through the pounding of blood in my ears, I hear her desperation. Despite the fuzziness of my dick-controlled brain, I'm conscious of her hands clamping down on the muscles of my back and her hips pushing into my thighs.

But it's the sound of her moan into my mouth as she nibbles and devours me like a woman deprived too long that destroys me. My brain stops, and I lift her off her feet, sweeping her into my arms and stomping down the hall to the last door. Banging it open with one foot, I carry her into my bedroom and slam the door behind us with the other foot.

The look in her eyes stutters my heart because she looks like an animal hungrier than I am, and I would have thought that was impossible. Her hair brushes against my cheek, soft and smelling sweet and exotic and fucking irresistible. I swear her scent alone makes my cock twitch.

"You're as strong as you look." Her breathy words make my head buzz. She runs a hand through my hair, giving me chills while I bring her to the bed. I stare at her glazed eyes and then her lips. They look like they've been bitten because they have, and I've never seen anything sexier in my life.

"Stronger." My voice quivers, and my eyes don't leave hers as I lower her. "Do you want to undress yourself, or do you want me to do it?" My heart races, but I pause a beat to watch her reaction.

If I was worried about her having second thoughts, I didn't need to. Her eyes go dark, and one corner of her mouth lifts in a tiny curve, the kind that almost makes my knees buckle with need. I hold back a growl. *A fucking growl.*

Instead, I heave a deep breath. "I have to warn you, if I undress you, your clothes may be shredded."

"You first. Let me watch you strip. I want to see if all your muscles are as big and strong as your arms."

I stop and flex my arms automatically as if they appreciate the compliment. I'm not sure if waiting another second to see her naked is punishment or enhanced reward—either way, every second that goes by until I'm inside her is pure exquisite torture. My cock throbs like fuck, and I don't think it's ever been this hard or big. But that could be the confines of my jeans, forcing it to push its will.

I grit my teeth.

"Anything you say, Buttercup. I'm all yours." I pull my shirt over my head, groaning as I realize I mean those words. She can make me do anything right now just so I can get a whiff of her pussy, a taste. If it's half as good as the scent of her hair or the taste of her mouth, I swear I'll explode like never before once I get inside her.

She sits up and reaches out to touch my pecs. "You make the statue of David look like kindergarten art. Look at those fucking muscles ripple."

Her words douse me with more encouragement than I need as I watch her. She turns me on like a faucet. I swear I feel like a teenager, like I haven't felt in ten years.

"Jesus, Buttercup." I grind out the words as she caresses me, pinching my nipples and running her hands down my abs to the fly of my jeans. I'm about to tell her to take it slow, to push her back down to the mattress, but she flicks my button open, pulls down the zipper, and frees my cock from my pants and boxers in a quick and sure move that has me seeing spots.

"Fuck." The rasp of my voice disturbs the air, unsettling it and overpowering the room, leaving no doubt of the state I'm in.

She chuckles softly and rises to her knees in front of me, moving close so I have no choice but to hold her, to run my hands up her ribs to the luscious mounds of her breasts. I literally drool. Then she moans and leans into me, and when I think I have control back, she pushes my jeans down and takes my cock in her two hands. It jumps, and I reflexively squeeze her breasts.

She moans louder.

"Sorry, I didn't mean—"

"That's too bad," she whispers. "I like it. Don't think you need to be gentle with me. I'm not fragile."

"Good to know." She tightens her hands around my cock,

stroking me up and down, and I jerk, grabbing her hand and pulling it off me. "Not so fast, babe." My voice is dense with the effort to hold back my raging need.

She smirks, and I push her back to the bed, rolling until she's under me. "I need something from you first."

"What's that big boy?" Her sexy whisper heightens my already edgy arousal.

"I need to taste you, to drink every ounce of honey in you, to drain you and make you beg for my cock inside you, to make you desperate for me."

"I'm already starting to feel a little desperate. I love your dirty talk. You have a talent for it."

I let my hands wander down her body and slip one between her legs. I swipe a finger down the seam of her pussy, and I swear it pulses, enveloping me with wet heat. *God almighty*. I imagine my cock being swallowed by her paradise.

"Fuck. You are so ready." I don't wait another second before kissing my way down her body, fast and hard, the need in me building to lick her pussy, to have her in my mouth and feel her writhe in my arms.

My hand shakes as it slides over her hips, and down her thighs. They're tight and solid, and as I lower myself between her legs, I slip my arms under each thigh and lift them over my shoulders.

"Your legs are amazing, babe, so firm and strong and perfect." I stop to study her face, and she's watching me, her lips parted, her eyes half-lidded with those sexy thick eyelashes, and my heart bobbles in my chest at the sight. "I don't think I've ever seen anything sexier than you right now."

"I could say the same." She reaches a hand out to touch my face, scraping across my stubbled jaw. She slips a finger in my mouth, and I suck it, tasting her. She pulls it out, and I lean forward, pushing her back down as I lower my face to her pussy, inhaling deeply, the scent of her arousal making my mouth water.

"You're driving me crazy, Zak. Take me in your mouth—"

I do as she asks, and she sucks in a breath as I lick her and nuzzle her pussy, getting my fill of the aroma and the taste of her juices, oozing from her delicious swollen flesh.

"Oh my god," I whisper and hold her ass cheeks in my hands, bringing her fully exposed and glistening. I can't help slowing down to take in her beauty. She squirms and moans. I chuckle and glance up at her. Her face is pink and flushed, and her breasts heave with her labored breathing. She smiles, one side of her mouth lifted higher at a sassy tilt, testing the limits of my already maxed restraint.

Shutting my eyes, I take a deep breath and picture the locker room filled with my teammates, anything to tamp down my rising orgasm. I need her to come all over my tongue, to watch and hear and feel her fall apart under me.

"Zak, I…" Her words are breathless as she pushes her hips up and winds her hands in my hair to press my mouth to her, and I oblige. Opening my mouth wide, I suck on her delicious pussy as the blood rushes in my ears, and she cries out. I flick my tongue over her clit, back and forth and around, as it plumps up like a marble, slick and round and hard and ripe. She pumps her hips and squeezes her thighs as she shouts my name, holding onto me while I suck her exploding clit into my mouth and nip it with my teeth.

She jerks under me, my name a keening song, loud and shrill from deep down inside her. Lapping up every bit of the butter from her cup, I'm dizzy either from lack of air or her heady scent and taste driving me crazy. Licking her as she vibrates with the kind of intensity I've never seen, I hold her until the need to see her face moves me.

Loosening the clench of her thighs, I push my way up and take her face in my hands, needing to see those eyes, to see that look of ecstasy and complete surrender. She doesn't disappoint me, wrapping her arms around me, glowing and spent.

"Oh my God, oh my God." She whispers the words as I kiss

her mouth, cheeks, and temples, then move the strands of hair stuck to her face.

"Do you have any idea how beautiful you are?" My voice is low with the reverence I feel, and my heart hammers. This is fucking crazy. I've never seen a woman so devastatingly gorgeous and destroyed. I want to hold her until she calms, so I wrap her in my arms. She wraps her arms and legs around me and kisses my face, licks my lips, and murmurs too softly to hear. All I know is that her voice warms me.

We lie wrapped up in each other for a while, and I'm in no rush to untangle myself. My dick is hard but calm, and my heartbeat matches hers. Something about that synchronized rhythm compels me and keeps me in the moment.

She nibbles on my earlobe and takes in a deep shuddering breath.

"That was unbelievably earth-shattering." She takes my face in her hands. "I mean it. I truly do not believe it." She smiles, and I chuckle, a shot of warmth zipping through me, waking up my resting dick.

Do I lie and tell her this was nothing? That it's like this all the time? Because that would be one of the biggest fucking lies of my life.

"Glad you enjoyed yourself. I kind of liked your buttercup, too."

She grins. "What's with the *buttercup*?"

I reach down and cup her pussy. "It's you. It's how I think of you. Don't worry, Buttercup; it's all good. Fucking good." Too fucking good. Maybe she's right—unbelievable.

She laughs. "Whatever you say. I can't complain about anything right now, can I?"

"That would be bad manners," I drawl.

"Your turn, now, big boy." She slips her hand down to my cock. "Let's see if I can swallow that cock of yours. It's so tempting and beautiful and... I won't lie, large."

"You afraid?" I can't help teasing her even as her scorching hot words stir my blood, forcing my heart to pump in a wild rage.

"I would be if I weren't the kind of woman who likes a challenge. But I'm not intimidated." She tightens her grip and strokes me.

"Rylee…" Her name comes out as a groan, and I can't remember being so turned on, so primed with anticipation to be in a woman's mouth, to be inside her, to have her own me. "Sweet fucking…"

In a quick heart-stopping move, she rises and throws a leg over my body, giving me an eyeful of her ass, and goes down fast and hard, sucking half my cock into her mouth at once as she holds onto the base. My hands clench her thighs in a reflexive move, and I grit my teeth hard in an effort to hold onto my control.

"What the fuck." I grind out the words to distract myself from her hot mouth moving on me, up and down, as her fingers slip under my balls. "You are a fucking miracle."

I struggle to breathe and gain control, but I do, and I knead her ass, finding her pussy from behind, plump and soaked, ripe for another orgasm. When I stroke her, my fingers finding her clit, she jumps and moans with her mouth full.

The satisfaction ratchets up my arousal, bringing me close to the edge. Then she glides her mouth to my head, her hands clamped on my shaft, and sucks so hard I see stars and feel the dizzying zip of pulses run down my spine and to the base of my cock.

"I'm going to come." I half groan, half shout the words like I'm warning her about a cataclysmic event because that's how it feels. Pumping my hips toward her mouth, my hands shake as I fist her hair, and the rush of my cum erupts from me, leaving me blind and dizzy and feeling like I'm living on a knife's edge—perched perfectly, precariously, and about to fall into the abyss of aftermath. Instead, my body shakes with aftershocks, and I watch my cum spill onto Rylee's face as agonizing bliss spasms through me again. She welcomes my cum like a bath, spreading it over her skin.

"Jesus fucking Christ," I hiss, yanking her up from between my legs and dragging her mouth to meet mine, desperate to taste her, to taste myself on her, to lick her face, to share every intimacy, exchange every bodily fluid possible.

She murmurs and runs her hands through my hair and over my bunched shoulders and back in a constant motion, her words unintelligible, and I hold her while I continue to kiss her in between heaving air in and out of my lungs.

Eventually, our breathing synchronizes to a calm rate, and she shifts, so I loosen my hold.

She aims those spectacular eyes at me for a beat, and I have no idea what she's going to say, but my pulse picks up, waiting to hear it.

"You're something else Zak. What you have going on here is gold." She blows out a breath, then lies back on the pillow next to me and sinks into it.

I let out a short chuckle. "You're not so bad yourself. In fact, I think you win our unofficial competition."

"Gracious of you to admit it."

"You admit we were competing?"

Her mouth curves in a lazy smile, and she swats me. "Life is a competition whether we admit it or not."

I nod and wonder where she came from—then stop myself before I wonder where she's been all my life. Because that's stupid. She's a one-night-only hookup. She's a stranger, and she's going to stay that way no matter how intriguing, no matter how compelling, no matter how much my dick cries bloody hell.

After taking turns cleaning up in the bathroom, this is where I would normally say good night and send her on her way. Instead, I return to bed and slip in next to her. She doesn't look any readier than I feel for this night to end.

"What are you smiling about?" I ask because I know the

answer and need to hear her admit it like a proud conqueror, like an ass.

"You're as good as your word. You made me forget all about my ankle."

Her words settle through me like a shot of well-being. This must be what an addict feels like when they get that fix they're desperate for. *I could become addicted to her if....* But there's no danger of that. *One night only.*

"I'm glad. How's the ankle now?" It strikes me that her answer matters as I wait for it.

"I'm not sure. I'm not moving it—letting sleeping dogs lie and all that."

"Good plan for now. But if you start feeling it again, let me know. I'll get you more ice."

"You're such a good host." She laughs. "Are you in the hospitality business?"

"No." I'm on my side facing her while she lies on her back, sheets tangled around her middle, breasts exposed and tempting me. I lean down to kiss each nipple.

She half laughs, half groans, her fingers running through my hair. "What do you do?"

I raise my head. "What?" I don't like this question. The specter of the Bachelor of the Year secret shame being exposed rises. To distract her, I dip my head again to kiss her, but she stops me.

"What do you do?" Her eyes, bright and compelling and expectant, force me to answer her.

I can't explain why, but she makes me feel like I owe her an answer, like we have an intimate connection that requires it. Which is crazy because no matter how much intimacy we've shared tonight, it's only for tonight. *Right?*

"I'm a ... banker. Boring, but there's money in it." *A banker?* Could I have come up with a more ridiculous lie? I'm not into lying, obviously. And I don't want to get into it. Guilt tightens my chest, and I clam up. My mind goes blank when I need it to come up with a new subject. *Fuck*. I don't know what the hell she thinks, whether she believes me or not, but her smile goes saucy, and she clears her throat.

"I'm so sorry I brought up such a boring subject. How about if we talk about where you're ticklish?"

Relief loosens the tightness in my chest. "Go for it. I'm not ticklish. But I'll enjoy you touching me."

She promptly tests my belly with the lightest, most sensitive touch I've ever felt, and damn, my gut clenches in a ticklish spasm. Oh my God. She's so hot and so tuned to me. I needed the subject changed, and she changes it. But fuck, she's tickling me, and I'm not supposed to be ticklish. I spasm again, more intensely.

"Stop. You win. Uncle," I half laugh between my words.

"You admit I'm the best in the world?"

"Whatever you want, Buttercup. You are the best. In the whole damn world."

I turn on her, pinning her down underneath me, taking no chances as I hold her two wrists above her head. "How is it possible? How could you create a ticklish spot I've never had before?"

She licks her lips, one of the many ways she taunts me. Her very existence, her breathing, her scent, every damn thing about her reaches out and grabs me by the balls, making me want her.

"The trick is," she says in a whisper, "to barely touch the fine hairs on your body and move them just a whisper to activate the most intense sensors."

"How do you know that? Who are you?"

She laughs. "I'm a connoisseur of the male body."

"Is that right?" Something about that statement hits me the wrong way, smacking me right in the dick and making me edgy. How many male bodies would it take to be a connoisseur?

"I'm not a person for rules, Buttercup. But if I had one, it would be that a woman is never allowed to mention other men, even in a general, vague reference, when she's in bed with me." Am

I actually feeling jealous? Did I expect she was a virgin, or am I being an ass?

Her hand shoots to my face, cupping my cheek. "I'm so sorry. I had no idea you were the sensitive type." Her eyes are dark, the blue barely showing beneath those lush lashes, but I see the hint of a tease. I deserve that. Like everything about her seems to do, her teasing me turns me on, raising my temperature and sending the blood rushing to my cock yet again.

"Are you testing my stamina?" I ask, my voice deepening.

The pleased look on her face, like I've awarded her the grand prize, shoots me back into the zone of need.

I press my body into hers, closing the gap between our mouths, and my cock presses into her belly as I take her mouth and suck it into mine then nibble, small light bites, to taste her, to feel the give in her flesh, to absorb all her sexy bodily fluids and mix them with mine, to be with her so closely and so intimately that nothing is left to wonder. In this moment, she'll know that she fully belongs to me, and I belong to her.

She moans. "Zak... You make me feel so good, so wanted, and so vulnerable. I don't know how you do it."

I move my mouth to her ear and suck on her earlobe, watching her shiver, and feeling a jolt of fire. Then I whisper, words tumbling straight from my gut, "I own you, and you own me. For the time we're together, we're completely together. I throw myself into you with total abandon; everything I have is spent in our love-making. Nothing is left when we're done."

"I can't help myself," she says. "I don't want to, but I need to give you everything right now. All of me in this moment. You have me."

"That's right, Buttercup. That's the only way, the best way."

"Come inside me. I need you."

A tense jolt stiffens all my muscles. I lift myself and stare into those glazed, heart-stopping eyes. All at once, my heart thunders with urgency.

"Let me get a—" With a shaky hand, I reach for my nightstand drawer for a foil pack, but she grabs my wrist and stops me.

"No. I want you bare."

What? I stare at her. I couldn't have heard her right. She caresses my face, running her fingers down my jawline. Her touch calms me and, at the same time, raises my body temperature to the red zone.

"It's okay. I have an IUD."

I freeze. There's no mistaking her meaning, and her words send a thrill of lust combined with fear down my spine. My cock stiffens to granite.

"You trust me?"

She nods her head.

Can I trust her?

"I've never had bare sex." I feel like I'm confessing my virginity.

A slow sexy smile splits her face. "Let me be the one. You're so perfect and so big, and I need to feel alive tonight."

I have no idea what that's all about except that I feel the desperation of her need. And for myself, I feel the edge of being more alive than I have in—I don't know how long. A *take the world by storm and go for it* surge fills me, and I want—no need— to be inside her bare like I need to breathe.

"I trust you." I don't know why or how, but I know she wouldn't lie about something important.

I swear I feel it. My instincts tell me she's a decent, honest, and giving person. And she's mine tonight, for just this one night, to blow up everything I thought I knew about living life to its fullest and feeling every single one of my cells teaming with vitality.

Live for today because tomorrow may never come. The words would be a meaningless cliché, except they're the ironic words from my best friend Bill's suicide note, and they come to mind now, making me fumble as I move between her legs. Fuck.

"Everything okay?"

I stare at her face, at the dark fringe of her eyelashes contrasting with those bright blue eyes, at the genuine concern in those eyes, and her dark hair spread around her head on the pillow. My cock pulses, pushing every other thought from my head except her. I'm consumed by her and my need to have her skin-to-skin everywhere.

"Fantastic." *Is it a lie?* I can't answer that, can't let myself think about that or anything else except for this moment and feeling my cock as she sucks me inside her impossibly tight wet pussy.

I groan low from somewhere deep inside me as the sensations hit my nerve endings, ping-ponging with frenetic speed through my system, driving my blood in a blinding rush to fill my cock past its capacity.

"Oh God…" I breathe the words as I hold myself over her, plunging in and then out. Beads of sweat drip from my face to hers while I watch her face, her eyes glazed, her lips parted and panting small puffs of whiskey and mint-laced air that hits my nostrils and fills me with knowledge of her, piling onto the endless barrage of sensations from our connection.

"Baby, you're so fucking sexy." The words tear from my throat, ripping my skin and veins open, as if her body is becoming part of mine, exposing me down to my bones, down to my soul.

"Yeeesss." The one syllable she utters, long and hard, as I move faster, in and out, out of control like a rogue locomotive rocketing to the ultimate crash at the end of the tunnel, fires me into oblivion.

Without warning, I explode in a thrust driven by a deep primal force, devoid of thought or plans or talk or anything but a guttural cry, loud and violent, as I shudder with world-ending black-out ecstasy.

SOME TIME or no time later, when my mind flashes back to the here and now, I find my hand between her thighs and her hips bucking against me as I twirl my thumb around her marble-like clit. My heart beats wildly, and she pants with urgency, her wanton eyes glassy, close to release.

I press my thumb down hard on her clit until it pops, and her juice spreads over my fingers as I watch her face, the silent scream, the delirious pain of bliss creasing her forehead, her hair stuck to her glowing skin.

On instinct, my body surrounds her; my arms and legs envelop her, absorbing her spasms. My mouth covers hers, taking in her scream, my name shattering the space between us as I swallow it, feeling like she's given me her whole self as if we've melded together, and the separation between us is impossible to find.

As the beating of our hearts and our breathing normalizes, I blink in the semi-darkness of the room as her clothes tossed randomly on a chair across the room come into focus. I let go of her, suddenly self-conscious of our connection, unsure of the experience I just had, and trying to fit it somewhere in the realm of past exploits, anywhere familiar compared to other nights and other women.

My chest tightens with the slightly disoriented feeling, but when she leans up on an elbow, stares at me with those heart-stopping eyes, and strokes my jaw with a half-smile in place, a feeling of warmth loosens my tension.

"That," she says, her voice shaky and authentic, "was un-fuck-ing-forgettable."

"What she said." My grin matches hers, and my eyes feast on her as I let a hand wander down her body. Then I remember when I see the sheets tangled around her legs. "How's your ankle?"

She laughs. "What ankle?"

I laugh with her, but I sit up and untangle the sheets. "Let me take a look." I don't know why I feel compelled to play doctor, but I do, and I examine her ankle, gently touching it, feeling around the bones, and checking the swelling and bruising. She puts up with my exam with an amused look on her face.

Shit. The bruising is darker and has spread since earlier, and the swelling is up. It's probably sprained, and she might have an avulsion fracture, but I can't be the one to break the news. I'm not a doctor. I'm a fucking banker-slash-hockey player, and one charade a night is more than enough.

"You need x-rays and an ultrasound, Buttercup. I know a good doctor if you need one."

"No. Thank you, though." She yawns. "You're a very nice man, Zak. You know that?" She reaches up and strokes my chin again. Her hands are impossibly soft. She tugs at me to lie back down next to her.

I chalk her words up to exhaustion and resist her pull. Instead, I get out of bed to retrieve another ice pack from the kitchen. When I return, her eyes flutter as she watches me place another pillow under her foot and put the ice pack on her ankle.

"Rest," I say as I watch her lazy smile and her eyes flutter closed. I pull the covers over her to keep her warm against the ice.

"I need to leave soon. Can't stay," she murmurs.

I lie down beside her, leaning on one elbow. "I know."

Of course, she's not staying overnight. Especially not tonight. I have an early skate. But I don't budge as I watch her drift to sleep, listen to her light breathing, and watch the rise and fall of those magnificent breasts, the softness of her face, peaceful and carefree —those long dark lashes on her pale cheeks like a perfect doll. Unreal beauty. The only thing more gorgeous is when they're open and those smart sapphire eyes are staring at mine, the dark line of her lashes framing them like jewels. Shit.

This isn't good. Lying back, I pull her close with one hand resting on the soft, warm skin of her flat belly. Relaxing into the rhythm of her breathing, I close my eyes.

Fuck it. Why not? Why isn't this a good idea? Why can't I fall asleep with a woman in my arms? It's just one night...

I WAKE AT DAWN, and the first thing that hits me is the scent of a woman, the very specific scent of Rylee, aka Buttercup. Turning my head, I get an eyeful of dark, lush hair splayed on my shoulder and pillow. The warmth of her body, spreading the length of mine, hits me next.

After a deep inhale of her sexy scent, something sweet and exotic that I can't place, I shudder. What the fuck? I move, attempting to get some separation from her. What the fuck was I thinking? I can't believe I let her spend the night. *I can't believe she stayed.*

I don't remember the last time I spent all night with a woman. Not that it's a rule, but my experience says it's best to avoid the awkward morning after. Most—no, make that *all*—the women I know don't want a guy seeing them first thing in the morning anyway. And none of them wants to put on their clothes from the night before to go home.

Sitting up, I dislodge her from my side, and cold air immediately supplants the warmth of her body. God, this is torture. She stirs, but she's still asleep, looking so sinfully sexy and angelic at the same time. It's a fucking shame, but I have to wake her.

What do I say?

Shit. Who knows? This is why I don't do overnight stays or repeats, let alone relationships. Especially not this time, not with Rylee. She has no idea who I am, and it might be awkward if she found out I lied. Fuck. *Awkward?* I feel like a shit bastard for lying. I told her I was a fucking banker.

But it's not too late to avoid her discovering the lie. I was counting on this being a one-and-done event, and it still can be. Although the thought of not repeating last night's explosive connection and supercharged sex is slightly depressing.

No, make that *extremely* depressing. But never mind that. I'm a big boy, and I'll get over it, right?

Bracing myself for the awkward morning departure, I sit up and touch her shoulder. The spark instantly strikes me to the core, bringing back every electrifying moment of last night's mind-blowing...*activity*.

She wakes while I dick around watching her. Her dark lashes flutter open, and her eyes flick back and forth. She looks disoriented. Pushing the hair from her face and running her hand through the wild mane, her eyes finally land on mine. She looks like an angel when she smiles at me.

I smile back. "Good morning."

She moves in my direction, and I feel her heat, the scent of our sex wafting up from the covers. What the hell was I worried about? What awkward? I fist a hand in her hair and touch my lips to hers.

"Ouch, damn it." She pulls back, bites her lip, and grimaces. And just like that, the promise of morning sex—not that I can afford the time—disappears. She turns her attention to her ankle, bending her leg and raising it to get a closer look.

"Shit. I forgot about your ankle. It still looks swollen. Is it sore?"

She nods, clearly in pain. The ice I'd put on it last night is lost in the covers and warm by now.

"I don't remember it hurting last night." She tosses me an accusing look.

"I'll get you a fresh ice pack."

She waves me off.

"I need to get out of here and get home."

"Guess it's not so good a morning." No need to worry about Rylee wanting to linger or having stars in her eyes. But then, why should she have stars since I made sure she doesn't know I'm a pro hockey player? *Maybe because the sex was fucking amazing.*

She rises and, fully naked, valiantly tries to saunter to the bathroom, but she collapses into a limp after one and a half steps. I get out of bed and go to her. She turns and looks at me with dismay, pointing at my thigh.

"Where'd you get those bruises? They're massive."

I look down. Shit. I took a check into the boards and a puck to the thigh in last night's game. But that's not something I can share with her. I shrug.

"I need to get to work myself," I half murmur and wave her forward. "You can take this shower. I'll use the guest bathroom." A pang of regret hits me at her reluctance to turn away. I watch her chew her bottom lip like she's deciding something. Stupidly, I'm hoping she'll invite me to join her.

You don't have time for this, and you don't need complications. Keep it simple.

She turns away and limps to the bathroom before my good sense slips, and I invite myself. Fuck.

Before closing the door, she asks, "Why are you going to work this early? I thought bankers had easy hours."

Fuck. "They do. We do. I have a project to work on." I find my boxers on the floor and put them on before she comments on my more than casual interest in playing games with her despite my work obligations. I hate lying, and it's obvious I suck at it. So why the hell did I tell her I was a banker, for fuck's sake?

She shakes her head in dismissal and closes the door. I pick up my sweats and T-shirt and head for the guest bathroom.

By the time I emerge, she's dressed and heading for the door.

"What about the ice? Let me get you an icepack for the road." I try to hide my totally inappropriate disappointment that she was going to leave without saying goodbye. So what?

Dude, you're never going to see her again, right?

"You really are a thoughtful guy under all that massive hotness." She smiles, and the edge comes off her words, prodding my morning wood back to life. Then she reaches for the doorknob.

"No goodbye?" I stop her. Why the fuck I do that is a mystery since I want her to leave, don't I? I'm not looking for drama.

She flashes a sassy smile and bodies up to me, wrapping her arms around my waist. "It was a swell night, big boy." She stands on tiptoe, and I meet her halfway for a final kiss. And for a second, I allow myself to dive into her, to savor the softness of her lips, the sultry heat of her mouth, and the unforgettable seductive scent of her skin.

A small moan escapes her as she pulls away, ending the kiss. "There's your goodbye. I'm out of here," she says as if she wants me to argue, so I do.

"Why? You have an early start to work?" She doesn't answer, and her dreamy smile disappears. It occurs to me that I don't know what she does. I know nothing about this girl, and my curiosity surges like I swallowed that cat who got killed by curiosity and reincarnated in my psyche.

"What do you do?"

Chapter 4

RYLEE

What do I do?

I hold my smirk a few beats longer than is natural, my mind immediately spinning for something to say. Not that it matters, does it? This was one night only. All I need to do is walk out this door, and I'll never see him again. Cue the disappointment surging from my pussy.

"I don't do anything. I'm independently wealthy."

He laughs like he thinks I'm kidding. "No, really, what's your job?"

"I don't have one. Really." *Inward cringe.* I open the door and step into the hallway, pulling the door closed behind me as I watch his gorgeous face puzzle up.

The latch clicks, and it's over.

Fuck. I turn away from his door as if the ornate, raised hardwood panels are frowning in accusation. I hate lying. That's why I feel so bad right now. *No job?* It's technically true. Being an Olympic snowboarder isn't really a job. I am independently wealthy—using the word *wealthy* very loosely. I have enough money from sponsors to live independently. Barely.

Letting him know the truth, that I'm on the Olympic snowboarding team, would have only complicated things because he knows about my ankle injury. Besides, we're not a thing. I don't owe him anything. I don't want to owe anyone anything. Especially not him. He could be dangerous.

Dangerous? Him? *WTF.*

Zak is history, and I'm counting on it. Though, according to my crying lady parts, it's a damn shame. He has a knockout face and killer body, and he knows how to use it. A combination I'm experienced enough to know doesn't come around very often. And he's truly a nice human being—the biggest rarity of all.

Limping to the elevator, with each step, I'm literally and painfully reminded about why I'm here in Boston. Not for fun and games and not for a vacation. Partly to see a doctor about the ankle, under the radar of the Olympic team, and especially without my coach finding out. And partly to see Mama Cass, to find out in person how bad she's gotten. Now that I know, getting her to see a doctor is even more important.

Inside the elevator, I hit the down arrow and lean against the back wall. When my plane got in last night, I thought it a grand idea to get some release and spend one night stress-free from Olympic and family pressures. But one night will have to do, and I'll have to finesse the fact that I didn't come straight home last night to Mama and Suzie.

THE SUN IS SHINING, and it's still early as I pull to the curb in front of the house with my rental car. I manage to wrangle my overnight bag out of the trunk and drag it up the crumbling walk of my old foster home in a neighborhood on the border between legit Southie and respectable—somewhere in no man's land.

The past year since I've been back hasn't improved the place any. The usual flaking paint is now peeling away in layers. The steps were crumbled at the edges, but now, half the second step is missing, and I need to be extra careful I don't make a wrong move and end up making my sore ankle worse. It's down to a manageable throbbing now, but I wish to hell I let Zak give me that ice pack.

Zak. I sigh as I reach the door. The guy gave me enough last night in the form of multiple orgasms and a trip to the light fantastic well past the last planet and beyond. He's a very generous and attentive man; I'll say that for him. But I doubt very much he's a banker. In my experience, bankers don't have thighs like that, bulging with muscle and covered in bruises.

Shaking my head—as if that'll dispel the memory of him any time soon—I push open the front door and call out. "Suzie? Mama Cass, I'm home. Where's the Olympic welcoming committee? I don't hear any marching bands." Instead, I hear a hoot in response as I walk through the living room to the kitchen, where I smell freshly brewed coffee, and the sudden craving makes my ankle pain disappear. Something about coming home warms a person, even when said home is turning into a shithole, when you remember it as a comfortable haven from the harsh world out there.

"There you are." Suzie meets me on the threshold with a hug and takes my bag from me, thank God. "For some reason, I thought you were arriving last night."

I shake my head, return her hug, then head straight for Mama. She's sitting in her rocking chair overlooking the window where the sunshine streams in every morning. The sparkle in her eyes hits me first, followed closely by the sparkle of the oversized rhinestone-studded glasses she always wears. She puts down her coffee and gives me a big hug as she stands. I hug her formidable form and notice it's shrunk since last time. Or is she shorter?

I can't stay away this long again. But I've said this to myself every year since I left when I was eighteen and she promised to keep my room waiting untouched for as long as I wanted it, even if I had gray hair like hers.

"Your hair is longer and wilder," Suzie says as she hands me a cup of coffee. "I like it. Matches your personality." She's as gorgeous and model-thin as ever. Her classic face reminds me of old-fashioned movie star's and even with her bushy blond hair up in a ponytail, she's a stunner.

"The hair is courtesy of an all-nighter," I say, though I don't specify that said night was spent in a bed with a man who could win the Olympics in the sex-stud event. He'd get my vote anyway. Or maybe it would be a pairs event, and I could volunteer to be his partner...

"Sight for sore eyes," Mama says. "Have a seat and tell us the behind-the-scenes details about the Olympic snowboarding team. How's Chuck treating you?"

The mention of *Chuck*, aka Charles Banner, the Olympic snowboard team coach and a former fling, makes me groan inwardly, but I maintain a smile and sip my coffee. I take the seat, grateful to be sitting and wish I could put my foot up, but I don't want to draw attention or let them know about the ankle injury. With any luck, it'll fade away quietly and quickly, and I won't ever need to mention it.

"This coffee is so good. I've missed your coffee, Mama."

"So, what's going on?" Mama asks.

"The usual. I was shooting a promotion not far from The USANA Center for Excellence in Park City, Utah, where the team trains, and I had a chance to take a break, so I took it. The promotion pays good money. Better than usual."

"Answer my question, Rylee. Why visit now? You should be training like the rest of your team. The Olympic games start in less than two months."

Shit, but she's a wary old lady. Then again, she has every reason to be since I'm hiding the truth from her, for her own good.

"I needed a break from Chuck. I didn't come home at Christmas, so he owed me." It's a partial truth. I did need a break from my ex. He was my ill-advised fling from the national snowboard team, now appointed as the Olympic team's coach. I've been trying to explain to him that we were never supposed to be serious every time he tries to *re-kindle,* as he puts it, but I haven't convinced him yet.

Not that he would do me any favors because no one went home for Christmas for more than two days. I used Mama's health as my excuse for this trip. I probably should have come home at Christmas, but I didn't want to spend the extra money to fly at the most expensive time of year for a two-day visit. Though as I breathe in the homemade bread scent of the kitchen, albeit laced with a trace of cigarette smoke despite the air filter, I admit to myself that facetime is no substitute for being home in person.

She nods her head, immediately sympathetic. She only met Chuck once last winter when we had an event in Vermont, and that's all it took for her to form her opinion. She's a good judge of character.

"Too bad he's your coach. It's a real shame you have to answer to a dirtbag like that."

"He's not a dirtbag." I don't know why I'm defending him. "He's mildly aggressive, is all." I grin. "Who can blame the guy for wanting me."

She laughs. So does Suzie. But Mama's laugh quickly devolves into a cough, and she reaches for her ever-present glass of water to wash it away. It takes a minute. Her eyes are bloodshot and watery when it's all said and done. Suzie takes the pack of cigarettes from the kitchen table and, because she's as tall as a willow tree, she reaches up and tosses the pack into the cabinet above the refrigerator.

Mama scoffs. "You think that'll stop me? I got a stepladder, you know."

"Don't you dare climb on a ladder. You'll fall and hurt yourself, and then you'll have to go to the hospital." Suzie knows the hospital is what the old woman is determined to avoid at all costs. She squints her eyes and shakes her head.

"No good kids," she grumbles. The familiar words make me smile.

"Speaking of boyfriends, how's yours?" I ask Suzie. "I'd like to meet him while I'm in town."

"His name is Ted. You'll love him. He's a perfect doll." She beams, and I wonder if it's another crush or for real this time. She was always the boy-crazy one. Not me. I could take them or leave them. Boys were fun, but I was serious—still am—about making cake and making a name, and living life to the absolute fullest on my own terms.

I didn't spend all these years training, albeit having the time of my life, so I could settle down and become someone's wife and have a bunch of kids. That's not me. I never had a conventional family—or if I did, it was so long ago it doesn't count—so I don't feel any need to have one in the future. *Why bother? I can barely handle the ties I have with the makeshift pseudo-family I have now.*

"Ted?" The coincidence hits me. "That's funny. I just met a guy named Ted last night." *What are the odds?* Not remote. It absolutely has to be a coincidence.

"Maybe it was him. We went out for dinner, and I went home early. He said he was going home early, too, but you never know. Where did you meet him?"

"None of your business—besides, it doesn't matter. It wasn't him." I'll never see him or his gorgeous roommate Zak again. Whipping myself out of any kind of wistful thinking, I straighten and flinch with the spike in my ankle pain and prepare to grill Suzie because it's what a big sister—foster or not—does. "Tell me about Ted."

"He plays hockey for the Boston Brawlers—he's a rookie and a hunk. I'm showing him Boston and a good time."

"Hockey player? Really? You know better than to tangle with pro athletes."

Suzie waves me off. "You're so paranoid about men."

"No, I'm not. I like men. In small doses. No need for entanglements. Especially not with the kind with egos and complicated lifestyles."

"You know what else pro athletes have?" Suzie says. "Muscles. Ted has a killer body, and he's not afraid to use it."

"Stop it right there," Mama says, albeit tongue in cheek because she's never been shy about sharing her impressive past exploits. We both laugh.

"I don't need the details. It's not good for my heart." She flutters her hands, with her mouth twisted in mock pursed lips.

I laugh, but then it occurs to me that she and her heart aren't getting any younger. "Wait—is there something wrong with your heart?" A stab of panic runs through me before I can stop it, and my heart races like she shot a starting gun.

"Nothing. Relax. Suzie's right. You are paranoid."

"Concerned." I calm myself and purge the ghost of tragedy and pain past. Focus on the here and now. I can handle this. In fact, this is the opening I needed to ask my next question. "Have you called the doctor for an appointment? For your cough?"

"Don't start that again. It's just an irritation. Only happens when I smoke."

"Have you cut back on smoking?"

"Some." She eyes the overfilled antique ashtray next to where the pack of cigarettes was on the table. So do I.

"Tell me about the guy you spent the night with rather than coming straight home to mama," she says, calling me out on my night of release. The tough old lady is hard to fool.

I shrug, letting her change the subject because I don't want to argue. I've missed her too much to waste the visit arguing. Besides, there'd be no point. Suzie and I will find a way to get her to the doctor, whether she wants to or not at some point in the next two weeks before I leave.

"One night and done. He was hot, though." More than hot. I suffer a rare pang that I won't see him again, but with Mama's health, this injury, and keeping Chuck and the Olympic officials ignorant about it, my life is already complicated enough. My phone pings as if I need a reminder. I know it's Coach Chuck texting me again. Guess he wasn't satisfied with my two-word response last night. *I'm fine.*

"Tell us about him," Suzie says. "What did he look like? What does he do? Is there any possibility of a repeat?" She lights up like the true optimist she is. Not that I'm a pessimist, but I don't believe in the happily-ever-after scene. I've been taught the ultimate lesson: that no relationship is forever, that one minute—one tragic minute—can end everything.

My mantra is live for today first and plan for tomorrow if you have a spare minute. And always live life to the fullest. Last night was living for the moment, one hundred percent living life to the fullest and turning up the dial on that. Today is about taking care of tomorrow—for Mama Cass's tomorrows.

"How long you staying? It can't be long at this point in the season with the Olympic games so close." Mama stares at me through her rhinestone-rimmed glasses that make her eyes look like giant bloodshot marbles.

Fuck. She knows I'm hiding something.

"A couple of weeks. Didn't you date a pro athlete once in your younger days? You have that photo of that hunky-looking football player on your bureau. When are you going to finally tell us what happened with him?" She's told us plenty about other men, but strangely not that one. One more reason that has me wary about pro athletes, even for a fling. As if I needed another reason in addition to Chuck of the massive ego who doesn't believe rejection is possible.

"It's pretty obvious nothing happened with him—nothing lasting. But for a few short weeks, we had a fling. The kind a lady never forgets—and never talks about. That's my secret memory I take out on cold gray days and run through my mind like my own private movie. Never fails to warm me up."

"Ooh, I bet he was hot. It's a shame it didn't work out, but it was his loss, Mama." Suzie reaches out and covers Mama's hand with hers. The contrast between the veiny, bony and wrinkled leather of Mama's hand and Suzie's smooth, creamy, and firm hand jars me. Shit. Mama *is* getting old. My heart goes into overdrive and not in a good way, *not like last night*. No, this is fear, stark terrifying fear, that Mama is in decline.

If I thought having my parents ripped away from me unexpectedly and swiftly as a child was a nightmare, right now, I'm wondering if it was any worse than the nightmare of watching the woman I've reluctantly grown to love and cherish like a parent, disintegrate slowly before my eyes. Fuck. Get yourself together. She can be fixed up. She's not that old. She's only in her sixties.

It's the cigarettes doing all the damage. And that has to change. Starting with getting her into a doctor for her cough. If we can get her into shape, she should last another twenty years.

Who knows? Maybe by then, I'll be ready to deal with...*whatever*.

"The problem with pro athletes, in my humble opinion," Mama says, "is that they're fickle. They are literally like kids in a candy store, and I was—like any one of us are—just one more candy bar."

"Come on now, Mama. They're not all like that," Suzie says. Of course. "Ted is super, and we have a thing going on. It could turn into a special thing."

My Suzie alarm goes off. How do people deal with big families? I have my hands and heart full worrying about just these two.

"You watch out, Suzie. Don't make any grand plans." I can't help my frown.

"I know, I know. It could all get ripped away." She touches my arm with her other hand and squeezes. "Don't worry, Rylee. I'm a big girl. I can take disappointment if it happens."

I want to say, *how would you know?* She's never been tested, not really. Not since she was four, and she barely remembers her life before coming to live with Mama. Doesn't remember the god-awful group home where I met her, thank fuck. We were only there for two weeks, but it was long enough for me to know two things.

First, Suzie was a beautiful little girl who would never last in that environment without getting abused. Second, we needed to get out fast. I was only nine but smart and hyper-aware despite the shock of losing my parents in a car accident the month before. Or maybe because of it. I was told the group home was a temporary place for me until they got me a foster home, and I was told by the angel who worked for social services that it wouldn't be long because I wasn't a so-called *problem child*.

In the group home, I learned what a problem child was. Learned that some of them were older and less child-like and nastier than I ever imagined people could be. I learned how to be tough in the short time I spent there, and my top priority was protecting Suzie from the older predators.

When Mama came along, I was skeptical at first. She'd only planned to take me. I hadn't realized that Suzie was one of those problem children. Her mother was a heroin addict. She wasn't dead, and Suzie had no father. You would never know it, so I took a chance.

I told my angel social worker that I wouldn't go with Mama Cass unless she took Suzie, too. Mama stood there and studied me. The social worker gently reminded me it wasn't up to me, but I met Mama's stare and tried to tell her without words that I meant business.

"Not technically," Mama had said to the social worker. "But the last thing we want is for Rylee to be a runaway." The social worker agreed.

"What do you want to do then?" the social worker asked.

"I'll take them both. Rylee and Suzie. They can be sisters."

The clamp that had been squeezing my chest ever since that day my parents disappeared from the world released then, and I

49

cried like a baby as I threw myself at Mama Cass and hugged her, holding on for dear life.

I sniff the memory away because it's foolish to go back, to remember any of it. Nothing but the good times should stay in your soul—according to Mama Cass. Words I try to live by except when my fear takes hold. It's trying to take hold right now, but I'm fighting like mad.

Mama coughs, and I almost lose my battle, but she quiets it with a sip from her ever-present glass of water. I exchange a glance with Suzie. Her mouth is a flat line. She looks as grim as I feel.

"I have to get going," she says, taking a donut from the box I brought in with me. "I have dance practice in an hour, and I need to warm up. Why don't you come with me to the Garden to watch?" she invites me out of nowhere. She's a dancer for Boston's NBA team, and they practice in a facility near the Garden where the pro basketball and hockey teams also practice.

"I suppose I've got nothing better to do." In reality, we need to talk and make a plan to get Mama to see a doctor. I grab a donut and take a bite.

"That's where I met Ted—at the practice facility. Maybe you can meet him. And one of his friends. There are all kinds of hunky athletes wandering around there. Who knows? Maybe you can find one to hook up with." She winks and bites into her donut. I almost swallow mine whole as I realize the chances of finding another Zak-like experience are slim to none. Not even in a locker room full of hockey players.

At least, I don't think so.... *no*. Pro athletes are against the rules for a good reason.

"I'll come with you to watch you dance. I'm really proud of you making it as a dancer for Boston's NBA team. I predict you'll start getting top modeling jobs soon."

"It's very competitive, but I'm having lots of fun. And wait until you meet—"

I raise a hand to stop her. "No flirting with the hunks for me. I told you. I'm serious about my rule against pro athletes."

"Not all of them are like Chuck. You could have a fling while you're here, then you'd have the perfect exit excuse."

"No thanks. Not even a fling. Too much ego and competitive testosterone."

"What are you talking about? You're a pro, and you don't have an ego."

"Male athletes tend to have easily bruised egos when their fling can beat them at miniature golf. And they're wicked competitive."

"You're right about the competitive part. You're pretty competitive yourself."

"True. One competitive person in a bed is enough. Besides, who has the time or energy for a fling? I'm busy enough doing my own thing." I expel a long breath in relief when I see her resigned eye-roll that this argument is going nowhere.

"What time is practice?" I ask her.

"We should leave in the next fifteen minutes."

"Good," Mama says. "I need to clean up around here."

I've been managing to hide my limp so far since I didn't see either of them last night, but it's throbbing now. When I got off the plane, I threw my gear into my rental car and drove around Boston until I found a place to park near a bar. It wasn't the first time I've given into my impulse for adventure. What luck that I ended up at the fucking Tea Party.

I'm not sure yet if it was good or bad luck, but I did work out my frustrations during the night with one hot man who was surprisingly skilled at turning me on. My sigh comes out of nowhere.

"Wait 'til I get back, and I'll help you, Mama," Suzie says.

Looking around, I snort. "This place needs more than any of us can do for it. When I get my promo money, we can get you new floors for the kitchen."

"And maybe some new windows?" Suzie says.

Shit. The place is falling apart. I nod.

"Save your money for yourself," Mama says. "I'm fine here." She reaches into her apron pocket and pulls out a fresh pack of cigarettes, and it takes every ounce of my restraint not to rip it from her hands. But I tried that once, and it didn't go well, so I learned not to make the same mistake. She needs to quit by her own choice. Suzie and I can't make her do it.

She lights it up and blows a stream of smoke that floats up in front of her face, blurring her kind, glassy eyes.

It's clear, Mama is sick and house is in dire need of repairs, inside and out. It's also clear that I need the money from that promotion and the others that will follow if—*when* I medal at the Olympics. I've been nervous that GNU, the snowboard company, will cancel me because of the injury. Despite the fact that I told them I was fine, they were there and they saw it happen, and they heard the emergency med tech say it could take up to eight weeks to heal.

I swore up and down my ankle was fine, that it only needed a couple of weeks rest. I made it clear I wanted to keep the whole incident low-key because there was no real injury. When the producer and the promotional rep from GNU left, I told the med tech I was headed to Boston. He discretely gave me the card of a doctor he knows at Mass General. That card is now burning a hole in my pocket like some kind of bad luck talisman.

When I called Tanya Lu, my agent, on my way to the airport last night, I told her about the injury and that I was going home to lie low. She agreed that would be best and that we'd say I was going home because Mama had a medical emergency. We further agreed on two weeks. I'm determined to return to the halfpipe at the end of two weeks.

Ready or not. Shit. I can't even let myself imagine anything but the most positive outcome.

I'll be fine. I'll be in the Olympics. I'll win a medal and cash in on millions in promotional deals. GNU got me at a bargain price compared to what Tanya said I'll be getting if—*when* I medal.

In the meantime, she said she'd hold off scheduling more promotions. I swore under my breath at that because I could use the money. A small budget endorsement for a brand was big money for me. However, I could hardly argue with her since I wasn't in shape to do another promotional shoot if it involved me getting on a snowboard. One fall, one slight twist of my already hurting ankle, and I'd be toast. Out of the Olympics. *Burnt toast.*

My career would be over, and I'd be relegated to a has-been, no longer invited to compete at international events, demoted back to a ski resort instructor making a paltry living. Fuck.

That was not going to happen to me.

But my call with Tanya Lu made me uneasy. It's like I don't trust her to keep my ankle quiet—*hell, no, I don't.*

I don't trust her. She's young and ambitious and always gives me the impression she has bigger fish to fry. Plus, she's convinced that my appearance is my best attribute as long as I make the Olympic team. She insisted it's a fact that pretty women can get lots of promotional opportunities whether they have gold medals or not.

I'm not so sure about that, or about her as an agent, but as a relatively unproven commodity, with only a year competing in the World Snowboarding Tour, I don't exactly have hordes of top agents knocking down my door to replace her. Luckily, she wasn't at the shoot and doesn't know I insisted on doing my own stunt work—namely jumping from the copter. She didn't see the fall and my ankle afterward. But I know her, and she's going to talk to Chuck eventually.

Thank God, the swelling is down compared to when it first happened. I frown and wave a waft of smoke from in front of my face. Mama turns on the television with the volume low, some re-run of an old cop show plays in the background.

Maybe I should thank Zak for taking such good care of me last night. Another sigh seeps from somewhere deep down. Too bad I can't thank him. Because I have no idea who he is or how to get in touch with him, short of driving to his building and asking security which unit Zak and Ted live in. I know their apartment is on a high floor, but there are a lot of floors in that luxury condo tower overlooking Boston Harbor. Come to think of it, he must have a lot of money to afford to live there, even with a roommate.

My phone pings again, and I glance at it. Another text from Coach Chuck. That was the tougher phone call I made last night. I told him the same story about needing to go home to see to Mama's health emergency. But since Coach and I were an item for a few weeks—three to be exact—two weeks and six days too long —he knows me and has it in his head that we still might have something despite my best efforts to convince him otherwise.

He grilled me about the promotional shoot. My agent—or I should say *our* agent because Tanya reps both of us—must have told him. The little traitor. I knew having the same agent as him would come back to bite me in the ass eventually.

Of course, Chuck didn't want me to do the shoot because he thought it was dangerous. I won't lie—the danger part was what excited me about it. I wanted to jump from the helicopter onto the slope. It was the coolest thing I've done yet. It got my adrenaline going like nothing else except hitting a misty flip—an off-axis backside flip with a 540-degree rotation and a late nose grab on a clean pipe. And that's saying something.

That sex last night was something, too—but no need to go there. *One and done.*

"Is that Coach Chucky calling?" Suzie asks. "You think it's an official call, or is he still trying to convince you to get back with him?" Suzie doesn't like Chuck, either. She probably has better instincts about people than I do, mainly because she tries harder, and I tend to keep people at arms-length. Which doesn't explain why I wanted to befriend Sheila last night, but I did. I give a mental shrug.

Mama takes a long puff on her cigarette, and I hold my breath to no avail. She coughs and then sucks in a ragged breath, launching her into a massive fit of rough coughing. I jump to my feet—big mistake because I almost scream with the shot of pain to my ankle. Shit. I go to Mama anyway and massage her back. Suzie puts the glass of water to her lips. Mama's hand is shaky, and when there's a break in her coughing, she manages a sip of water.

"That does it, Mama. You need to see a doctor." I squeeze her in a quick hug, my heart pounding as she settles down.

"I'm not going to the doc because it costs more than smoking cigarettes, and if I have a choice, I'd rather stick with a sure thing."

"That makes no sense." I contemplate giving her a pill and carrying her to the car, but even with Suzie's help, my bum ankle rules that option out.

"When are you going to see a doctor for your ankle?" she asks.

Fuck. Mama has me. I contemplate denial but don't bother because I need ice and limp back to my chair.

"Tomorrow." I haven't called yet. I toy with the card the med tech gave me, taking it from my pocket and barely resisting the urge to crush it and toss it. "I already know what he's going to say. Ice and elevation and rest for two weeks."

"Go today."

"You can swing by Mass General Medical Center after you watch some of my practice," Suzie says.

"What makes you think my doctor is there?"

"It's where all the best doctors are." She saw the card. The brat always had eagle eyes. I slip it back into my pocket.

"How'd it happen?" Mama asks.

"I refused to let the stunt double have all the fun jumping out of the copter." That's as much as I'm going to say about it, but Mama is used to my smart-aleck attitude.

She grunts. Suzie shakes her head.

"I'm fine." But as I glance around the place, I realize that maybe Mama isn't so fine. She coughs again. A swell of responsibility and guilt assaults me. Shit. I need that promotional money and a whole lot more. I can't lose my spot on the team because of this damn ankle.

"You're going to the doctor for that cough," I say to Mama. She scowls at me, but I'm not going to let it go this time. "I'm making you an appointment."

"Go for it." She looks me up and down from behind her rhinestone glasses. "I doubt you can carry me out of here while I'm kicking and screaming." She clears her throat. "And especially with that fucking sprained ankle of yours." She raises a brow in challenge and triumph.

Fuck. "Who says I have a sprained ankle? It's a minor twist. I'm resting it while I'm here."

"You sure you're not here because you need to rest it?"

Bam. She nails me. A flush of anger, mostly at myself because she's right and I should be ashamed, makes me repent. "I'm here for you more than my ankle." It's true now that I see her condition for myself.

Her face softens. "I know you are, Rylee girl."

"I have to get to practice." Suzie glances at the Felix cat on the wall next to the calendar. "Coming?"

Even though I should stay home and put my ankle up, how can I turn down the look on her face? Big brown eyes, perfect creamy skin, and classic features framed in the kind of golden blond mane of hair that movie stars pay big money for, make her an unlikely candidate as my sister. She's soft, and I'm angles—physically, emotionally, and every which way there is for a person to be. "Absolutely."

I grab my jacket, and we say goodbye to Mama.

"Good. You two get out of here so I can get some peace and quiet. I need a nap already from all your drama."

I laugh and give her an extra squeeze.

"I'll drive," I say because I know Suzie normally takes the subway to save on parking.

"You sure? I don't have a parking pass."

"I'll splurge."

IN THE CAR, I'm about to talk to her about Mama, but she beats me to the conversation starter punch. "Tell me all about the promo shoot, Ry. I'd give anything to be in a televised promotion. All I ever get is in-person events. I want to hear everything. I bet it was exciting."

"It's a small deal for GNU, a snow board company, but anything that pays in the thousands is big for me. I think they paid extra because it involved parachuting out of a helicopter."

"Oh my God. I thought you were kidding about that." She laughs. "But that didn't scare you I suppose."

I wince involuntarily. "About that. I wasn't supposed to do the ad until after the Olympics, but since I need money now, I might have begged Chuck to allow it."

"You got him to go along with it?"

"He made me promise to use a stunt double. But when I got there, I told the director I'd be doing the jump myself because I want to be authentic. I'm no pretender. So he went along with it. The guy was thrilled because he was all over getting a shot of me in the air. Turns out he's wicked into authenticity, too. And that's the stupid sad story about why and how I hurt my ankle, shooting a commercial while sky diving onto a slope.

"How bad is it?"

"The slope-side emergency med tech said my ankle could take anywhere from two to eight weeks to heal. He said I'd need an ultrasound to determine the severity. Nothing I didn't already figure. I called my agent, and she said she can fudge a two-week injury with the official line that I'm in Boston for personal reasons —for Mama's health."

The drive only takes ten minutes, and I park in the Garden

practice facility's garage. When I head to the elevator, Suzie takes my arm.

"This way." We go through a door and down a stairwell and end up walking through a maze of underground hallways. My ankle starts complaining and I wish I'd wrapped it in an ace bandage, but I don't want to make a big deal of it with Suzie and Mama. "This is the short cut to the dance studio where we practice. We share the facility with the basketball and hockey teams."

"So, this is how you met Ted? Wandering around the hallways looking for your studio?" She pretend-pushes me, but giggles all the same. She has no shame about her love of men, which is all well and good, except she romanticizes them. Me? I love them for who they are—a decidedly unromantic lot with tempting bodies and lots of exciting hormones.

"In fact, yes, it is how I met him. The practice rink is right around that corner." She points in the direction of a hallway, and smiling, because she's incorrigible, I glance that way. There's a sign with an arrow that says *Brawlers Training Room* bolted to the cement wall.

And just beyond the sign, appearing from around the corner, a very large man dressed in a hockey uniform steps out, heading our way. I stop short to avoid colliding.

Then I look up.

And I almost run smack into my hunky dream from last night, standing real as day, tall on his skates and staring down at me. *Zak.* The so-called banker.

He's a fucking professional hockey player. And a liar.

Chapter 5

ZAK

W*hat the actual fuck? It's her.*
"What are you doing here?" Rylee asks, and I wonder if my sick imagination conjured her up because flickers of last night interrupted my flow all through the morning skate.

"What?" *Shit.* I'm holding a fucking hockey stick, caught red-handed as *not* a banker. I can't keep up the lie, but I'm not up for a messy explanation in the hallway near the locker rooms with my teammates lurking around either. So, I punt.

"I'm looking for the equipment manager. What the hell are you doing here?" I flick a look at her friend, and she looks familiar. Then I snap my fingers. "You're Nowicki's latest... You're with Nowicki, right?" Shit. I hate awkward scenes with women, especially women I don't know.

The short blond girl rolls her eyes. "Yes, I'm with Nowicki. We're actually dating if you want to know the truth. You're his roommate, right?"

Rylee stares at her friend in disbelief. "Of all the bars and all the hookups..." she mutters, then looks my way, folding her arms and looking like she'll wait all day for an explanation.

I shrug. "I'm a hockey player. For the Brawlers. Not a banker."

"I got that. Any reason you lied to me?"

"Probably the same reason you lied to me." I'm betting she's not an independently wealthy socialite and wondering what the hell she has to hide.

"So you two...hooked up?" Suzie starts laughing, and her laugh gains momentum.

After a few beats, Rylee smacks her on the back. "Calm down, Suzie. It's not that funny."

"Yes. It is. Especially after you—"

"Never mind." Rylee shoots her friend a glare, the kind with edge. And I'd be lying if I said I wasn't a little turned on. It's a different kind of edge than she had last night, but it reminds me.

Suzie pulls her phone from her pocket and reads a text. "It's Nowicki. We're going out tonight after the game." She looks up and winks at me. "We'll be out all night."

"Congratulations," Rylee says, re-folding her arms and standing with all her weight on one foot.

"Perfect," I say to Rylee, and her gaze grabs hold of me, bringing back every electrifying shot from last night. "How about if I get you a ticket to the game, and you stay over tonight?"

She turns her attention to me, her mouth opens, then shuts, wearing an expression like she thinks I escaped from the nearest alien spaceship.

My invitation hangs in the loaded air between us for an uncomfortable beat as my dick hardens, and I start to wonder what the fuck possessed me to invite her back. Especially now that she knows who I am.

Maybe it's because she was so thoroughly unimpressed to find out I'm a hockey player. In fact, she looks pissed and about to shut me down. Her frown signals rejection, and I should cut my losses, and walk away, but no. I see red like the proverbial bull. She may as well have slapped my face with the white glove of challenge. I smile.

Since when am I a glutton for punishment? Since when do I go after the girl who plays hard to get? I'm an easy-going guy, all about the easy-going non-relationships with women. I don't chase or beg or even take chances. Hockey is the challenge in my life; the rest of it is reserved for fun and games.

Not about trying to score a woman who lied to me, especially not for a second round. That spells complicated.

The opposite of what I need.

But apparently my dick brain doesn't care what the rest of me needs, and it has taken control. *I've fucking turned into an adolescent dick brain with something to prove.*

Chapter 6

RYLEE

Having a two-week fling with Zak while I'm recuperating tempts me far more than it should. But he's a liar, isn't he? He told me he was a banker. The bastard didn't want me to know he was a pro hockey player.

Of course, by that standard, I'm a liar, too. Because I didn't want him to know I'm an Olympic snowboarder. Still don't. I blurt out the excuse I've been using for every lie I've been telling, and they're piling up.

"What about Mama Cass?" I ask Suzie, ignoring the big guy and his compelling presence as best I can.

"I'll have the grump from next door come over and stay with her," Suzie says. "She'll be fine for one night."

"Mama Cass? Like from the Mamas and the Pappas? I thought she was dead?" Zak says.

"Right. We bought a stuffed version of her from a shop in Hollywood and keep her in our living room for fun," I dead pan.

His breaks into a grin, and Suzie pulls on my arm like she always did to get me to stop toying with people.

"She's our mama. Her name is Cassandra Mooney, but she

loved the Mamas and the Pappas—she was a regular flower child type. So, she loved being called Mama Cass, and it stuck."

"Cool. *Monday, Monday* is my favorite of theirs. My mom always had them playing on her CD player in an endless loop."

"You're a regular throwback," I say. Scanning him from head to foot and back to his long unruly, touchable hair, my belly flutters like a flirty cartoon character batting her eyelashes. "Come to think of it, you kind of look like you'd be a hippie if you weren't a hockey player."

He throws back his head and laughs. "Not me. My—" He stops talking abruptly and turns away. "Nope. Not even close. I was a gym rat and a rink rat all my life."

I lock on his face to distract myself from the sheer size and buffness of him, and my memories of last night. "I can see that. Good for you."

"You appreciate what you see? We can arrange for more of that —after the game."

I keep my mouth shut and flat, no smiling from me, no flirting. But I'm so damn tempted.

"You're not going to turn him down, are you?" Suzie is nearly incredulous, but keeps her voice within the polite range.

Her watch alarm goes off, saving me—saving us all.

"I have to get to dance practice. Talk later," she says over her shoulder as she takes off without me down the hallway.

My personal temptation with the killer body and some kind of irresistible sex aura takes a step closer until the pungent smell of his hockey uniform invades my nostrils. The scent should totally turn me off and have me running the other way, but it doesn't. Oh no, that manly scent is like catnip to my nose and has me leaning in. I'm a sicko.

"I should go too," I murmur.

"What are you afraid of?" he says like it's a dare.

That hits me in my Achilles heel hard and I toss back my hair. "What about my ankle?"

"What about it?"

"I need to keep off it."

"I'm not asking you to dance, honey."

I can't help the twitch in the corner of my mouth before I narrow my eyes at him. "Getting around in a hockey arena would be a bitch."

"I'll get you seats in a box with an elevator. No stairs."

"Everyone in the box will assume we're... something we're not."

"I'll tell them you're my sister."

"Something I'm not," I say sarcastically. "You have a sister no one's met?"

"As a matter of fact, I have three. No one's met the youngest. She just got out of high school."

I snort. "I'll be sure to wear my knee socks and put my hair in braids."

He eyes me like he likes the idea.

"You're not into dressing up and role-playing, are you?" I ask.

"What if I am?" he says without inflection, and I can't tell if he's joking or serious.

"A girl likes to come prepared is all."

He snorts, shaking his head, and I know he's joking. "You talk big, but are you going to show up?"

"Okay, you're on, big guy. Not for the sister act." I pause to catch my breath which seems to be in short supply in his presence. "I'm not afraid of another night with you. But I have some rules. First, I'm not going to your game."

Chapter 7

ZAK

"No game, no hook up," I say without thinking, as if it was a rule of my own. *Rule?* I have no fucking rules. But I do have some pride, and I'm fucking proud of playing hockey.

"Second, no feelings," she says, ignoring my rule completely.

Wow. It's like she stole my lines from the bachelor hook-up script. I should be thrilled. I am thrilled. Right?

"Like what kind of feelings? Give me an example?" Why the fuck did I bother asking? Who cares, right?

"No crying and no declarations of love—"

"Wait—you've had guys cry after hooking up with you?"

"No. They cry when I'm done hooking up with them."

Trying not to laugh, I stare her down, and she rolls her eyes. I don't even have to call her on her exaggeration before she confesses.

"Okay, so maybe it was only one guy, and maybe he didn't exactly cry, but he did tear up."

Now, I laugh. She's trying so hard to act tough, but for once I keep my mouth shut, and I don't ask her flat out why. And it's hard because I'd love nothing more than to spar with her, to give her a hard time even though she pretends she's the one giving me a hard time.

"Seriously. No drama allowed." She throws her hands on her hips and shoots fairy sparks from her eyes.

Raising my hands like I'm giving up, I say, "No drama from me. I'm cool with your rules if you're cool with mine." I fold my arms across my chest and watch her calculate how much she wants to hook up with me. And fuck if I haven't been this turned on by a woman in a long time.

I haven't had to work this hard to convince a woman in a long time. Never found it worth the bother. Until now.

She nods, and my dick wants to tear through my pants and hug her. I tighten my arms in place. "Anything else?" I'm almost hoping for more because negotiating with her is a better aphrodisiac than the best porn.

"One more." She looks me up and down.

"No seeing each other in public. No going out after the game. We go straight to your place."

"Oookay. So... What? I'm your dirty little secret?" Why do I feel excited yet offended at the same time?

"Think of it as being discrete. I don't want public drama with a..." she flicks her hand in my direction, "a professional athlete."

"I see. I should be offended, but I'm chalking it up to the idea that you're one eccentric chick." I say the words, and I should mean them. It's an odd request, and I should be jumping for joy because she's not a social climber using me, or a groupie looking for a notch in her bedpost or looking for stolen fame with a famous athlete in a viral video. Not that any of those things ever bothered me too much before, because I'm proud of being a famous athlete. But it does get old. I'm more than that, right?

And yet, there's something about her request that feels like a grain of sand in my sneaker. It shouldn't bother me, it's too small, but I know it's there, and it bothers me.

"In fact, I need some kind of cover—something believable, not that I'm your little high school sister—so the people in the box won't think we're together."

"What the fuck? You're serious? Like what? Aren't you being paranoid about what people might think?"

"Those are the rules, big guy. You want to find out exactly how much chemistry we have, you need to play by the rules."

"Oh, I know we have a fuck-load of chemistry. What makes you think I'll put up with a charade to sleep with you, when I could get any one of the groupies at the Tea Party—"

"You mean like Sheila?"

Jealousy sparks from her like she's a live wire and someone just flipped her switch—that someone would be me. She ignites my dick with those eyes. No surprise. Then she turns away to hide her emotional fireworks. The squeeze of excitement in my chest surprises me. Either way, I'm on board.

"Yeah. I like Sheila. Why? Does that bother you?"

She tries to laugh. "No. Why should it? Besides, Sheila is too good for you. She's not interested in seconds."

I step closer. "How about if Sheila is our cover? You're with her, and you're... a friend, a groupie."

Chapter 8

RYLEE

"A groupie?" I snort. "How is that a cover?" I step backwards as he gets close, and his scent makes my heart hammer. Good sense shouts at me to stop considering the idea, to back away from the danger of this highly flammable man. I'm supposed to be hiding out. But that fucking adventure-seeking part of me—because I refuse to call it risk taking like Mama Cass does—rises up to taunt me with the possibility of a secret fling and all that titillating adrenaline.

"No one will think we're *something we're not*. No one will think you're anything more than an acquaintance."

What he's saying is true, and I can't help feeling the sting on behalf of Sheila. Except, Sheila doesn't seem to care. She seems perfectly happy to have fun, and so should I because that's all this is about. A fun distraction while I hide in plain sight and heal without anyone in my world knowing there's a thing wrong.

My ankle disagrees loudly as I shift my weight. At least I hope there's nothing wrong. It's a damn twisted ankle is all. I'll go home and put it up with ice for the rest of the day.

"Fine," I say. "I have to go."

His already sizzling smile goes up a hundred watts, and I frown deeper in defense.

"I'll arrange two seats in the executive suite for you and Sheila. Check with the 'will call' window." The second his arm reaches out for me, I jerk away and start walking. I wish I could say I walked quickly, or even with dignity, but my bastard ankle fails me, and I feel every bit of the sharp pain that forces my limp.

"Put that foot up and ice it, Rylee," he calls after me. "Wouldn't want you to be hurting tonight."

I don't bother turning back or saying a word to him as I walk down the hall to find a different elevator, damn him. I raise my hand with a single finger showing. You can guess which one.

And yes, the bastard laughs. *And fuck yes, the sound gives me goosebumps*

ON THE WAY HOME, I order Uber Eats for lunch for me and Mama C. I'm not sure she'll thank me since it's not her usual KFC or BK style food. I haven't eaten that shit since high school when I started training seriously. All my competitors were into eating healthy, and I'd be damned if I was going to let any of them get an edge on me.

Now, it's part of life. Like boarding, the halfpipe, jumping, and snow. Fuck if I don't miss it already as I stumble inside the back door, not bothering to hide the sting in my ankle this time.

"Welcome back. You gonna make it, Rylee girl?" Mama C gets up from her rocker on the forward swing and goes to the freezer. I'm tempted to take her place in the rocker, but she's earned the most comfortable seat in the house. Instead, I sit in a wooden kitchen chair and lift my foot up onto the table.

She hands me the ice pack and takes a look at the ankle.

"You call the doc yet for that? It doesn't look better. It looks worse. I can dig out some old crutches—"

"No crutches." That's all I'd need is for someone to recognize me walking around on crutches tonight. One more reason I shouldn't go. But that horse is out of the barn, and my anticipation is already well on its way to heaven.

"Call the doctor," she says.

"You call the doctor," I say, and we have a showdown of stubborn staring. Unfortunately, I have a feeling I know where it's going to lead. Tit for tat.

She doesn't blink from behind those oversized glasses. My chest tightens. Her cough is quiet for the moment, and the ashtray is empty. Fuck.

I slap the ice on my ankle and give in. "You win. I'll call and make a doctor appointment right now. One for each of us."

She nods and sits back in her rocker, her gaze still on me. "Go ahead. I'm watching you."

Taking in a deep breath, I pull out the bent card for the doc and my phone. I tap the number in and listen to the ringing as my heart rate spikes. I do not want any bad news. After a few rings, a voice comes on that the office is closed and to call back during regular office hours. While the voice drones on about the hours, relief fills me like I've just landed my first trick of the day.

Taking advantage of the reprieve, I talk into the phone as if I've confirmed my appointment and then disconnect. I glance at Mama C, and she nods. Without wasting a second, I search my contacts for her doctor's name and tap it on. Luckily, the receptionist answers, and the appointment I make for Mama C is for real.

With business taken care of, I force myself to rest the ankle and catch up with Mama C and the neighborhood. Mostly, she talks about the grump next door, Mr. Argyle. I haven't seen him in a couple of years.

"We watched you on TV. It was the qualifying rounds I think," she says. "He's impressed and worried for you going so high in the air like that. I told him you can take care of yourself. You always could."

"Thank you, Mama." It's true, and I'm truly relieved to hear her say it because I don't want her to worry.

After lunch is delivered and I suffer two more rounds with the ice pack, my ankle feels better. The swelling is down. Two weeks—or rather one week and six days—and I'll be fine. Mama clears the table, and my phone pings. Again.

"What's with your phone? Aren't you going to answer all that pinging?"

I check the phone. Another text from coach Chuck. Without bothering to read it, I ignore it same as the last two. The text from Tanya Lu, my agent, is tougher to ignore, giving me a pang of something, a tightness in my chest, but I ignore it just the same because I'm determined to be here for Mama Cass just as I planned to be, and to see to her health.

At least she had the good grace—or good sense—not to smoke for the past couple of hours in my presence.

The house phone rings, startling me. "It's been a while since I heard a house phone."

"Works the same as always." She puts some things in the dishwasher. I should be the one doing the work, but my foot is still up, and I know I need to stay off it. I know she'll yell at me if I don't.

"Aren't you going to answer it?" I tease her.

"Why should I? It's only the grump next door checking on me. He had the nerve to call earlier to ask me about the strange rental car out front. I told him it was you. Not that it's any of his business. Now, he probably wants to come over to fawn all over you and get your autograph."

I laugh. "So, let him."

She swats the air with her hand. "I'm keeping you all to myself this visit. Who knows when—" She cuts herself off and hands me a fresh bottle of water.

"What?"

"Never mind. I'm so proud of you, Rylee girl. If all I saw of you was watching you win snowboard competitions on TV for the rest of my life, I'd be perfectly happy."

"You'll get more than that. I'll be home in the early summer between circuits. It's just that this past year was an Olympic training year, and I had to—"

"I told you how proud I am. I wouldn't want you to do anything differently."

Shit. I can't go tonight. I need to stay home and spend the night with Mama. But I don't have either Sheila or Zak's number to let them know. Shit. Fuck it. I don't owe them anything. Not really. Do I? So what if I don't show up? It was only supposed to ever be a one-night thing.

I watch Mama mix a meatloaf, giving me the play-by-play of the ingredients like she's doing a cooking show when Suzie comes in the back door.

"So, did you agree to the date tonight?" She doesn't even take off her coat before she asks me. Mama stops what she's doing and runs an accusing look through me like a dagger.

"You been holding out on me, Rylee girl? You got a hot date tonight?"

"No."

"You turned down the hottest bachelor in Boston?" Suzie says laughing and shrugging out of her coat as she shoves her duffel and coat in a closet.

"He'll get over it," I mutter. Shame makes me feel like I'm sitting on a literal hot seat. It's one thing lying to strangers, but I don't lie to my family. These two people are the only ones who mean everything in the world to me, and I've already fibbed to Mama about my doctor's appointment, and now I'm not being straight about my so-called date with Zak.

Suzie shakes her head. "You're crazy. I don't see the harm in having some fun with the guy."

"What she said," Mama says.

"I'm here to visit you guys, not have fun."

Suzie's eyebrows rise. "Nice."

I scowl. "You know what I mean."

"I insist you go out with this hot guy," Mama says. "It'll do you good. Make you forget the ankle. Just stay off your feet." She pauses and points her finger at me. "Just stay clear of any whiff of commitment. You remember you're an independent woman."

I snort a laugh. "It's only a night out, Mama. No worries."

"So, you're going, then?" Suzie says. "I'm going to the game, too. Nowicki gave me a ticket."

"Terrific. You going out after the game?"

She nods. "We're going to dinner and staying at the Bostonian for the night."

Mama shakes her head. "You watch out for this Nowicki fella. He's only a rookie and unreliable. Too young and unproven."

"What is that supposed to mean?" Suzie says.

"You need someone who can take good care of you—in case this dancing and modeling doesn't work out for you."

"Since when do I need a caretaker and Rylee doesn't?"

"Since forever," Mama says.

I see the hesitation on Suzie's face. "You'll be fine, Suzie. Mama just worries."

Suzie slides me an uneasy glance as she paces a circle. "The thing is," she says, "I worry, too. Maybe I should go after a more reliable career."

"Either you need a reliable way to make money or a reliable man," Mama says. "Though you could make the argument they're the same thing."

I laugh. Suzie tries not to, then she bursts into a grin.

"You're forever the practical one, Mama." She leans in and hugs the old woman, and I stand to join them and make it a three-way hug. This is something we used to do all the time. The tug in my chest literally feels like my heart's being ripped loose, and I straighten. Mama breaks the hug when she coughs. I hand her a water and sit back down with my foot up again. One last round of ice while I watch her get the cough under control.

"I don't know about you, but I'm going the independent route," I say to Suzie. "I'm going to make it on my own and be one hundred percent fully in charge of my own life." I pause. Suzie gives me a pensive look. "I think it's easier and a hell of a lot safer," I add.

"Maybe," Suzie says. "But it sounds a hell of a lot lonelier, and I'm too much of a romantic for that." She shrugs.

"So, tell me about this hot date," Mama says.

"He's a professional hockey player," Suzie says, laughing at my expense.

Her gaze swings to me. "So now, you decided you can handle a professional athlete after all?"

"It's only for two weeks. What could go wrong?"

Mama snorts. "Nothing, as long as you stay off your ankle."

Suzie giggles. "She won't be doing much standing tonight, Mama."

"Okay—I don't need the details about what you're doing, but tell me something about the man. He's not the kind to hold you back, is he?"

"There doesn't exist the kind of man who can hold me back, Mama."

She smiles and nods her approval, and I take that cue to go get ready. I head to the room I shared with Suzie growing up. Two twin beds, one small dresser, and a small closet for both of us. I never minded the cramped conditions, and for a while after I left, I missed the closeness. Now, all I have is the few items of clothes in my overnight bag and a few personal items to call my own, and Suzie has taken up all the space in the room, including under both beds, to store her things.

As I rummage through the bag, which takes thirty seconds, I wish I had something to impress Zak. This is the first time I've ever worried about impressing a man, aside from competition judges. I don't worry about impressing anyone. Shit.

Don't lose your mojo now, Rylee. Of course not. It's the damn ankle injury cutting into my self-confidence. I toss the bag aside and head for the shower, minor wobble shaken off.

After all, it's not like I'll be wearing my clothes for long tonight.

Chapter 9

RYLEE

"Have you been in the executive suite before?" Sheila asks me in a jittery voice.

"No, but I'm not afraid of fancy."

She looks me over with her brow arched. I'm wearing jeans, an alpine wool sweater, and my sturdiest lightweight hiking boots—courtesy of Moon Boot, an Italian snow boot and après ski wear brand. They generously outfitted the entire U.S. ski and snow-board teams in anticipation of the upcoming Olympics in Italy. The boots are comfortable and help support my ankle while hiding the ace bandage I have wrapped around it.

I push open the door to the suite since Sheila is reluctant and walk inside, keeping low-key without compromising my self-respect. My usual M.O. I don't hide in corners, but I don't make a spectacle. The people who need to find me seem to find me—like coaches, scouts, and promotors. Mostly, my performance in the halfpipe and the jump get me all the notice I need even though I was late to the party, not getting my start with the real competition until I was seventeen because I lived in the city and not the mountains.

But I've caught up since then, boarding five out of seven days a week, weight training, and practicing with my high school gymnastics team on their skill cushions and practice mats, tumbling and practicing my landings mostly off the vault to simulate the air and get my body movements in synch.

Now, I'm known for my exceptional body control in doing my tricks off the halfpipe and big air jumps. The poor high school gymnastics coach begged me to switch to gymnastics from boarding, but I'll take the wildness of the mountain and the big outdoors over the confines of a gym. Plus, I felt sorry for the gymnasts because of the excessive attention to body size they put up with.

Eyes are on us now, and I crack a Mona Lisa type smile, not too enthusiastic, but enough so you can't complain that I'm unfriendly.

"Ladies." A man nods. "Welcome. I understand you're guests of Mr. Tomas."

Sheila bobs her head as she squeezes my arm.

"Don't mind us. We'll just take our seats over here," I say. I flash my smile wider to lessen the blow that I want nothing to do with them, especially a conversation about how we know *Mr. Tomas.* A woman wraps her arm around the older man, steering his attention away from us, and she's my new angel.

Sheila takes a seat next to me after helping herself to a pile of food and drinks that she brings with her.

"Don't you want something to drink?"

"No." I stop myself from saying that I don't even really want to be here at all, but the Zambonis finally leave the rink, and that must be a cue of some sort because Brawlers players shoot out of the gate onto the ice with surprising speed. They glide around the rink one after the other while the fans cheer. My gut tumbles as if I care when I spot Zak, number eight.

When he stops near the goal and tilts his helmet back from his face to glance in our direction, it's my heart that tumbles next like a domino. For no good reason.

"There's Zak," Sheila says, waving as if he can see us.

Who knows? Maybe he can. The thought makes me stiffen as I keep my hands in my lap even as my eyes stay pinned to him.

She nudges me with her elbow. "I wonder if he can see us. This is exciting. These seats are awesome. This box is rad-iculous. I hope they win. I hope Zak scores a goal. Do you think he'll take us out somewhere fancy after the game? I was so surprised to get his text about the tickets. I wasn't surprised that he gave one to you—"

"Wow, woah, there Sheila. Slow down. Did you swallow a fast-talking auctioneer before you came tonight?"

She laughs. "No, but I wouldn't mind swallowing—"

"Never mind. I don't want to know."

She nudges me again. "You must have had a good time with Zak the other night." She wiggles her brows, aiming an expectant glance at me.

I nod. I'm not a kiss and tell type. But oddly, I like Sheila. She's cool in a very uncool way, raw and full of enthusiasm. She watches me, still waiting for me to elaborate.

"What?" I say, turning my eyes back to the ice, I can't keep my eyes off him because I feel this unbroken invisible thread keeping us connected. The tug of that same connection I've felt since I first sat on his lap tethers me to him now, and I wonder how or why.

Then I force myself to look away when Sheila sighs.

"Guess you're not going to talk details, are you?"

"No. But then, you already have your own first-hand experi-ence, so there's no need."

"Not exactly," she says slowly. Surprise lifts my brows, quickly followed by skepticism. She goes on. "I went home with him once a while back, and we tumbled around a little, but as soon as he real-ized I was a little more than tipsy, he refused to do anything but give me coffee and a cab ride home. I wish I remembered more details, but the night's a little fuzzy."

"Gotcha." What I got from her words is that Zak Tomas is an honorable guy. *The bastard*. I'm not interested in anything but his body. And maybe his sense of humor. I could care less that he's honorable…except that it's good to know he won't try to take advantage of me—I say *try* because that would never happen. I would never let it happen because I'm always in control.

One hundred percent in control. At all times… Sort of. The exception is when he has me exactly at that moment of release…

The horn blows, grabbing my attention as the teams file off the ice to the bench while the Zambonis return for a quick run around, and then the players line up at center ice for the national anthem. From that moment, with my eyes trained on Zak lined up on the Brawlers blue line, the column of nerves along my spine trills a warning before I clamp down.

The puck drops, and Sheila watches the game like a cheerleader, arms pumping, shouting and jumping from her seat with frequency. The rest of the room doesn't match her enthusiasm, but they're far from quiet. In fact, I'm the anomaly.

Aside from the fact that I'm the only one not wearing team gear, I'm also the only one who did not jump from my seat when Zak scored both the first and last goal of the game, giving the Brawlers a three-to-one win. I'd blame it on my ankle, but I'm not the jump up and fist pump kind of girl.

There's a reason I was never a cheerleader. It's called the stark reality of my past instilling too much wariness to allow enthusiasm to get a foothold.

When the final horn blows, Sheila gives me a hug, and I roll my eyes. Some of the others in the box turn their attention to the large screen TV which has been on in the background. They turn up the sound.

"Let's watch the post-game interviews," Sheila says.

I shrug. "Why not?" I have a half hour to wait for Zak now, and then I'm supposed to take the elevator down to the basement to meet him somewhere outside the locker room.

The others from the box, whose names I've already forgotten, watch as the sportscaster introduces Zak.

"He's on fire as a defenseman scoring two goals in one game."

"The second goal was an empty netter. It doesn't count," Zak says, his half grin showing one sexy dimple.

I stop moving and try not to stare too hard.

"That killer slap shot from the blueline certainly counts. It was extraordinarily accurate," the sportscaster says.

"I practice. A lot." Zak expands his grin, looking straight into the camera, and I take in his face, the sweat trickling down his temples, his hair disheveled as he swings it back, the bulge of his Adam's apple as it bobs when he takes a gulp from his water bottle, and I hope to God from her close proximity next to me that Sheila doesn't notice the rise in my body temperature.

After smiling at Zak's modest response, the sportscaster continues. "Some say your slap shot is reminiscent of Bobby Hull's. That you're a lot like Hull only bigger and a defenseman." The man shoves the microphone back in Zak's face.

He laughs. "You mean, I'm nothing like Bobby Hull."

"Except for the killer slap shot."

Zak looks pleased and embarrassed at the same time, and I'm mesmerized. "This guy is wicked authentic, wearing it all on his sleeve," I whisper to Sheila.

"That's Zak," she says.

I glance her way. "Hey, you're not really into him, right?"

"Of course not. He's all yours."

"That's not how it is." I continue to whisper even as some of the other patrons drift away from the TV and start putting on their coats.

"Then how is it, Rylee? Because I've never seen him go to so much trouble over a girl before."

"And?"

"And I wouldn't want you to hurt him—"

"Hurt him? How? He's impervious. All he wants is a good time. Believe me." I turn away from Sheila and watch the sportscaster move on to interview someone else. Exhaling, I loosen up.

"I suppose you're right," Sheila says. "How's your ankle holding up? You never did say how it happened."

The son of a bitch is throbbing. I should have put it up, but no way I'm admitting to that. I have eight days for it to heal enough to snowboard. Shit. I might need a shot of cortisone.

"It's fine. I told you I twisted it jumping out of a helicopter."

She laughs, clearly not believing me, as I knew she wouldn't. Someone turns off the TV, and the consensus in the room is that it's time to leave. We exchange polite murmurs about the great game, and I walk without the limp, feeling every ounce of pressure I put on it as we file into the elevator.

Following the crowd, we meet Zak downstairs outside the locker room. He hugs Sheila like an old friend. He winks at me. I stand out of reach with my ball cap pulled down, wishing it didn't have a Burton logo. Who wears a ski and board brand to a hockey game?

"Let's get out of here before another reporter gets to me," Zak says under his breath.

I back up another step before he snags me, leveling a warning look at him. He smirks and walks away. Sheila and I follow him to the parking garage exit at a plausible distance. If Sheila thinks it odd, she doesn't say, but it's obvious I don't want to be seen with him. I can't tell her it's because I don't want to be noticed at all by the media, hat or no hat. She walks slowly, considerate of my ankle.

"You're a skittish one, aren't you?" she says. "Camera shy?"

"You have no idea."

She nods her head knowingly when she doesn't truly know a thing. And I need to keep it that way, though for some reason I feel a twinge of something for being so closed. Internally, I snort since I'm always closed, and this is nothing new. It's how I live my life. It's who I am. I keep to myself and conduct the business of my life.

Maybe someday, I'll be able to afford the luxury of normal friendships. In the meantime, I have my family and my teammates, competitive peers and business partners, which are more than enough relationships to handle.

Talk about the details of the game dominates the ride home, and I don't contribute much more than a nod here and there. However, Zak is so animated and full of life—and likely leftover adrenaline—as he talks, that I doubt he notices.

I know what he's feeling. I feel the same high I feel after I nail a halfpipe run or a big air jump. Only difference is, I channel my energy differently than he does. Sure, I hug teammates and celebrate with my coach. Maybe that's what got me into trouble with Chuck. I was vulnerable to him mistaking my post-trick high as genuine enthusiasm for a relationship with him.

Once Zak drops Sheila off at her house in Revere, I turn the radio on to fill the silence as we drive back into the city to the parking garage at his place.

He jumps out of the SUV, and as I'm opening my door, he comes around and helps me from the car to a soft landing.

"Well, aren't you the gentleman."

"I try. Don't sound so surprised."

"I shouldn't be, since you've been so good about tending to my ankle, but I find it best to keep my expectations low." I don't mention that they're especially low when it comes to pro athletes who are more used to others giving them deferential treatment. I promise myself again that no matter what achievements, how much fame or how much money I make, that I'll never turn into the kind of person who takes people for granted. Like Chuck, among others.

"Normally, I'd agree that's a wise policy." He wraps an arm around my shoulders and walks me toward the nearby elevator.

"I sense a but..."

"But I'm going to prove to be the exception to the rule, so be prepared to change your mind." He flips the cap off my head and lowers his mouth to mine as we reach the glass-enclosed mini-lobby of the building.

Surprise ignites the dormant flame that's been kindling ever since I woke up this morning and saw his face, felt his warmth, and not to mention the hard-as-fuck boner he had waiting for me. He devours my mouth like he's hungry, and I'm on his menu for dessert. I return his enthusiasm, exploring everywhere my tongue can reach, sucking and nibbling and trying to get as much of that intoxicating taste of him as I can. He's minty and salty and earthy, and the sensual fullness of his lips drives me crazy.

The elevator doors slide open, startling me into my senses, and I jump away. He quietly chuckles, shielding me from view of whoever it is who got off the elevator and discretely walked in the other direction.

"We should go upstairs…" His coarse voice and hot breath on my neck ripples across my nerve endings, and I shudder. He puts the cap back on my head and chuckles softly. Wrapping me up in his arms, he backs me onto the elevator like I'm his captive. A role, according to the sudden heat in my panties, I wouldn't mind playing.

After a short intimate ride, we switch elevators in the lobby, and the night security guard greets him. He hides me from view as he slows down to talk with the man.

"How's business, Claude? Slow, I hope."

"Yeah," the man chuckles. "No lock out emergencies tonight."

"No cat burglars?"

The man laughs. "You have a good night."

Zak salutes the man, sweeps me onto another elevator, and presses the button for the penthouse while I let out a breath.

"That's the one flaw of this building. You need to switch elevators from the garage," he says, holding me close against him as he leans into the back wall. Close enough so I can feel his excitement hardening against the V of my thighs.

"Not so bad," I say, my words breathier than they should be.

"To tell the truth, I never thought about it until tonight. Until

I needed to bring a woman up to my penthouse without anyone knowing who she is. Like she's some kind of mystery V.I.P."

He stares at me, and I stare back, my heart pounding now, knowing I'm going to need to tell him who I am and wondering why the hell I'm so afraid to do it. It's no big deal, is it? He's not going to call the press and tell them an Olympic snowboarder got herself injured jumping out of a helicopter doing a stunt in a promotional shoot she wasn't supposed to do.

I clear my throat, though I have no idea what I'm about to say. But it doesn't matter because the elevator doors glide open, the sound a discrete whisper, leaving us at the posh entryway leading to two doors. He leads me to the one on the right, and I remember it well as he lets us in with an electronic code.

"Before we do anything else, let's get you some ice for your ankle." He guides me to the kitchen, holding onto my hand. His hand is large and strong and without softness, but not without remarkable talent as I recall.

"And there you go again, being kind and gentlemanly. Just when I thought you were going to eat me alive..." I catch up to him and reach a hand up to touch his mouth for no other reason than it's there, and it's irresistible. He sucks my finger in and nips it.

He ducks his head down to my ear and whispers, "I am going to eat you alive, Buttercup."

I shiver, and my nerves scream that they can't wait. My pussy begs me to forget about the ankle, but he opens the freezer door and retrieves an icepack. I notice he has a stack of them inside.

"Do you need an icepack?" I ask. "Any injuries? How about your hip from that time you slammed into the boards?"

He laughs. "I'm always slamming into the boards. That's what they make hockey pants and pads for—to minimize the damage." He stops talking, standing in front of me with the icepack in one hand and the other holding my hand as he pulls me in, releasing my hand and cupping my ass snug against him so I can feel every big of his intention, big and hard and grinding where I want it.

Then he kisses my eyes after staring hard, first one then the other. The gesture surprises me, stirs something that makes me feel uncomfortable like he's crossed some line, gone too far on the intimacy scale, and I pull back.

"Your eyes are so..." He says and shakes his head. "Don't mind me. I'm hooked on your eyes." He takes a deep breath. "They take my breath away."

I don't know what to say to that, so I grab the icepack from his hand and turn away. I don't get far.

"Let me help you with that."

He lifts me onto the kitchen island, takes the ice pack from me and retrieves an ace bandage from a drawer.

I laugh. "Your kitchen is like a nurse's station."

"Gotta be prepared in my business." He unlaces my boots and takes them off. "Fancy shoes. You a fan of winter sports?"

"Like hockey?" I try to deter him from talking about me. For as long as possible. Though I'm not sure I'll ever trust him no matter how illogical or irrational I'm being.

"Sure. You a fan?" He looks eager, like he wants my approval, like it matters.

I laugh. "Duh. You think I'm going to tell you I'm not?"

"Anyone else, that's an easy answer. But you? You're a puzzle, a mystery lady with a twisted ankle, fancy boots, and the sweetest pussy I ever—" I smack him on the shoulder as he laughs. "Sensitive about your—"

"Where's your gentlemanly sense of decorum now? Besides, I thought it was my eyes that you adored."

"True. There's so much to like. You have a lot of gifts, Rylee."

I smile. Those are the words Mama Cass said to me nearly every day of my life growing up. "You are a very nice man, Zak Tomas."

"I'll remind you of that sometime in the future when you're having doubts."

Future? "Oh no, there won't be some future time. I'm here in

Boston for two weeks—or rather a week and six days. Then I'm off."

"Off to where?"

"How about if we're off to the bedroom. Right now. Are you up to carrying me?"

His face lights up, and he scoops me from the island countertop, ice pack ace-bandaged in place, and carries me through the dining room and great room and down the hallway, same as I remember from last night, to his bedroom. He gently places me on his bed and sits next to me.

"You rest while I get out of these clothes." He's dressed in a suit and tie but has no trouble getting it all off and strewn into an orderly pile on a chair until all he has left are his boxers. Boxers with a giant tent protruding from the front and aimed my way.

"Nice show, though you might want to slow it down next time."

"Next time, I'll let you do the honors since you think I didn't do it right." He sits on the bed again and leans over me, pinning me with his broad chest and those arms sculpted to perfection. I'm afraid I'm staring too long, but really, I don't give a crap as I caress the hard bulges of his torso. I plan to work my way down to the bulging temptation in his boxers when he lowers his face to mine.

"How about if I take your clothes off in the meantime?" He nibbles my lips and makes his way down my jaw to my earlobe, and I shudder with pure pleasure. He has so many ways of turning me on.

"You're so sensual, so fucking good at this," I say.

He gives a muffled chuckle as his mouth reaches my neck and lower. "That's my line, Buttercup. You tempt me in so many ways that I can't even decide where to start right now." He glances up at me, and I see it as my duty to solve his problem.

"Let me help you decide." I drag his hand from the side of my face where he planted it to my breasts, and he wastes no time slipping it under my sweater to find the plump needy nipples and tweak them through my sheer bra. I let out a needy moan and press myself into him.

He captures my mouth, swallowing my next moan as he kneads my breasts and then lowers his hand, fluttering his fingertips across the hypersensitive skin of my abdomen.

I groan. "You're doing it... the way I did it to you."

"Except you're not laughing."

"Because you're doing a lot better than tickling me," I admit. He shifts to sit up, and in one smooth motion, lifts my sweater off, then unhooks my bra and releases my breasts, removing the garment and tossing it away.

"You have the most perfect tits I've ever seen, and I consider myself a connoisseur."

"Is that right?" My long-held wary instincts tell me not to believe him, to chalk it up to dirty talk in the moment, the kinds of things a guy says to a woman he's about to fuck into oblivion. But something in me buds, pokes through the wariness and wants to believe him—before I smash the dangerous bud, pulverizing it before it does any harm.

"I HAVE all kinds of interesting body parts if you want to take the rest of my clothes off and see."

He growls in response and kisses his way down from my nipples to my belly button, licking it like it's a treasure he's claiming, raising the hairs of my tender skin there, and all the nerve endings attached to them dance like wild ballerinas.

"I'm starving for a taste of you." His mouth reaches the edge of my groomed pussy, and he inhales deeply. "You smell like the best meal of my life. You're so hot and juicy." He looks up. "I think I've acquired a taste for the rare delicacy of Rylee..." He frowns. "I don't even know your last name."

I grip the back of his head and press his face into my lower belly. "Never mind the distraction. I need you to eat me like I'm your last meal." He chuckles as he opens his mouth over my mound, and his tongue darts over my seam, flicking my clit and sending a spasm of pure ecstasy through my nervous system.

"You're like a fucking drug, so damn addictive, so…"

I suck in a breath as he goes from kissing to laving my swollen and needy folds, making appreciative noises as his tongue darts around, circling the central bundle of hot nerves like they're a live wire to be avoided.

"Pleeease…" I can't stand the desperation in my voice, and maybe he hears it, too, because he grips my thighs and presses his mouth down, kissing and then sucking the hypersensitive nub into his mouth, nipping and then licking and making me shudder as the sensations rise in me to that impossibly satisfying crescendo like hitting the peak of a big air jump, and I come crashing down, blind and frozen in the throes of electrifying pleasure.

He licks me once more from top to bottom, sucks every drop left from me and then rises, climbing up my body, his arm and chest muscles bulging as they work, until his face hovers above mine, his mouth glistening with my juices. I automatically reach out to touch his face, to wrap an arm around him to hold him to me a he lowers his mouth into a kiss. I'm surprised he doesn't have some wise guy quip, but I'm not disappointed as his warm lush lips rain kisses on my mouth and cheeks and eyes.

"Come inside me," I say, breathless from his shower of affection, drained from my orgasm, but still needy, still wanting everything he has to offer. I'm all too aware that there's a clock ticking on this pleasure train, an end of the line when I'll have to jump off.

His mouth reaches my earlobe, and he nibbles, and like everything he does to me, it sends my nerves skittering, makes me want more.

"What makes you think I'm ready?" he says, his hot breath fanning my ear and raising gooseflesh all over my neck. My pussy gets the message he's sending, pulsing with anticipation.

I reach a hand down and take his cock, long and like silk-covered iron as it throbs in my hand. My fingers go to his tip where I find creamy pre-cum, and I groan as I spread it around and squeeze. He groans.

"I officially pronounce you ready."

"Buttercup, you have no idea." He covers my hand with his and removes it. "I want to be inside you before I explode." He lifts himself slightly and reaches over me to his nightstand. I pull him back.

"What are you doing? No condoms. That's not our thing. I thought we agreed." My heart speeds up faster than before, and harder, like it's going to hammer through my rib cage if I don't calm down. I have no idea what I'm saying or why. We don't have a *thing*. Because that would mean there's an *us*. And there's not.

He stops and watches me, and I have no idea what he's seeing or thinking, except his eyes are troubled. I reach up and caress his face as he settles back down, half over me, half beside me, our skin sticking together and the heat of it against me reminding me of what I want.

"I mean—"

"I know what you mean." He takes a quick breath. "And I like it. I'm all in—so to speak." Then he beams that infectious grin, and relief mixes with concern that we're on a different page than I had planned, than we should be, or that he thinks we are. I'm sure about where I am with him. Here and now. That's it.

He proves me right by settling between my legs then lifting me and rolling us so I'm on top, perfectly poised atop his stiff and ready cock.

"You ready to go for a ride, Buttercup?"

"I'm so ready I don't even mind that you keep calling me Buttercup." I smirk and he chuckles. Then he gets serious and lifts me, maneuvering himself to spear me right through the pussy, and I feel every hard inch of him glide inside, feel myself closing around him all the way until he hits my wall, and I see stars. I let out a gasp and lean forward.

His hands are on my hips and his eyes on my face, intense and glassy. He lifts his head and kisses me. Surprised, I don't know what to think because it feels so good, but it's too much. I sit up, lean back, and wriggle my hips to take back control. Pins of pleasure shoot through me in all directions.

"That's it. Ride me." His voice is hoarse, and he moves me up, pulling his shaft from me, and the buzz ripples through me.

"Oh my God. Zak don't stop." I slam back down on him. "I want more. Harder." I can hardly talk now because I'm concentrating on the sensations, staying in the here and now of life, taking in every feeling of being in the moment.

He growls as he does what I ask, moving me and moving his hips in a hurried rhythm. I open my eyes to take him in, his intense expression revealing that border between pain and bliss, alive to the extreme, energy pouring from him, sweat pouring, his muscles straining, the tension of his every fiber permeating the air.

The circles of sensation at my center tighten, and I slam harder and faster, and he keeps up.

"Fuuuck. Rylee..." The strain in his voice drives me harder, and I ride him like he's indestructible, like I need to try my best to destroy him, to destroy us both.

His hand comes between us, and his thumb presses exactly on the swollen nub on the verge of explosion. I throw back my head, coiling my thigh muscles as tight as they'll go, and close my eyes, screaming bloody murder as if my life depends on this orgasm that rises inside me. I picture myself rising in the air inside the halfpipe, ready to emerge above the world, higher than everything as the explosion hits me from the inside, and I let out a scream that only I can hear.

I find myself collapsed on top of him, breathing like I've been on top of Mt. Everest, gasping and gulping air. His arms shake as they wrap around me, and I would wonder if he came because I was oblivious, except I feel the hot sticky evidence seeping between us.

"Rylee..."

"What happened to Buttercup?" I don't want to talk. I don't want to share more than bodily fluids tonight. Or ever. Buttercup is safer.

He chuckles softly, and I dart a glance to see his exhaustion. "You played a hockey game tonight—and that was nothing compared to—"

"Having you play with my stick?" He smirks.

"Go to sleep, Zak." He chuckles again, but there's no energy in it, and I feel his body settle into relaxation and then sleep before I rise to clean up.

When I come back from the bathroom, I glance at my clothes and then back at his sleeping form. He really is a gorgeous specimen. There's no harm in spending the night, is there? Especially not if it means morning sex.

My conscience soothed, I get back into bed and fall asleep next to him, close enough to feel his warmth, but separate.

SOMETHING SMACKS me in the face, and I hear a moan as I wake, sitting bolt upright in the dark. It's him. It's Zak, and as I get oriented in the shadowy room, I realize the indistinct moaning is him, his body writhing, and alarm zips through me, shutting down all but the instinct hard-wired in my brain to help someone in trouble.

Leaning over him, I know he's asleep, and when I touch his face, it's wet. He must be having a nightmare. Sweet Jesus. It's like the group home all over again. Only it's not me crying in agony. It's Zak.

There are fucking tears on his cheeks.

Chapter 10

ZAK

As I come awake, I grip the arms holding me and the hand on my face, but the burning in my chest doesn't let me breathe.

"Zak, it's okay. You're alright. Wake up. You're having a nightmare. You're okay." The sweet breathy voice goes on like that as I struggle to completely escape the confines of sleep. I grip a tangle of hair that brushes my arm and hold on.

"Take it easy, Zak. You're okay. Everything is fine." The soft familiar voice penetrates the panicked fuzziness in my head, and I finally shake off the remnants of the nightmare and open my eyes fully.

I see her in the dim light and loosen my grip on her hair and arm. The here and now hits me all at once, the warmth of her skin against mine, those gorgeous dark-lashed eyes, her sensual scent, the night, falling asleep with her—and fuck, the nightmare.

"Sorry," I croak, feeling like I swallowed a desert.

"No need to be sorry. Must have been a bad nightmare." She softly caresses my cheek, wiping the tears I know are there. Fuck. This has only ever happened a handful of times in my life—since Billy's death. I have no fucking idea what the trigger is, and that's the worst fucking part because I'd sure as hell avoid it at all cost if I knew.

I give her a weak version of my usual smirk because I'm not quite feeling it yet, but I am feeling her, so I pull her close so she's draped along my side, looking down at me, her warm curvy, killer body up against mine, her energy seeping into me. And she has a damn mountain of energy.

"You okay? You're heart's beating real fast."

Now my smirk goes to full wattage. "That's not from the nightmare, Buttercup."

She laughs, and I hear some relief in it. "Now, I know you're fine." There's an awkward beat of silence, and I doubt she'll ask me what it was all about. After all, it's probably against her stupid rules. No feelings. No crying.

"Fuck. I just broke your number one rule." I grin at her. "I cried."

Her eyes go wide, and then she cracks up into a peel of laughter. "Oh my God. You did. That's so ridiculous. I never thought— I mean." She laughs again and then settles down. "Seriously, you know I didn't mean you couldn't cry about something unrelated to me, to our... to..."

"To our non-relationship?"

She nods and still doesn't ask what the nightmare was about.

"Who says my nightmare wasn't about us? Maybe I was crying because I didn't want you to leave in the morning."

She raises her brows in challenge, but she still doesn't ask.

"Okay, if you really want to know, I'll tell you what it was about. But I have to warn you, it's a downer."

"You don't have to tell me—"

"What if I want to? What if I need to talk about it to get rid of the despairing after effects?" I'm serious as the pope now as I realize it's true. I need to dispel the gloom, expose all the dark thoughts to the light of day—so to speak since it's still dark. I glance at my phone. Five a.m. Not for long.

"I'll listen to you then. Tell me."

I watch her physically brace herself, withdrawing from me as if she doesn't want to catch the bad vibes. But her eyes stay on me, compassion still lighting them, a softness like empathy showing through. I take a deep breath.

Unsure of what I'm going to say, I let go, only sure that I need to tell her, that I can't help telling her, even if it means showing her who I am, exposing everything. It's only for two weeks. It's safe. Right?

But my racing heart tells me it's about more than that, whether I want to listen or not. I don't listen. I talk.

"I come from a good home. The best. I have two loving parents and three pesky sisters who would walk on fire for me." She nods slightly like it's what she guessed. "So, my nightmare isn't about some dark childhood. I glided through life without ever having a problem. I was gifted and lucky."

"Past tense?"

"Still am." I flash a smirk, but it's weak. My heart protests with faster thudding than before, knocking around my rib cage like an animal that needs escape. My hand automatically goes to my chest. Then I clear my throat and swipe my hand through my hair, pretending I'm cool. I don't know why I bother since I'm about to bare myself, become more vulnerable than I've ever been.

But it's like a dip in the icy ocean; you're in and out in a flash. No harm, no foul. Right?

I don't wait for my conscience to answer while my heart continues to clatter.

"I'm still very lucky. What brought this home to me was the day after I turned eighteen, the day after I accepted a full boat to Minnesota to play hockey. Me and my best friend Bill were supposed to meet at Tony's Pizza, our town's local hang out, to celebrate." I pause and take a breath, willing my heart to quiet, trying to get control of my jumping nerves. But when I speak again, my voice catches, and then watching her, staring into those perfect eyes that speak to me, saying all the things I've ever wanted to hear, I continue.

"He never showed. Because that was the day Bill committed suicide."

She sucks in her breath and goes still. I reach out and touch her because I need to. When she doesn't back away, I realize I half expected her to.

"I'm sorry." Her words are an agonized whisper, matching the feeling in my gut. I look away. Swiping an unsteady hand through my hair again, I force a deep breath like, if I don't, my body will give up breathing.

I nod. "The thing is, I never realized Bill had mental illness... depression. I never knew how my own fucking best friend suffered." I swipe my hand, rearranging my mop of hair again and clear my throat. "We were close. We played hockey together since we were pee-wees, and he was madly proud of me for getting the scholarship. So stoked." Facing down, away from her eyes raw with emotion, reflecting how I feel, I shake my head. Still to this day, I'm in disbelief that he would take his life over a fucking girl.

"I knew he was down about his girlfriend, but... his mom told me later that Bill had sunk into a depression after their breakup. According to her, it was the last straw but not the cause. But I don't know. Bill was obsessed with Nora. Another symptom of the mental illness, I'm told. All I know is that even though he was sad about Nora, he laughed when he was with me, was psyched about me going to Minnesota, and already angling for tickets to every game."

"You were only a kid. You wouldn't know," she says, sounding wistful, like she was never a kid.

"No. But the thing is, I still don't understand it. Maybe I never will." I reach up and pull at my hair because I can't stand thinking about this. She reaches out and touches my face. Some of my tension dissipates. She brings me back to the here and now, where I belong. I hold her and drag her back down into the pillows. My chest relaxes as I breathe in her scent.

Live every day of life to the fullest. Do not look for problems; do not let life get complicated. Do not let a girl own me. Not the way Bill did.

"I'm sorry you lost your friend that way. Mental illness is a bitch."

"No kidding. I do what I can. Charity functions to benefit research and facilities for the mentally ill, and I donate heavily to group homes."

"Group homes?" She sounds interested and wary like I hit a nerve.

"Yeah. I didn't know it at the time, but Bill was supposed to check into the local Newport Institute for treatment. The next day. He never made it." My chest tightens until my breaths become shallow, and I know if I don't do something, it'll get worse. I'll hyperventilate. It's happened before. After the nightmare.

"Are you fucking with me?"

Her blurted words startle me, and I suck in a deep breath. "What are you talking about?"

"That's the group home where I met Suzie. Or one of them. We were put there because DSS had nowhere else to put us until they had a foster home."

"What the fuck? You're from a foster home?"

"Long story, and we've had enough stories. It's starting to get light out already." She waves at the window and the purple horizon. She doesn't want to talk, but my curiosity is amped.

She moves her leg and grimaces.

"How's your ankle?" I'd almost forgotten about her injury.

"Sore as hell now that the anesthetic of sex has worn off."

I check it out, and it's still as swollen as yesterday.

"Stay put. I'll get you some ice." When I get out of bed, I'm reminded of that check into the boards last night, and I stifle a groan as I retrieve another ice pack from my supply, returning the warm one.

"You didn't have anywhere to go today, did you? It's Sunday. You should stay right where you are and rest." I sit on the edge of the bed and re-wrap the ace bandage around the fresh ice pack while she watches, naked and unselfconscious about it. I toss a blanket over her, knowing the ice will make her cold. She takes it and wraps herself in it.

"Stay with me."

"Of course, I have nowhere to go. I'm a woman of leisure."

"Seriously, what did the doctor say about the ankle."

She gives me a blank stare.

"Wait—you haven't been to a doctor, have you? No ultrasound?"

"I had a med tech look at it. He said it would be fine—"

"Like hell. You need an MRI."

"Thank you, Doctor Hockey." She gives me a sassy look that translates as *mind your fucking business*. Then she adds, "I plan to call."

"Do you need the name of a specialist?" She probably has no clue about who to see for this kind of injury.

"I have a referral to see a Dr. Oliver Yancey. I'm told he's a good orthopedic specialist."

"How the fuck did you get his name? He's the top orthopedic guy in sports medicine in Boston. His practice is exclusively professional athletes."

She shrugs.

"What aren't you telling me?" She's so fucking secretive it's extreme. She doesn't say a word. "You're an Olympic gold medalist at keeping secrets, aren't you?"

Her head whips up, and she glares. "Why the fuck would you say that?"

Now, that hit a raw nerve, and I like it. My surge of excitement is perverse as fuck. She's a complicated beauty, and I should be running the other way right now. But I needed a distraction from contract negotiations, didn't I? That must be what triggered the nightmare.

Fuck. As rationalizations go, I don't think a weaker one exists, but I don't care.

"Tell me, Rylee. What's your story? The real one."

Chapter 11

"We've already broken enough rules, haven't we?" I stall because guilt has me by the throat, imploring me to share, telling me it's only fair after all he's told me.

But I didn't ask for it. I didn't want to know all about him, about his secret fears and past tragedy.

"Your rules. But I have a rule. Never sleep with a girl who keeps too many secrets."

"That horse is out of the barn."

"Rylee, damn it." He's more than frustrated. He might even be angry, but I still see the hunger in his snapping stare.

"I'm a snowboarder. That's what I do. I didn't lie. It's not a job."

"It's not a life of leisure either." He exhales, and I see relief relax every muscle, including his jaw, and that lazy smile returns.

"There money in snowboarding?" He looks me up and down, paying special attention to my thighs as he runs a hand down my body with new appreciation.

I hold in a shudder, cursing my body's response to this man. He makes it hard for a girl to stay in control or even want to bother.

"There is if you're on the U.S. Olympic team."

His eyes dart back to examine my face. "You're shitting me? Do not shit me."

"For real."

"So the ankle..." He glances back down my body to my injured ankle with the ice pack, and he sits up to take a closer look. "This could be a real problem. The Olympics are six weeks away."

He turns to me for confirmation of his lightbulb moment, and I smirk at him. "Bingo."

"You're lying low so no one will find out about the injury. But why?"

"Duh. I don't want to get tossed off the team and replaced by the next boarder in line who doesn't have a bum ankle." Who isn't a defiant rule breaker and doesn't do stupid things because they can't resist a challenge.

"You're not telling me something. Again."

I push him away. "What do you need? My life story?"

"You didn't hurt your ankle jumping out of a helicopter?" He sounds unsure.

I laugh. "You know something? That was the one thing that was the God's honest truth."

"You fucking jumped out of a helicopter weeks before the Olympics? Fuck. Do they know?" He swipes a hand through his hair and looks more worried about my predicament than I feel.

"No, Sherlock. That's why I'm hiding. I don't need my coach or anyone on the team or associated with the Olympics to find out I took that risk."

"Why did you?"

"That's the most complicated question you've asked." I take a deep breath, my heart beating fast like I need to run or push back. My fight or flight response is hair-trigger with people I don't know though it's been quiet with him. Until now. Shit.

"What made you take the risk, Rylee?"

"You should go back to calling me Buttercup and quit the interrogation." I move to get out of bed.

He grabs my wrist and tugs me back into his naked body, and the singe of his warm skin causes a stutter in my wild heartbeat. Fuck.

"Buttercup, I'm not going to spill any of your secrets. And if you're a risk taker, I want to know all about it because we just had unprotected sex—"

"Shut the fuck up. I'm not some kind of—"

He lowers his mouth and covers mine, cutting me off, and his sensual salty taste calms my nerves when it should panic me. However, his words seep in past my defenses. He has a point.

He lifts his mouth, his eyes slightly glazed but no less penetrating. "I know you wouldn't set me up like that. Don't ask me how. But I'd like to know what's going on with you."

"Why? You could send me home now and have nothing to do with me ever again."

"Call me greedy, but I want the full two weeks."

"One week and five days."

"Tell me about growing up in a foster home. Tell me why you ended up in a foster home." He's not asking. He's commanding, compelling me as if he has some magical power over me and I'll comply. I deride myself. *His magical hockey stick is his power*. And maybe I'm greedy enough to want more of him, too.

"Not much to tell." I shrug, but my chest tightens, and my gut roils like I'm going to be sick. "I ended up in the foster system because my parents died in a car accident when I was seven, and they couldn't find my aunt. They put me in a group home until they could find a foster family, and that's where I met Suzie. She was only four. We ended up with Mama Cass in Southie. I was lucky—we were lucky—to land with a great foster mom."

"Lucky." I hear the irony in his comment and ignore the suffocating tightness of my chest to drag in a deep defiant breath. I go on like I need to prove my point, that he doesn't need to feel bad for this girl.

"Me and Suzie grew up together like sisters. Mama Cass got me in a snowboarding program at eight, and I went straight for the halfpipe and jumps and on from there to every extreme sport I could find. Skate boarding, surfing, ziplining. I stayed with snowboarding long enough to win some prizes and got on a team to compete. I competed nationally in high school and earned a spot on the Olympic team when I was seventeen, but I wasn't close to the medal box."

"The Olympic Team. Fuck, that's amazing. That's every kid's dream."

"It wasn't mine. Not at first. I started with the basic dream of surviving without my parents and helping Suzie survive. Then when things settled in with Mama Cass, I got greedier in my ambitions. I wanted to really feel alive."

"So, you're an adventurer at heart. I can identify with that. What other adventures do you have?" He gives me a sexy smirk, but I'm still in a defiant mood, so I disappoint him.

"At one of the competitions, I met some boarders who were into parachuting onto a ski slope in South America, and I went with them. Some people call me reckless." I lift my chin, inviting him to register his opinion.

"Not me. You have to live life to the fullest."

"All in. Every day."

He nods. My chest tightens again at the way he's looking at me, like he sees me, like he likes what he sees. I clear my throat.

"Suzie was sent to a theater camp. Now, she's trying to break into modeling and acting. So far, there's not much money in that."

"What about you? You have any promotional deals yet?"

I shake my head. "I have enough sponsorships to get by, but my competition resume is light compared to others on the circuit and on the Olympic team. I kind of came out of nowhere. But I can live on very little money. It doesn't matter." *Or it never mattered until now.*

"I'm like you," I admit. "I have an appreciation for the value of life, the need to live every day to the fullest. I figure I've been on borrowed time since the accident. I should've died with my parents —" *Fuck, where did that come from?*

"Don't say that. Don't even fucking think that," he says, clamping his hand around my arm.

"But I didn't die, so here I am living in the moment and making the most of life. It could all end in a flash." I shrug, but my heart moves to my throat, and I shove my hair from my face with a shaky hand. Why the hell am I sharing so much? I don't want him to get the wrong idea, so I add, "That's why I'm not interested in relationships. Why bother?"

He gives me a hard look. "I get your logic, and I understand— but still... There's something not right about it. Makes you sound, I don't know...tragic."

I scoff and slap his back. "Don't worry about me, Zak. I'm doing just fine."

"I believe you."

"Except for money." Fuck. It's like I'm drunk on sex and can't keep my mouth shut. Something that's never happened before.

He narrows his eyes like he's wary, suddenly unsure about me. That stirs my indignation.

"I'm not asking you for money. I'm not that girl. I'm an independent woman and proud of it."

"Again, I believe you. What's the problem? Why do you need money?"

"Mama needs to see a doctor. Her health is falling apart because she smokes like a chimney and won't quit. Her house is ramshackle and needs fixing up. She says she won't go to the doc because it costs more than smoking cigarettes, and if she has a choice, she'd rather stick with the sure thing. Have you ever heard of anything more ridiculous?"

He gives a deep sigh, then clutches a fistful of my hair and pulls my face to his. With his mouth a whisper away from his, he says, "Everything about you is ridiculous, Buttercup. Ridiculously sexy—"

My chest tries to squeeze the life out of me because I get the feeling he was going to say more. I don't want to hear it, so I plant my mouth on his, taking in his lips, thrusting my tongue as deep as it'll go, running it along his teeth, his tongue, and every succulent part of his mouth, savoring his taste and losing myself.

His breathing is ragged when he pulls his mouth from mine, and he tangles himself around me, his hands palming my ass and pressing. Hard.

"Top or bottom, Buttercup?"

I laugh, and a slow smile spreads with the excited tingle in my pussy that's flooding with heat and anticipation.

"That all you got?" I straddle him then, with my ass facing him and my mouth watering as I lean down to suck his ready cock.

WE SPEND all day in bed, but half of it is sleeping, and only hunger forces us to leave the bedroom at four in the afternoon.

"I'm going home to have dinner with Mama before she wonders if you've kidnapped me."

"You told her you were with me?"

"Sure. Who do you think talked me out of standing you up?"

He's blocking the door of his condo or apartment or whatever it is, dressed in a T-shirt and sweats that make him look even sexier than he is naked. The ripple of his muscles shows plainly as he pulls me close. I'm fully clothed, jacket and all, but I feel his ever-ready cock hard against me all the same.

"When do I see you again?"

"I don't' know…" My hesitation is genuine, and my heart races, having nothing to do with the twitch in his damn cock.

"What's the harm? It's all over in two weeks, right?"

"One week and five days."

He laughs, but his eyes aren't in it.

"When you get back from your road game, give me a call."

"We're not leaving until Tuesday."

"That works. I have something to do tomorrow. I got Mama Cass a doctor's appointment, and I want to spend time with her."

"You're a good daughter."

"Foster daughter."

He shrugs like it doesn't matter.

Chapter 12

RYLEE

"I 'll meet you there," Suzie says as she leaves for dance practice. She's smiling, but there's a crease of worry on her forehead.

We're meeting at the doctor's office near Mass General. Mama Cass frowns at me.

"You sure this is necessary? So what if I cough?"

I shake my head. There's no sense in answering her because she already knows and doesn't want to acknowledge there's a problem. I kind of get it. After all, I haven't bothered to get the MRI for my ankle yet, have I? No news is good news. Ignorance is bliss.

Fuck. I know better. All the ignorance in the world won't change the reality when the hammer comes down on your head, will it?

"Let's get you dressed and ready to go," I cajole.

"I can dress myself fine."

"Then do it. I'm ready now." I'm wearing clothes I left behind from when I was in high school, but jeans never go out of style. Even if they are tighter than they should be for my circulation. The sweater fits well. It's red-white-and-blue. Very patriotic. I should take it back to Utah to the Olympic training camp when I go.

❋

I'M PACING around the waiting room while Mama sits watching me when Suzie finally shows up.

"What took you—" I stop talking because she's not alone.

Nowicki follows her in, which is unexpected but not outrageous. But the last person I expected to see following him into the waiting room was Zak. My normal cool rattles, and I feel the cracks in my resolve to remain detached before I stiffen.

"What the hell are you doing here?" I'm not usually an ungracious bitch, but doubling down on my defenses calls for drastic measures.

His smirky half-grin falters, but only for a millisecond. Long enough to turn my gut inside out and make me feel like a fucking miserable queen bitch, the kind of person I least want to be even in my wariest people-avoiding state. Mama always said you catch more flies with honey than vinegar. Right now, I taste pure revolting vinegar in my mouth as it rises from my churning gut.

"Don't mind her," Suzie says, stepping between me and the two men and greeting them each with a hug as if they're family members and belong here. Shit.

Mama stands and joins Suzie, not bothering to give me the glare of disapproval she usually does if I'm rude. That hasn't happened since my hormone-ridden adolescence, the time in life when every newly minted teenager is at their confused angry-at-the-world peak. My only excuse now is stress and confusion.

I wish I could say that the stress over Mama's health and my Olympic-threatening injury were the biggest part of my problem. But no. I'm staring right at the fucking motherlode of the biggest problem threatening my well-being right now.

Unfortunately, he looks so good that my traitorous body melts down, making it tougher to be tough, to resist the pull of him beyond the scope of fling status. Shit.

He hugs Mama, telling her he's glad to meet her and has heard wonderful things about her, all of which sound more sincere than most people when they utter the same trite words. I watch and feel like I'm being torn into two pieces, fear forcing resistance, and at the same time, need pulling me into his orbit.

But what kind of need is this? I'm not a boy-crazy needy woman. And I've never depended solely on men for sexual satisfaction either, thank you very much to my trusty vibrator.

When Zak turns to me with a confident, warm smile firmly in place, my heart leaps to my throat, but I immediately calm myself as if I'm at the top of a halfpipe and ready to jump in, about to attempt risky, injury-defying tricks where I need a cool head detached from emotional turmoil like fear or hope, allowing only the thrill of the moment to register with my icy cold concentration.

"I thought I'd come by in case you wanted company," he says.

I sweep a pointed glance in the direction of my sister. "You didn't need to bother. I hope you didn't have anything else—"

"Nothing that couldn't wait." He steps closer as the others take seats on the other side of the room. He lowers his voice. "I know this is important and stressful for you and thought you could use moral support."

I snort. "Since when does being my sex toy qualify you to provide moral support?" I mean the words to cut him, so I'm taken aback by his response.

"Sex toy, eh?" His mouth twitches at the corners, and his eyes go dark with that heavy-lidded sexy look that undoes me—or would undo me if we were in a bedroom or any other place besides a fucking doctor's office.

I'm about to issue a scathing retort about the sorry filthy state of the male brain—never mind that I was the one who called him my sex toy in the first place—when a nurse comes in and calls my mother's name.

"Cassandra Mooney, please come this way with me."

Suzie helps Mama to a stand because she's visibly shaken, and all my focus shifts to her. Zak Tomas could be a stick of furniture right now for all the attention I pay to him. Every nerve I have is on alert with fear, determination, and goddamn useless hope that these doctors can help Mama.

I join Suzie, and we follow the nurse into the examining room, leaving Ted and Zak behind without a second glance.

THE DOCTOR, a woman named Marion Zola, snaps her gloves off at the conclusion of the thorough exam. The nurse took blood samples, but the toughest part of the process was watching Mama try to breathe deeply. And the coughing. We all return to the waiting room, but only for a moment.

"Please come to my office," the doctor says from the doorway. She nods in the direction of Ted and Zak and summons them to join us. With my arm around Mama, I use all my concentration to follow the doctor into her office and have no fucks to give about Zak right now.

"I'll cut straight to the chase, Ms. Mooney. We'll need to wait for the chest X-rays to confirm a diagnosis of emphysema, also known as COPD, and rule out other lung conditions. And we'll run Arterial Blood Gases Analysis. These blood tests measure how well your lungs transfer oxygen to your bloodstream and remove carbon dioxide. But there's little doubt that you have emphysema."

"So?" Mama says.

I pat her back as my chest tightens, ironically constricting my ability to breathe. "What does that mean?" I manage to say. "What can you do for her?" My heart pounds, and I force my lungs to work, deepening my breathing to calm myself as I stare at the doctor, certain she has an answer, foolishly or not.

"We can do a V/Q lung scan, or ventilation/perfusion scintigraphy, a type of medical imaging using scintigraphy and medical isotopes to evaluate air and blood circulation within the lungs in order to determine the ventilation/perfusion ratio.

"Depending on the results, we can possibly do a broncho-scopic thermal vapor ablation. This surgery uses heated water vapor to target affected lobe regions of the lung—the damage can cause permanent fibrosis and volume reduction. The procedure can target individual lobe segments and be carried out regardless of collateral ventilation. The ablation can be repeated with the natural advance of emphysema."

"Advance?" Suzie's voice squeaks, and I hear the emotion. Nowicki puts an arm around her.

The doctor nods. "Yes. This isn't a curable disease. We can treat it to slow the progress, but lung damage from emphysema is irreversible."

The silence that follows her words booms through my head, and the room goes dark as a buzzing sounds in my ears. The sensation of falling startles me until arms wrap around me violently, and my eyes pop open.

Zak's strong arms hold me, and I'm leaning against him, all eyes on me. I pant, unable to speak.

"Are you all right, Rylee?" Mama says, touching me, her eyes wide and larger than usual behind her glasses. "Everything's going to be fine. You heard the doc. I'll get treatment." She coughs.

Tears spring to my eyes, but I squeeze them shut and break free from Zak's hold to throw my arms around Mama.

"Of course, you'll be fine." I rein in the tears that threaten and straighten. *You're the strong one, aren't you? Haven't you always been? Mama and Suzie don't need you to turn into a simpering puddle.*

I dart a glance at Suzie to see her swipe a tear from her face as she leans into Ted's side. He kisses her temple and murmurs something.

"It's a lot to take in," Dr. Zola says. "I'll write you a prescription for a bronchodilator to help with the coughing, and we'll make an appointment for you to come back next week after we get the results of the tests."

"What happens then?" I ask with a slight shake to my voice. I don't want to know, but I need to know. Fear has me wanting to bolt or to hide in Mama's arms, or to bury myself in Zak's arms and let him bury himself in me, to lose myself in the moment of bliss... Shit.

"We'll likely do the V/Q lung scan and then possibly the bronchoscopic thermal vapor ablation. But first steps first." She turns to Mama and puts a stern look on her face, all clinical neutrality gone. "You need to quit smoking. As of today. As of right now."

Mama stares back at the doctor, and her mouth quivers for a second, but then she lifts her chin and nods. "See you next week."

Everyone files out of the doctor's office, but I hang back. There's a question drumming in my head, relentlessly demanding an answer and getting louder and more insistent. I face the doctor as she sits behind her desk, typing some notes.

"Doctor Zola," I say, my voice strong and calm and insistent with my need for an answer despite the stark fear pulling at the periphery of my awareness. I shove the fear aside for this one moment and allow the bravery to make me vulnerable to devastation. My need for the real-real, for dealing in truth and danger, overrides the emotional residue of my past. I'm on borrowed time, right? This is what life is about, meeting every minute of it on real terms and not living in some cocoon of illusions.

"What is it, Ms. Flynn?" The startle of how she knows my name doesn't derail me, but I take an extra breath of life for reinforcement.

"What is her long-term prognosis?" I close my eyes and give myself shit. Then I rephrase my question. "How long does she have to live?"

"The average life expectancy of someone your mother's age is approximately five years." She stops talking although she looks like she has more to say, all kinds of qualifiers and exceptions no doubt, but she can see that I don't want the bullshit.

The news hits me, and I nod, absorbing the shock like a numb person, and allowing it to bounce off me. In my detached state, I can see the future moment when the reality might sink in, might pain me like a stab to the heart, but I can't feel it right now. Can't do anything about that. It's like I've given myself an anesthetic. Maybe my body is instinctively wiser than my mind.

"Thank you."

I walk out of her office to find everyone waiting. Zak comes to me without hesitation.

"I'm so sorry, Rylee," he murmurs in my ear.

"I have to go. To take Mama home." I sound like a robot, and I don't like it. When I look into his eyes and I see the empathy, the emotion, I feel myself buckle, so I pull away from him. Not now. Not here.

"I'll call you," he says.

I don't care. I walk away with Mama and Suzie, our family closing ranks to lean on each other, to handle the damage. Temporarily.

Chapter 13

Practice was a bitch. I walk off the ice with my head down. My concentration sucked, and I let every guy on offense get by me right down to the fourth liners—some of them more than once.

Finn lumbers past me and taps my shin pads with his badass goalie stick—and not gently. "Where's your head at? You made the rookie look good today. You trying to boost his morale or test my puck-stopping skills by letting every mother fucker on offense get a shot at me?"

"Sorry. Rough morning. My head's somewhere else." I take a deep breath because this is unacceptable. "I'll be fine. Wait 'til tomorrow night's game."

He nods. "That's good. I bet your agent will be happy." He juts his chin in the direction of a few men in suits, and one of them is Ham Jett, my agent. Fuck. "You're making his job tough. Isn't he in the middle of negotiating your contract?"

"Fuck."

"You in contract negotiations?"

I nod.

"Your rookie contract's expiring. You should be excited. This is your chance to negotiate for big bucks."

"More like nerve-wracking."

Jett waves at me and points to his watch. He wants to see me later. Double fuck.

In the locker room, I undress in record time because I need to wash away the stink of this practice—and not to mention the gloom of this morning's doctor visit—before I face Jett. My clothes shed, I wrap a towel around my waist to head to the shower, but Nowicki, still half-dressed in hockey gear sans skates, parks himself on the bench in front of me and spreads his legs blocking me.

"That was a sucky morning. Sorry I dragged you with me."

"Not your fault. I volunteered. At least we were there for Suzie and Rylee."

"Yeah," Nowicki scoffs. "Like that'll do a lot of good. Suzie texted me. She's done a lot of online research since the doc spoke to us, and she's freaking out because it doesn't look good. Doesn't look like the old lady has a long life ahead of her."

"Thank you so much for the cheery update," I say. "I need a shower."

"You need a lot more than that after the practice you had. You gonna be okay, or are you freaked out, too?"

"Why would I be freaked out?" I stop in my tracks and stare him down. This rookie has a lot of balls.

He shrugs. "I don't know. Maybe you care."

"What's that supposed to mean?"

"Hell, if you don't know that—"

"Know what?" Finn says, walking past us in his towel. He stops and waits expectantly. Nowicki keeps his mouth shut. For once. But I don't have anything to hide.

"About relationships," I say. "He thinks I don't know anything about them."

"The female kind? If so, I'd say he's right."

"Fuck you." He could be right, but it doesn't matter, does it? Because I'm not in a relationship, and I'm not interested in a relationship. I smirk and shove Finn ahead of me in the direction of the showers.

As I let the hot water do its magic, I drain my head and meditate. It's the best way I know to deal with stress.

Unfortunately, when I emerge from the locker room, I run into double the dose of stress in the form of two people. Jett, I expected, but I did not expect him to be standing there waiting for me and laughing with Candice-fucking-Montgomery, author of my Bachelor of the Year debacle.

Nowicki joins them, and then Finn, and I wonder if this is a party I ought to bypass, but that would be the chicken's way out. Besides, I have business to discuss with Jett. So, I stride over to the lively group and join them.

"How's our Bachelor of the Year doing? Any new conquests? Have you been snagged yet by some lucky young lady?"

"Hello, Candice." That's about all I have to say to her.

"I think he may have been snagged," Nowicki says. "No more Bachelor of the Year. He's been seeing a super-hot chick and—"

Alarmed, I elbow Nowicki in the gut. "Whether I've been seeing someone or not is no one's business."

Finn laughs. "Is this true, Zak?" He grins, not exactly believing Nowicki.

Jett and Candice both look on with interest, and I hope to God she hasn't been filling Jett's head with notions of publicity and promotional deals related to the B.O.Y. thing.

"Jett, I told you," Candice says, "a follow-up article and event would be perfect."

Shit. "She's a fling with an expiration date. She's leaving in two —one week and five days."

"Why? Where's she going?" Finn asks.

I'm not about to tell him she's in the fucking Olympics. "It doesn't matter. Gone is gone." The words sink into my gut and don't sit too well. Fucking hell.

"This is all very interesting," Jett says, "but Zak and I have pressing business to discuss. I have reservations for dinner, Zak— unless you have other plans?" He grins, and Nowicki snickers. Candice stares at me with expectation—it's her permanent expression, I think, and it unnerves me, and not in a good way.

"No other plans. Sounds fucking fabulous."

As we walk away, Candice calls out, "Don't forget to talk about my offer to do a follow-up article and photoshoot of you with your new girlfriend, whoever she is."

I cringe. "Ignore her," I say to Jett under my breath as we walk out the lobby door to the street.

"Don't worry. Unless the article comes with a lucrative promotional sponsorship for something like...I don't know...a cologne brand maybe, we're not interested."

"Cologne? Unless they pay north of a million, I'm still not interested. Her fucking award put a target on my back, and it's ruined my previously happy love life. I had it all going on. I loved women and had no problems. Now, women are a pain in the ass because their expectations have been ruined by Candice and her whole Bachelor of the Year deal."

"Oh? I thought you had a fling going on?"

"Yeah. There is that," I admit as we walk. It's a cold day, and there aren't a lot of people on the streets in the fading light. "But I'm in hiding, and when she leaves..." I shrug, an uncomfortable clench in my chest.

Jett opens the door when we arrive at his usual dinner place near the Garden, West End Johnnie's. We're seated right away. The smells of rich Italian food permeate the air and soothe me better than meditation. Better than anything except maybe sex. No, definitely not better than sex. Especially not sex with Rylee. That's a whole 'nother level of *soothing*.

"I have news for you that may help distract you from the woes of your love life."

His casual use of the term *love life* shouldn't strike a nerve. It's an innocuous and commonplace phrase, right? But the words *love life* trumpet in my mind like a blaring alarm.

He puts down his menu and stares at me. "Aren't you interested?"

"Yeah. Sure I am. What's up?" I try to focus on the business at hand, namely my contract, which should be of more than mild interest since it's everything. I need the Brawlers to renew because I fucking love playing for this team, and I love Boston; everything about this gig is perfect. My life here is perfect. *Was* perfect.

The waiter takes our order and brings a drink for Jett.

"You're not drinking?" he asks.

"I'm a professional athlete, a well-oiled machine."

"Sure. You only drink after games, right?"

"How would you know? You spying?"

He shrugs. "I know people in this city. It's my home town. The owner of The Tea Party is a good friend."

The server brings our steaks and a side of pasta for me because this well-oiled machine requires a massive amount of protein and calories to run efficiently. We start eating, and I'm glad for the reprieve from talking business, but it doesn't last long.

"Brawlers management made an offer, but I want to hold out for more." He names the number they want to pay. My eyes widen, and I blow out a breath.

"I'm impressed." Thrilled like a teenager in a brothel is more like it, but I try to play it cool.

"I think we can get another ten percent, but I'll ask for fifteen."

"I don't know." Discomfort lodges in my gut where the food should be going, and I'm suddenly not hungry when I should be starving. I force another bite of steak.

"Look, I know talking about negotiations isn't your favorite thing, but I have an obligation to look out for your best interests."

"It's just... Look, I don't care so much about the money. I want to play for the Brawlers." I wouldn't admit this to my teammates, but I trust Jett. I'm lucky to be on my dream team.

"I understand where you're coming from, kid, but don't worry. They want you. We'll work it out. Don't worry about a thing. I'll take care of you. You'll be on the team you want and paid what you deserve." He slaps my back. "I'll make sure you're wealthier than ever."

The thought that Rylee needs money drifts through my head. I have no business worrying about her. I finish eating the steak without tasting it. Besides, she'll be fine. She has a lot going for her, chiefly a take-no-prisoners attitude. We finish dinner, and I dismiss her from my head as I exchange a bro-hug with Jett, then head home. We have an early departure in the morning for our game in Carolina tomorrow night.

ONLY ONE WEEK and four days left to enjoy Rylee's company. That should not be what's on my mind as I hit the bed alone in my hotel room, but it is. Without thinking—because apparently, I've lost my fucking mind—I grab my phone from the nightstand and tap on her number, which happens to be at the top of my favorites list because, yes, I am that pathetic right now.

After one ring, my senses return, and I'm moving the phone off my ear to end the call when I hear her voice. It's quiet and sleepy and sexy as hell. A picture of her in bed fills the previously empty space between my ears, and I clutch the phone to my ear again at the insistence of my dick—and the other instinct in me, whatever that's made of.

"Did I wake you?"

"Is that what you called and woke me to ask?"

I laugh as her sarcasm does its magical levitation trick on my dick. Holy shit, am I easy. "We lost our game tonight. Did you watch?"

She yawns. I'm unsure if it's a fake yawn, but I grin.

"I might have. If I did, I would've noticed your two penalties and the minus-three performance when you managed to stay on the ice."

I laugh when I should be wounded. "Hey, you're supposed to be consoling me."

"You called the wrong girl for that. Unless..."

My pulse spikes, all my blood suddenly rushing south to my already stiff dick, and I know there's no returning from this boner without some satisfaction.

"Unless what, Buttercup?" I slide my hand down and free my dick from the boxers.

"You wouldn't be interested in some dirty talk, would you? Nah, not you..."

I chuckle at her tease and take hold of my dick. "It's not me. But my dick misses you terribly."

"Tell your dick I miss him, too. Tell him I'm getting hot thinking about you palming him right now."

I inhale a shuddering breath and move my hand from the bottom to the top of my shaft. Stroking the tip, I spread the pre-cum back down and squeeze. Shit. I need her, and I wish to fuck she was in this bed right now.

"My dick and I are all about following your instructions." I keep stroking, but I need more from her. "How about you and your pussy?"

"I'm bored and half asleep, but my pussy is a lively little girl." I hear her suck in a breath, and my dick jolts. "She's swollen and wet and needs consolation because she's missing out on all that Zak-dick fun. She might even be jealous of your hand right now. Mmmm... but..."

My hand pumps harder because I know she's touching herself,

and I can feel the silky pulse of her around me with each slide of my hand.

"Tell me more." My words are a ragged command.

"I... I'm busy...you tell me..."

"My cock is hard and crying for you, but I'm doing my best to beat the fuck out of it... Jesus..."

"Are you close? Are you pulling fast?" She lets out a moan. "I'm so... my clit is weeping, and no matter how much I flick...it needs...*oooh*."

"What? Tell me." I pump hard, my hand tight, and I manage to put the phone on speaker and drop it because I need two hands. Shit. "I'm getting close."

"I'm... I... Oh my God... Zak." She lets out a moan, and then my reception is muffled.

And that's all I need because I know she's gone over the top, and I pump my hips and hands and let go as my orgasm shoots like a geyser onto my belly, and I groan, gritting my teeth to keep it low. Fuck, I wish she was here.

My chest heaving, I gulp in breaths to calm down as my heart pounds fast, clattering harder than it did in tonight's game with the effort. Fuck. That's not good.

"Buttercup...you with me?"

"I...let me catch my breath." She's struggling to speak, and that brings a grin that stretches my mouth wide. "So, tell me why you called?"

"To check up on you. How's Mama?"

She chuckles and takes a few deep breaths. So do I.

"She quit smoking like the doctor ordered, so we had to hide the kitchen knives for fear of our lives."

"Put her in a bad mood, did it?"

She snorts. "I can handle it."

"What are you doing tomorrow?"

"I'm busy."

"Tomorrow night?"

"Still busy."

"You sure you can't squeeze me in—so to speak?" I refuse to be discouraged, not after this call.

She groans, and I picture her eye-roll. "I'm going shopping with Suzie to buy some things for the house, and then Mama's making us a big dinner." She pauses and lowers her voice. "I want to spend time with her."

Shit. "Of course. I get it."

"Maybe the day after tomorrow."

"That'll leave us only a week and two days."

She laughs. Predictably. "I promise I'll make it up to you."

"I have a game that night. Come to it, and we'll disappear afterward."

"I'll go to your little game, but not the executive suite. I'll blend in better with the regular crowd."

"How's your ankle?"

There's a pause, and my gut sinks. Not a good sign.

She answers me after another beat. "The same. I think I have to make that doctor's appointment."

"When? I'll come with you."

She laughs again, and I frown at the phone. "What?"

"It's not like you can help or change the outcome, killer."

"You've never heard of moral support?"

"Suit yourself. I'll keep you posted." She pauses again. "But Zak, don't start thinking like this is a relationship."

"One week and two days. Got it."

"Good." She ends the call, and I toss my phone.

Fuck. Maybe I am starting to feel like this is a relationship. Because what I feel right now is concern for her sick mother, her damn injury, and the consequences for her Olympic team status.

THE COACH WORKED our asses off, so I feel good about this game. We're playing the Devils, and they aren't the toughest opponent. I'm dressed and head to the hallway with some of the others to build up some energy for the game. We're bouncing off each other, shouting, and generally getting rowdy.

"Let's give these motherfuckers a Brawler's lesson," Nowicki shouts, and I almost laugh, but I shout back the requisite mean shit, manufacturing the necessary anger to pound some bodies into the board every time they touch the puck.

O'Rourke, the captain and a long-time veteran on the team, leads us through the tunnel to the ice for pre-game warm-ups. There's a rumor this is his last year. The notion of anyone's last anything doesn't sit right with me, so I dismiss the thought.

Then I look into the stands for the antidote to all wrinkles in my life, the poster girl for feeling alive and living in the moment. My eyes scan the seats near the top of the first section looking for Rylee, when I hear tapping on the glass. I look down rink-side, and there she is.

I skate over, and when I get close, I notice what she's wearing, and my chest tightens, my pulse going erratic before I let out a breath. She's standing there at the glass with a half-smile and Sheila. And Rylee's wearing a Brawlers jersey with my name on it. And fuck, it shouldn't give me the kick that it does, but my big fat grin doesn't lie, and some stupid kid inside me makes me pick up a puck and toss it over the glass to her. Then, going on instinct, I find myself touching the glass where she stands, staring at her, willing her to touch the other side.

Instead, Sheila touches the glass—and Rylee? She raises a brow and shakes her head. Then they disappear.

I watch her go, her limp more pronounced. Fuck. She's wearing a Brawlers cap to blend in, and her hair looks different. But I don't have any problem following her with my eyes. If she thinks no one will recognize her, she'd be mistaken. It's her eyes that will give her away. They're recognizable all day long. If the right person—that's anyone who's into watching snowboarding competitions or the pre-winter Olympics coverage—gets one look at her face, they'll recognize her.

AT THE BENCH, Coach stops us just before we're about to take the ice for the national anthem. "This game has to go better than the last one. No excuses." He flicks his gaze to me and holds my stare for a couple of ticks too long. My motor is already revving, but now I lock in tight.

It doesn't take long from the puck drop at center ice for me to check the Devils' best player in open ice as he's carrying the puck on a two-on-one. I steal the puck and pass it up to O'Rourke at the blue line, and he takes off. I follow, pushing myself to the max. We take control in the Devils end of the rink, and the puck gets passed around.

O'Rourke takes a hard wrist shot, and as the rebound bounces out, time slows down, and I surge forward, catching the puck on the tip of my stick and flicking it back toward the goal. Nowicki redirects it, and the goalie has no chance. As I collide with a defenseman, I don't care about the pain in my hip as I hit the ice because the red goal light goes off.

Adrenaline takes over from that point, and the team huddles in celebration, backslapping and hugging. Sometimes, it only takes one play, and I know from that second we'll win this game.

THE SIREN SOUNDS to end the game, and I skate full speed from the bench straight to the goal, along with the rest of the team, to congratulate Finn on the four-to-nothing shut-out.

"That was more like it," he says as I tap him on the pads. "We were beasts tonight."

"You were in the zone," I tell him, and in truth, I felt like we both were because we were in synch and tough as bears in the defensive end.

In the locker room, I'm all business and get showered and dressed within twenty minutes. Rylee's waiting for me outside, and I know there's media lurking around, so I head straight for her as soon as I emerge from the locker room.

A reporter jogs after me as I reach Rylee. I turn to block her from view as she stiffens next to me. This reporter is from ESPN, and he has a camera following him. It's Jonesy. Shit.

"Zak, can I have a word with you?"

I give him a big grin. "What's up?"

"Your contract is expiring at the end of the season. Have you started negotiations?"

"I leave that kind of thing to my agent."

"You want me to call your agent?"

"Sure. Let him earn his money." Shit. I'd better warn Jett and hope he doesn't poison my meal next time I see him.

Jonesy leans sideways and takes a look at Rylee.

"Who's this lovely young lady."

Fuck. This is precisely what Rylee didn't want to happen. It's the last thing she needs.

I manage to maintain my professional smile. "A friend. We were just leaving."

Jonesy steps around me and takes a closer look, like I'm hiding something. Shit. He probably figures that out because I am hiding someone, and I'm a terrible fucking actor.

"Hi there, I'm Jonesy. Nice to meet you. I bet you're proud of Zak. He's having a hell of a season."

"Sure." Rylee reluctantly replies. But she stands straight with only her ball cap to protect her from recognition as she meets his stare. Hiding behind me wasn't helping. Shit. She's never going to come to a game again after this.

"And you are?" Jonesy says, back to reporter mode. The

camera is off, but still close by.

"Look, we're running late," I say. "We have to get going—"

"Of course. Sorry to keep you, Zak. It's just…your friend looks familiar, and I usually never forget a face."

I smile, albeit with my teeth gritted, and wrap an arm around Rylee. "See you around, Jonesy." I sweep her away to the garage and don't breathe a sigh of relief until I shut the door of my SUV behind me.

"Fuck." She looks at me. "I'm fucked if he remembers where he saw me before."

"He won't. The Olympics aren't his beat. Even if he does, you can stick to your story that you're in town for your mother." I stop. "How is she by the way? Still out of sorts without the smokes?" I start the car and pull out of the garage.

Rylee snorts. "And still waiting for the results of her tests. Still coughing like there's no tomorrow." She takes in a shuddering breath.

I pull her in for a hug and kiss the top of her head. "Don't worry. We'll make sure she's seeing the best doctors—"

"We? There's no we. I'll see that she gets the best care. No matter what it costs." She looks part defiant and part scared shitless.

"Right." I drive the short distance to my building and pull into my spot in the garage near the elevator. Catching her before she has a chance to open the door, I kiss her on the lips this time, a long, lingering soft kiss, while my heart pounds madly because she's wrong. There is a *we*. At least as far as I'm concerned.

And that lightbulb thought has me scared shitless.

Rylee's phone pings, and she pulls back to check her phone. "Shit. I have to take this call."

"Who is it?" The look on her face tells me she'd rather tango with a toad than talk to whomever it is. I watch her put the phone to her ear.

"Hello, Chuck."

Chapter 14

RYLEE

"Finally. Why the fuck have you been avoiding me? Do you know how many texts I've sent you that went unanswered?" Chuck is pissed, but it's hard for me to separate Chuck, the over-bearing asshole, from Chuck, the coach, so whatever guilt I should be feeling is buried deep.

"I'll assume that's a rhetorical question."

"What the hell's going on, Rylee?"

"I'm taking care of Mama Cass. We saw a doctor, and she has emphysema. It's terminal." I flinch as I say the words, and Zak's hand goes to my thigh and holds on like he means it, like it means something other than foreplay.

"I'll be there tomorrow." He pauses, and my fear alarm spikes.

The last thing I want is for him to see me limping around. He clears his throat, and I know he has more to say. I dread what it might be. I close my eyes as if that'll protect me.

"How's your ankle?"

Shit.

"Fine. What did Tanya tell you?"

"Enough to know it's not fine. You see a doctor yet? I have the name—"

"I have my own doctor, damn it. And I'll see him when I'm damn well ready. What is it with men trying to nose in—"

"Men? What *men*?"

Fuck. I open my eyes to see Zak giving me the kind of stare that would rattle a girl if she cared. Fiery anger, hurt, and concern war in those deep dark eyes. I wish I could say I didn't feel a small pinch of conscience.

"Never mind. I don't need you coming to Boston." I watch as Zak's eyes go cold and angry and he motions for me to end the call. He can hear every word Chuck says, and he doesn't like it. Well, that makes two of us, but I can handle it.

"I'll be on the next flight I can catch," Chuck says before I can come up with a way to convince him otherwise. "I'll call you when I get in."

I jab the "end call" button and toss the phone, feeling like I could fry someone with the heat flying from me I'm so mad.

"What did you mean by 'what the fuck is it with controlling overbearing men?'"

"You tell me." For once, Zak isn't smiling or even smirking. The easy-going expression he usually wears has been replaced by a tight, wary look. His eyes study me with uncomfortable intensity. "Chuck's your coach? Charles Banner?"

I nod. Of course, he knows who the Olympic snowboarding coach is. He's probably googled the shit out of the Winter Olympics since he found out I'm on the team. The idea should bother me, but all I feel is a hint of satisfaction. I'm an idiot. I put my hand on the door handle as I answer him, and he doesn't stop me. "I don't want him to know about my ankle, but I don't have any choice in the matter."

"When's your appointment?"

"Tomorrow morning."

"You going to tell Chuck about it?"

"I don't want to, but—"

"You need to. I'll be there with you."

"Don't you have practice or something?" I should be telling him I don't need him there, don't want him there, but I can't bring myself to say any of those things. Probably because it'll send Chuck a message that we're over. So, I tell him, "I'd appreciate if you could."

"That was a sudden change of tune."

"I'm fickle. Sue me."

He laughs and then his face softens. "What are you going to do if your ankle takes more than two weeks to heal."

"It won't." I want no part of this conversation.

I reach up, take his face in my hands, and kiss him. This is what we're all about. Pure carnal lust and satisfaction. I let my physical instincts take over, breathe him in as I plant myself in the present, with him and his hot sensual mouth.

We're both panting when he breaks away.

"Not in the car, Buttercup. I want you naked and spread out in my bed."

His words mix up any residual anger and channel it to the lower half of my body, far away from any thinking.

SOMETIME EARLY IN THE MORNING, the sunrise wakes me. Or maybe it's the feel of a hard cock pressed against my rear, fitting perfectly and tantalizing me. Or it could be the heavily muscled arm draped over me, with a large calloused hand clutched to my breast. A light shiver of desire runs through me, and a chuckle automatically escapes before I have a chance to examine my predicament or how I feel about it. I was supposed to go home last night.

"Good morning, Buttercup." The lazy drawl of his crackly morning voice scrapes over my sensitive nerves, lighting me up like gasoline on embers. My pussy clenches like I'm Pavlov's dog.

I groan. "I can't. My doctor's appointment is at eight, and I need to—"

"Get dressed. I'll make us coffee and breakfast."

"You cook?" That's what I have to say in response? Not, *you're out of your mind. I'm outta here?*

"I'm no cook, but I can manage eggs and English muffins." He leans in and nibbles my earlobe. "Before I cook, how about joining me in the shower?"

"You're worse than the devil, tempting me every chance you get."

"No, Buttercup. You have it all wrong. You're the temptation around here. You're like a drug, and I'm addicted." He pulls away the covers, scoops his arms under me, and throws me over his shoulder as he rises from the bed.

You'd think I'd put up more of a struggle, but I fight like a five-year-old girl, mostly giggling and too turned on to resist as he carries me into the shower with his hand on my ass, caressing and making my toes curl.

EVEN THOUGH I'M wearing my clothes from last night—his jersey because I let Sheila talk me into it—I feel fresh and relaxed from the shower. It's not until Zak parks the car and we're walking into the medical building that my nerves seize up in panic.

Zak tugs on my hand. I pull it away.

"We're not in a hand-holding relationship," I snap. "Especially not in public." I pull my hat lower.

He inhales deeply. "Don't worry, Rylee. You can handle whatever the news is. You've handled worse setbacks."

I look up at him. His face is soft, his eyes filled with compassion. I should never have told him about my past. What the hell was that about?

"Quit it, will you?"

He snorts. "I'm not even going to ask." He opens the door for me, and we walk into an empty waiting room because I'm the first appointment. A measure of relief loosens me. The receptionist thanks me for filling out the online form and tells me someone will be out in a minute to get me. I pull my cap down.

Standing in the middle of the room, I don't bother to take a seat. Zak throws an arm around me and nuzzles my neck. He's hatless, and I frown, pulling away, but not with enough force or conviction because I'm a slave to my greedy sex hormones today. *Every day, every time, I'm in Zak's presence.*

"Relax," he says with a smirk, and I'm about to smack him in the chest when the door opens.

Panic that I'll be caught grips me almost as hard as Zak grips me, like he thinks I'm going to flee, and maybe he's not wrong.

Until I see who walks into the room.

Suzie and Sheila. *Sheila?* Suzie rushes over and gives me a hug and kiss on the cheek. She whispers, "Don't be mad." Then she steps away. I'm confused until the door opens again and in walks the last person I want to see.

"Chuck? What the hell are you doing here?"

"I told you I'd be here. When I called the house, I was told you were here."

"And you took it upon yourself to show up at my doctor's office?"

He looks around at Suzie and Sheila, and when his eyes meet Zak's, he scowls.

"I have as much right to be here as he does. Who the hell are you?" He shoves his hands on his hips and glares at Zak.

Zak glares back, and when it's about to get really awkward, Sheila hands me a bunch of flowers. "This is from the group." She gives me a hug, and it makes me almost cry with relief at her intervention. I hate drama.

"Who is this?" Chuck turns to me, gesturing toward Sheila.

"She's with me," Zak says.

Chuck frowns with confusion. Suzie nearly laughs.

"Really?" Sheila says. "News to me." She pats Zack's chest. "We're among friends here, big guy." She turns to me. "Aren't we?"

I nod. "Zak is with me, and I'm with Sheila and her group—"

"Groupies for the Boston Brawlers, to be exact," Sheila says. "President of their naughtiest fan club."

Zak snorts a laugh, and a sizzle of jealousy-inspired desire kicks through my system like a lightning strike. I wonder if my hair is standing on end.

"None of this makes sense," Chuck says. "All I know is you're going to have to work the ankle to get back on the slopes in less than two weeks, or I can't save your spot on the Olympic team."

All the air is sucked out of the room by the collective sharp inhales of everyone in the room except the asshole who dropped the bomb.

"She'll be back," Zak says, shocking me into a coughing fit.

No one calls him on his preposterous prediction, not even me.

I was about to make the same crazy claim myself. I only hope he has something besides my sheer brash willfulness to back up his belief.

A man in a white lab coat with a stethoscope hanging around his neck comes through the office door, and we all turn to stare at him.

"Rylee Flynn, you're up. Doctor Yancey will take a look at your ankle, and then we'll do an ultrasound. Follow me."

I'm amazed that I follow the guy's instructions instead of running the other way like every instinct in me screams to do.

He checks out the ankle and doesn't say much, and I don't prompt him. All he says is that the ultrasound will confirm the course of treatment and brings out the ultrasound machine from the corner, rubs gel on my ankle, and proceeds. It's my first ultrasound, and I watch intently as I lie on the bed. He moves the cold do-hickey around on my ankle and watches the black-and-white screen like he's seeing something.

Whatever it is eludes me, and my heart speeds up. It's the damn outcome that has me so scared I'm thinking about praying —something I haven't done since my parents died in that crash.

Closing my eyes, in my mind, I reach across the abyss between alive and dead and ask my parents to send me whatever positive energy, Karma, grace, prayers, or whatever they can—I'm trying to cover all possible bases—because I need a break here, some good luck to bail me out, even though it was my own stupid, foolish bravado that got me into trouble.

I promise I'll be more careful in the future. I won't take stupid unnecessary risks, no matter how enticing they seem. As long as I can get out of this and keep my spot on the Olympic team. As long as I can compete. I know I can win a medal because I need to. I need the promotional money for Mama.

After he's finished, he tells me to dress and meet him in his office. I don't know how long it's been, but I hope everyone out in the waiting room, except maybe Suzie, will have left to do whatever better things they have to do. The assistant knocks on my door as I finish tying my boots, and he leads me to an office.

Dr. Yancy sits behind a desk staring at a computer and looks up when I limp inside.

"Have a seat. You need to keep off your feet as much as possible. When you walk, use crutches for the next five days." He opens his drawer, pulls out a compression brace, and hands it to me. "Wear this for the next ten to fourteen days." He smiles. "I would also wear it when you go back to your *regular* activity."

I take off my boot and put the compression brace on my ankle. My heart races, and I clear my throat as if that will dredge up some courage. But I remember where I came from and what I've been through and speak up, "How long am I going to be out of commission?"

He turns away from his computer, shuts it off, then folds his hands on the desk and gives me another smile. "The ultrasound results confirm my exam that you have a severe, grade-two sprain, meaning that the ligament is more than fifty percent torn but not completely torn. If you stress it before it's healed, it will not only be unstable and therefore unsafe, but the injury could worsen, and you could have a chronically unstable ankle."

"How long?"

"If you take good care of it with ice baths, wear the compression brace, and stay off it completely, I'd say you could be ready in fourteen to eighteen days."

A breath whooshes from my lungs, and my heart calms. I might be able to work with that by the skin of my teeth, if Chuck will cover for me.

"Thanks, doc."

"And when you do go back to the half pipe, use this gel to manage the pain." He hands me a tube of Voltaren gel.

Chapter 15

ZAK

Chuck and I are the only two left in the waiting room when Rylee finally comes through the door. On fucking crutches.

"Are you all right?" I get to her side first, but just barely. The asshole coach is quick. He's a former pro athlete. Of course, he is.

"What did the doctor say?" Chuck grips her arm, and I want to rip his arm off.

"What are you two still doing here?" She looks from me to Chuck and back again. "Where's Suzie?"

"She left," I say. "Sheila had work, and Suzie had practice, so I told her to go, that I would stay because I have the morning off." It's not a lie. I didn't mention that I had to ask for the time off, claiming I had pressing personal business. The only reason coach went along with it was my performance last night. He warned me not to slip and make him regret it.

"I told him he shouldn't stay," Chuck says, still gripping her arm. "We have official Olympic business to discuss."

She rips her arm away from him, and the only thing more satisfying would have been if she'd hit him with the crutch. She glares at him. "I came with Zak."

"I'll drive you home." It's my knee-jerk response, and as I think

134

it over, I wouldn't change it based on the look on Chuck's face alone.

"We have to talk, Rylee."

"Not here. Not now." She heads for the door.

"Not at your house," he says, following her out of the office and to the garage. "Let's get lunch at my hotel." He juts his chin in my direction. "He can drop you off. I'll take care of you from there."

Something about Chuck hits me the wrong fucking way. Who am I kidding? Everything about him hits me the wrong way. His very presence makes me want to punch someone. Plus, the way he treats Rylee like he owns her, doesn't sit right. Okay, it's the main fucking thing and more than enough to boil my blood. Because even though we're only having a temporary fling, she's mine for the moment, and it doesn't sit well when some asshole moves in.

"I'm staying with her," I say. "Especially if she's going to your hotel." I grit my teeth in a hostile smile.

He ignores me. "Let's go, Rylee. We'll talk over lunch, and you can catch the next flight back to Park City with me. You can take advantage of the state-of-the-art medical and training facilities and—"

"No," I say at the same time as Rylee. My heart bumps hard into my chest wall at that. I thought I might have to fight her.

She looks at me, surprise registering before she frowns. "That's asking for trouble with all the media there constantly asking questions. Tell the Olympic officials I'm away on personal leave, taking care of my mother because it's true. I'm not leaving Mama right now. She's going to have surgery."

"She's your foster mother," Chuck says. Is that a hint of disdain in the asshole's voice?

Rylee stiffens and drifts in my direction, and I'm not even sure she realizes it, but I put an arm around her, crutches and all.

"Rylee will be fine here," I add. "I'll see to it."

"Who the fuck are you?"

135

"It doesn't matter who he is," Rylee says, and I'm not sure if she's coming to my defense or sweeping me under the rug.

"I'm the guy who knows all the best doctors, PTs, and trainers in Boston, and I can get her access to state-of-the-art facilities like ice baths and whatever the hell else she needs."

Chuck snorts and raises one brow in serious skepticism.

"I'm staying," she says. "Tell the officials I'm caring for my *mother* for the next ten to fourteen days." She nearly spits the words at Chuck. He stares at her, his mouth in a grim line, ignoring me.

"I am an Olympic official, Rylee."

Her chin goes up, and everything on her face screams defiance.

I hold her closer, tighter.

"And?"

He stares at her, his face turning red in frustration and anger. I want to sweep her away, but he is an Olympic official as a coach, and we have to deal with him. So, I wait him out until he heaves out a long breath.

"Have the doctor forward me a full report. You have twelve days. Don't take another minute, or you're off the team. And at the end of that time, I want a follow-up visit with the doc and a copy of that report verifying that you're good to compete."

"What about my *mother*?"

"What about her, Rylee? You want to compete in the Olympics or not?" He waves a hand. "She has Suzie. Let Suzie take care of her."

"Fuck you, Chuck—"

"She'll be ready," I say, and now I sweep Rylee away to the garage elevator and my car.

"You had no right to tell him I'd be ready." Her eyes burn holes in the side of my head while I drive the car.

"You're not wrong. But no harm, no foul. If you're ready, then you go to the Olympics. If not, then you tell him in twelve days you're not going."

"Shut up, you jerk." She covers her face with her hands.

"It's okay, Buttercup. I was trying to look out for you, but it's not because I don't think you can take care of yourself."

"Then why?" she asks, looking at me through her fingers.

I almost laugh but think better of it and look away to hide a grin. "Because you've taken some serious blows in the past... however many days...since I've known you. And Chuck didn't seem to care."

"You are such a jerk. A big fat *nice* jerk."

Now, I laugh. "Where to?"

"My house." She rattles off the address, and I put it in my navigator. It only takes twenty minutes to get there after one wrong turn, where she takes the opportunity to call me out.

When I pull to the curb in front of the ramshackle house, I ask, "Do I get to come in and say hello to Mama Cass?"

"No." She softens the blow with a smile. "There could be crying and drama, and I know how you hate that."

"Right. How about if I pick you up later?"

"You never know."

Fuck. I get out of the car and help her out, then walk her to the door, ignoring her protest.

"Don't worry. I won't barge in."

As we reach the door, it opens, and the older woman with her gray helmet hair and oversized rhinestone glasses stands there, grinning as she stares at me.

"If it isn't the handsome hockey hunk I'm dying to talk to—no pun intended. Come right in."

I almost choke on her dark humor. "If it isn't the beautiful and kind Mama Cass," I say.

"Don't—" Rylee doesn't get any further before Mama shushes her, and I bite down hard on my lip to stop myself from laughing. I help Rylee inside, and Mama Cass takes me by the hand, pulling me through the cozy living room to an old-fashioned kitchen. It reminds me of my grandma's house.

An older gentleman smiles at me and introduces himself as Mr. Argyle. He seems to be at home, bustling around doing someting at the sink.

Mama makes Rylee sit in the rocking chair and sits at the table with me after getting us each a drink of something. I don't ask what.

"Your ankle?" she asks Rylee.

"I'll live. Probably snowboard."

"The Olympics?"

"Hell yeah. They're not going to keep me from that if I have to go to a rogue doctor for a faked report to get it done."

I smile, though her attitude is on the edge of frightening. Mama Cass turns to me.

"And what about you, Mr. Hockey Player? What exactly are your intentions toward my daughter?"

Having picked the exact wrong moment to pick up my glass of unknown liquid, I try to swallow it and half choke, half spit it on the table. My eyes water.

"What is that?"

Chapter 16

ZAK

"It's my special lemonade," she says, smiling. "Don't you like it?"

"It's delicious," I croak. I'm worried about my voice ever returning to normal. I don't bother to ask what else is in it besides lemons.

"Answer my question. What are your intentions?"

Rylee stares at me, a tick in the corner of her mouth threatening to rebel into a grin.

"Strictly honorable."

"Bullshit. You're in it for the fun—and by fun, I mean sex—same as her."

My watery eyes feel like they're going to pop from my head, but I blink to reassure myself they're still intact as I try to respond to that. A guy in the corner of the kitchen I didn't notice before steps forward, lays a hand on Mama's shoulder, and comes to my rescue in a quiet, dignified voice.

"Mama, leave the poor boy alone," Mr. Argyle says. "He's clearly in love with the girl. I've never seen a more solid case of reluctant love as I have in this pair."

Shit. "No—"

"You have no idea what you're talking about, Mr. Argyle." Rylee throws her hands on her hips and then turns to me. "Ignore him. He doesn't know me. He's our neighbor."

"Don't be so rude, Rylee girl." Mama sounds breathless, and I wonder if she should sit down or something when Mr. Argyle hands her an inhaler.

Rylee helps her into a chair. "Sit, Mama. Enough excitement." She looks up at me accusingly. "You should go."

"You should go with him," Mama says.

"What are you talking about?" I've never seen Rylee lose her cool before. She collapses back into the rocker. "I thought we—"

"Can't you see I'm fixing to have a romantic evening with my man here?" She gestures in the direction of Mr. Argyle. He nods, looking slightly embarrassed.

"Maybe we can include—" he says.

"Not on your life," Mama says, harrumphing. "You think I want to eat dinner with these two setting off sparks all night?"

"That's it, Mama." Rylee stands from the rocker. I see the flinch on her face when she plants her foot. "You have it all wrong about me, but if you want a night alone, go for it. I'm not going to stop you." She hugs the old woman, then looks around. "What about Suzie?"

"She's out for the night. She didn't give me a hard time." Mama grins.

Rylee laughs and squeezes the old woman tight one more time. Mama shoos her, then gives me the side-eye as I follow Rylee to the back door.

"I'm counting on you, Mr. Hockey Big Shot."

"Yes, ma'am."

ONCE WE'RE BACK in my SUV, I turn to Rylee. "Where to, Buttercup?"

"Don't be a wise guy."

"My place, it is. But what if Suzie and Nowicki are there?" I wouldn't care, but she might, and right now, I'm all about pleasing her. Whether that's a lost cause or not is a puck flip. Whether or not I'm crazy is a sure thing because I've lost my mind and let my runaway dick take over. My previously perfect control of my bachelorhood-style emotions has evaporated into a distant memory.

The thing that scares me most is whether or not it's my addicted dick or my sorry excuse for a heart that's driving the Zamboni.

"Shit. Take me to a hotel."

"You got it." Both my dick and my heart leap for joy at her words, and I head to the Bostonian. She's silent and gazing out the window like the winter gray cityscape of Boston holds the keys to the universe. I know she's worried.

Keeping my voice soft, I have to ask, "When's Mama's surgery?"

"In ten days." She doesn't face me. "I have my follow-up appointment with Yancey the next day, and if all goes well with Mama, I leave for Park City the day after that."

My heart climbs to my throat. I don't remember the last time I felt this uncomfortable about the end of a... relationship—*call it what it is*. The next question pops into my head and can't be held back. "When do you leave for Italy?"

"Soon after that. Not sure. All I know is I'm cutting it close."

I gulp down my emotion and try to match her calm. "You think Chuck will keep his end of the bargain and keep your ankle injury quiet until then?"

"Yes. Unless someone else blows it up and I get the attention of other Olympic officials. Then they might question him, and I'm not sure he'll hold up...whether he'll back me. I wouldn't if I were him. There's no upside to it, and it would make no sense—"

"Sometimes, guys do things that make no fucking sense."

"You speaking from experience?"

"Not yet."

I relinquish the car to the valet, and she gets out with the crutches before I have a chance to come around and help her.

When I catch up with her, she stops and says, "You don't need to stay with me."

"What are you talking about?"

"I have a lot on my mind. I'm bad company right now."

"I'm staying with you."

She laughs with a derisive edge.

"I'm only trying to be helpful. I swear."

"That's always the cure for you, isn't it? Fuck the problem away?"

Ignoring her comment, I head to the registration desk without her and check in. The woman recognizes me with a big smile, but I don't smile back. Who knows what the fuck she's going to make of me getting a hotel room in a city where I live—without a bag. I glance at Rylee, and she's sitting with her ever-present ball cap low and a magazine in front of her face. When I'm finished, I walk to the elevator, and she meets me there, punching the up button.

Facing her, I keep my voice low. "This isn't about fucking. I want to talk." It's the truth. Mostly. But her earlier words cut close to the bone. "We need to talk about your problem."

She snorts. "Which one?"

"Your money problem," I whisper as we get on the elevator, alone, thank God.

The door slides closed, and her mouth turns grim. "What about you? Why don't we talk about what's wrong with you?"

"I don't have anything that needs curing." My chest tightens in protest as if I'm lying.

She looks at me, her mouth turned in a skeptical twist like I smell bad. Or my statement smells like a lie.

"I don't," I insist.

"Whatever you say, *Mr. Life is a Beach.*"

We get to the hotel room on the top floor, and I let her in. She heads straight for the lone king-sized bed and lies down, fluffing the pillows behind her head and closing her eyes. I sit on the edge of the bed next to her.

"I thought you weren't going to tell Chuck about your ankle?" It's a detail that's been bothering me, like everything else about the guy.

"My agent told him."

"What the fuck? That doesn't sound ethical to me—"

She opens her eyes and looks at me squarely. "She's Chuck's agent, too."

I open my mouth, and I have no words for a full three beats, then, "Fire her fucking ass. I don't care if she's fucking Jerry Maguire come to life."

"Then who do I replace her with, smart guy? I didn't have a bevy of agents banging down my door before I had a bad ankle, and I'm counting on some kind of quick promotional deal to help pay Mama's medical bills."

"I have a solution."

"What's that?" Skepticism oozes from her.

"I'll call my agent and ask him to take you on. Maybe do joint promotions with you."

Her eyes flash wide, but she says nothing, and I'm not sure if it's shock or whether she's calculating the consequences of working with me.

"I'll call him now." I stand and grab my phone.

Before I have a chance to call Jett, my phone rings. I check the caller. "Fuck."

"Who is it?"

"Candice Montgomery, the woman who crowned me Bachelor of the Year for Boston Magazine and a fucking thorn in my side."

Rylee laughs. Relief floods me because this is the first time I've heard her laugh in too long.

"I didn't figure you for a wimp, big boy." Challenge lights her face, prompting me to hit the green button to talk to the one woman I never want to talk to.

I stand and hold Rylee's stare as I speak. "Hello, Candice."

"Great news, Zak!"

"I doubt it."

"Now, don't be that way. I spoke to Ms. Delaney, the Brawlers—"

"I know who she is." All my muscles tighten as if in preparation for a kick to the balls because, if there's one thing Delaney is known for, it's being a ball buster.

"She loves the idea of a follow-up article that follows you on a date with your new someone special. Of course, we'll include a video for the online magazine and social media, too. That was Delaney's idea."

"Of course, it was." *Is it possible to feel your blood pressure rising?*

"What do you think?"

"You know what I think."

"No, really—tell me."

I'm watching Rylee watch me as she listens. Her eyebrows lift, curiosity in those sensational eyes of hers. She licks her lips, and I lose my train of thought, distracted for a second as my gaze wanders from her mouth and slides over her naked breasts...

"Zak? You there?"

My attention snaps back to the phone. "You know I don't want my personal life out there, that I never wanted my love life put up for speculation by the world at large." It's bad enough when my mom and sisters bug me about my bachelorhood, never mind every woman on the street who's read the magazine—not to mention how the whole B.O.Y. thing has given my teammates an excuse to taunt me relentlessly.

"Oh, don't worry about that. You're so sensitive. It's just one night. Besides, it's been approved by the Brawlers, and all we need to do is determine who will join you on your date. That's up to you, of course, but I think Rylee Flynn would be perfect."

"No."

"Then who?"

I close my eyes for a second, then open them and lock my gaze with Rylee. "Sheila Brown"

"Have it your way. I'll let you know when and where."

I end the call and meet Rylee's stare. Those damn eyes make my heart stutter. What else is new?

"I heard my name mentioned. Thank you for rejecting me." She gives me an ironic smirk. "You're going on a date with Sheila?"

"I had no choice. It's not a real date. It's nothing—"

She snort-laughs. "Don't worry about it."

"We said that while we're together, we own each other."

"True, but I was aware you could change your mind at any minute. Especially with all the women you have throwing themselves at you."

"Like who? I've been with you every spare minute I have."

She smiles. "Maybe I own you...for now. But I'm not forgetting that it's temporary." She focuses her amazing eyes on me, and I nearly stop breathing. "Are you?"

I swallow hard and give a reluctant shake of my head. *Fuck.* I haven't forgotten that we're temporary because it's always lurking in a dark corner of my mind, making me uneasy because I dread the expiration date.

She bites her bottom lip. "Are you still going to call your agent for me?"

"Are you still willing to work with me on a promotional deal?" I wait for a beat for her to nod. "You must be desperate for money because I'm sure this breaks all your fucking rules."

She lifts her chin, but the defiance fades, and she squeezes her eyes shut. Not before I see the heart-breaking desperation there. And maybe something else, maybe regret or something softer? Or maybe I'm fucking wishful thinking that she has feelings for me beyond a *friendly sex partner*.

"Make the call," she says when she opens those eyes again.

All I see now is determination. The kind I'm familiar with, the kind that 99% of professional athletes—and Olympians—have in them in order to get where they are. I nod.

Then I stab the speed dial button with Jett's icon because I want to help her, whether that makes me a fool or not. "Excuse me." I step out of the room for privacy because I have no idea what his reaction will be or what I'll need to promise him to do me this favor.

It takes only two seconds for him to answer his phone. It doesn't take much more time than that to convince him to take Rylee as a client.

"You sure you don't need a few minutes to think it over?" I pace up and down the hallway outside my bedroom, glancing at the closed door.

"No, I'm quick-minded that way. What I am thinking is that you two could make a great promotional duo—the ultimate winter sports power couple. I can think of a whole range of products you could promote together."

He chuckles. I wince. But I don't put a damper on his notion even though *couple* doesn't exactly describe what we are because the deal could help Rylee. Though when she finds out about the power couple idea, I doubt she'll like it.

"The catch is you'd be sharing the spotlight and the fee," he says. "It won't be as lucrative for you as a solo promo, but, hopefully, you'll be getting more offers to offset that."

"You know I only have so much time for promos." In truth, I'm not a fan of televised promotions. I feel like an idiot reading from a script.

"True. It's up to you. I don't think I'll be able to do much for her otherwise until after the Olympics. And then, we're gambling on her medaling."

I stop pacing. "Fine. Set something up. The sooner, the better. Whatever you can get for the biggest bucks."

I can hear cash register bells ringing on his end of the phone, and I bet his eyes are lit up.

I should probably tell him that, to quote her ceaseless reminders, we don't have a relationship. We aren't a couple, and I doubt she'd be willing to play one on TV commercials. But that problem can wait for another day.

Pushing open my bedroom door, I find Rylee sitting on the bed, dressed and ready to go. My gut falls to my feet like I swallowed a cartoon anvil.

"The Jett Agency has agreed to take you as a client." I toss my phone on the bed and approach her. "He'll call you."

"Thank you." She stands inches from me, and with no pride, no sense of dignity or thought of waiting for her to thank me, I wrap my arms around her and pull her close until I feel every part of her against my body and lower my mouth toward hers.

"You going somewhere?" Because I'm a chickenshit bastard, I don't wait for her answer. I cover her mouth and shamelessly do my best to change her mind about leaving the best way I know how. The only way I know might work. My gut knots up with this truth, but I plunge deeper into the kiss anyway.

Until a phone rings a minute later.

"It's my phone." Rylee separates from me and grabs her phone. "It's Jett."

Fucking Jett.

She looks stunned but stabs the call button and puts the phone to her ear with a relieved grin. A wave of pleasure trips through me, watching her.

That's when I know I did the right thing no matter what else happens—or doesn't happen—between us.

Chaper 17

RYLEE

"Rylee? Hamish Jett here. I just spoke with Zak Tomas and wanted to give you a call. I'd like to represent you, and I have a few ideas to hit you with."

As Jett describes the so-called couple promotions he has in mind, naming specific brands where he has contacts, and it's like I feel the walls of a relationship closing in on me. I sit on the edge of the bed and stare at the floor—away from Zak as he stands in front of me.

"How does that sound? I can get something started for next week before you go back to Park City if that works."

"To tell the truth, it sounds wonderful—and terrible. I don't feel comfortable with the couple image."

I ignore Zak as he sits on the bed next to me.

"Don't worry about it. We can do something different—maybe a frenemies thing like Howie Long and Teri Hatcher used to do. Could be lucrative, and I can ask for a fee upfront."

"I don't know what to say. Sounds like a dream." I laugh to dispel my unease, but it doesn't work. "Naturally, I'm skeptical," I admit. "Why would anyone give an unknown quantity like me money upfront?"

He laughs, and it sounds real. "I'll be honest with you, they wouldn't. They'd be paying for Zak and willing to give you a shot on the strength of his and my reputation."

The truth punches me in the gut, powerful and nasty and knee bending in its demonstration of Zak's generosity and kindness. "Fuck."

Zak stiffens, and I dart a look at him, moving away, confused and struggling with emotions—need, self-respect, and fear all pulling me in different directions.

"You could say that."

"Jesus, I didn't mean to say that out loud. I don't know if I can accept that kind of charity."

"Don't be a fool," Zak says, reaching for the phone, but I'm as quick as he is, and I pull it away.

"I don't like the idea of being so dependent—"

"You won't be," Jett says, his reasonable voice a contrast with the stormy look on Zak's face and the storm of chaos inside my head. "You'll prove us right and do a great job. Sell some products."

"Let me think about it—"

"In case it influences your decision, we're talking about fifty-thousand dollars upfront, Rylee."

"Shit. I..." His words slice through my confusion with the knife of practical reality. The out-of-pocket costs for Mama's surgery, not to mention her ongoing medications and care, press on me, and I swear I can do whatever I have to do no matter how scary, for Mama. "Okay. It's a deal. I won't disappoint you." I'm looking at Zak as I say the words and beg him not to make a big deal of this because the fact that I owe him stings me like bad medicine, and I hate it.

He owns me—for real. This isn't some temporary fling we're talking about.

"I'll email you the contract and schedule something to be shot pre-Olympics for airing the opening week," he says.

"Thank you." We end the call, and I'm faced with Zak.

His mouth quirks up on one side like he's not sure if he should be pleased, but he is anyway. Thrilled that I owe him.

"I predict we'll have more promotional offers than we can manage," he says, "and you'll get a percentage of—"

"You mean, you'll require the poor suckers to include me in a promo if they want you for it and then take a reduction in your percentage."

His eyebrows rise. "Are you serious? Have you looked in a mirror? They'll jump at the chance to have you, and you'll earn your fifty-fifty split."

I turn away from him because he can't be as good as he looks. "I don't want things to get messy between us."

"No mess. Everything will be strictly by the contract."

I eye him. "What do you get out of this?" My voice is quiet because I almost don't want to hear the answer, almost wish his answer will be exactly what it can't be, that he wants *me*. But then, I'd have to end everything.

"Don't worry. We both know this is short-term. Until you win a medal in the Olympics. Then, you'll be able to get deals on your own."

"Except we'll still be connected by the deals we do together."

"That's business."

"It was business between me and coach. Until it wasn't."

"I'm not him."

"You're worse."

"How do you figure?"

I can't tell him it's because our chemistry is off the charts, nothing like I've experienced before, or because I crave his touch, because I want to tell him all my secrets. Worst of all, I can't tell him it's because a part of me wants to cave in and have him take care of everything, which goes against everything I've ever stood for, all the independence.

I don't need another soul. All the survival instincts in me, that have been bred in me forever since I lost my parents, scream at me to remember this whenever I'm around him. Because that's when I weaken.

"You're too risky." *But I'm the daredevil, aren't I?* If so, that makes him the devil.

"Come on," he says, unhappy with my answer. "You're a go-for-the-brass-ring kind of woman, aren't you? Take a chance."

"Not that kind of chance. The consequences could be too..." I wave a hand, unable to expose myself any further to him, or to myself.

"What's this about?" With gentle hands, he pulls me closer to him on the bed. He's so fucking hard to resist when he's *nice*, when he shows the other side of him that has nothing to do with fun and sex, when my heart melts with wanting more of all of him.

Do I bare my one last secret, about my parents? Maybe he already figures the worst since I'm a foster kid.

"I don't like being tied to people, okay? I don't come from a happy home like you did."

"How do you know about my happy home?"

"You're right. You suffered a great tragedy when your friend died, but you had your parents and your sisters. Everything about you shouts happy childhood and family sprinkled with pixie dust and poof, right out of college, your hockey career dreams come true. Me? I struggled to make the Olympic team for six years, missed it four years ago, and just when I make the team a few months ago, I stupidly injure myself and could lose it all."

"You'll recover," he says.

"That's it? That's all you got?"

"I got you a deal." He pauses, his face softens, and he leans closer. "And I have me. I'll be here for you if you want me. There's something in you that makes me believe you can do anything."

Those are the most devastating words any man has ever said to me.

"You're ridiculous. You can't promise you'll always be there for me, can you?"

"No, I—"

Reality reasserts itself, erasing the absurd fairytale of happy-ever-after he's trying to sell. I wave my hands between us. "This... thing between us, it's not permanent. It's temporary until I get back on my snowboard and then I'm off, out of here."

His soft expression disappears, and his mouth flatlines as he turns away from me. "I get it. You think I want something permanent?" he scoffs. "Not on your life. I enjoy my bachelor lifestyle. I'm on top of the world where I am, happy as a clam and plan to stay that way." He smirks, but I can tell it's forced. His eyes don't show the happy crinkles at the corners.

"Forever?" I don't know what makes me ask the question, but it's a stupid one because why do I care?

"I don't know." He lowers his voice until it vibrates, and I strain to hear. "If I didn't want to stay a bachelor, would that be so terrible?"

I'm startled, and my heart stumbles. It feels like something's tearing at my chest, and I don't know if it's something terrible trying to get in or something destructive trying to get out.

I back away. "It would be scary. Something I want no part of." I hug my arms around my chest and force air in and out.

He pulls back, and for the first time, I see real trouble in his eyes, something deep and panicked. Pain glistens in his eyes and leaps across that connection we have to lodge in my chest, making the previous terrible, destructive scary thing residing there seem like a ripple compared to the seismic cracks I feel now.

Some buried caring instinct in me rears up, the same one that made me protective of Suzie all those years ago, and I feel an overwhelming need to protect him from that pain I see and feel, to make things right for him.

Taking his hand, I pull him down onto the bed, and wrapping him in my arms, I kiss him. I kiss his mouth, his eyes, his cheeks, everywhere on his face, and his temples. I don't know what I'm doing or exactly why except I want him to have all my strength and passion because I need to undo whatever pain I've caused.

His powerful arms hug me back, and he whispers near my ear, "That's always the cure for you, isn't it? Fuck the problem away?"

I feel his smile as he tosses my words back at me. His low voice rumbles through me, settling me. "It's worked so far. Let's keep doing it until it stops working. Deal?"

"I can take that deal."

I sigh as he rolls on top of me, mostly because the feel of his calloused palms cruising down my body to the promised land have me on the edge of anticipation so fast that I've almost forgotten that troubled look in his eyes, the one that tells me he's on the edge of needing more from me.

Maybe more than I have to give.

Chapter 18

ZAK

Driving Rylee back home at the crack of dawn so I could get back for the morning skate sucked. But what sucks more is the ticking clock in my head, the countdown to the expiration date of our *non*-relationship. One week and one day. I toss my sneakers into my locker and sit on the bench to lace up my skates.

"What's with you? Your sneakers bite you?" Nowicki sits next to me.

I ignore him.

"Where'd you go last night?"

"None of your business." I finish tying my skates and stand.

"You spent the night with Rylee." He sounds confident. I stare him down. He grins.

"What makes you think that? I could've been with someone else."

He shakes his head. "It's your mood. A random girl wouldn't put you in a sucky mood."

I snort and head for the door. "I'm not looking forward to the road-trip, that's all."

He snorts back at me as he follows me to the rink. It's true. We'll be away for three days for two games. The only good thing about the trip, besides playing hockey, is that my parents and sisters will be at the game in Minnesota, and I'll get to spend some time with them afterwards.

Once I step onto the ice, I soak in the cold air and pump my legs fast to feel the breeze on my face, to smell that combination of cold air, Zamboni fumes, and man-sweat that permeates the rink. It smells like home, my haven. The one place where I can leave the rest of the world behind and automatically feel alive, one hundred percent present and in charge.

After practice, we dress up in suits. Some of the guys take their fashion seriously and get creative since we have cameras aimed at us everywhere we go for social media. I'm not that guy. I wear a dark suit and tie—in fact, I probably look like a banker, except I'm sure bankers don't smirk as much as I do. My only requirement in a suit is that it fits and it's comfortable. Maybe I should do a promo for State & Liberty athletic fit stretch suits. As we parade past some fans on the way to the bus, they're holding up their phones for videos and pics. Some of them call out and others whistle. I look plenty sharp in my charcoal suit and Brawlers black and gold tie.

WE WIN THE FIRST GAME, but according to coach, Minnesota is a tougher opponent as he goes over some key matchups and quirks to look out for.

"You," he points to me, "I'm counting on you to stick to their big right winger every time he's on our end. Don't let him breathe, much less take a shot."

"Yes, sir." I give him my game-shark smile, and my adrenaline starts pumping. This is the kind of assignment I live for.

"And don't get hurt. I don't care if you get a penalty or two, but no injuries. You hear me?" I nod, and he moves on, giving O'Rourke some game-time handy tips.

"What's he worried about you getting hurt for?" Nowicki

whispers as we sit on the bench in the no-frills visitor locker room, ready to go. He's antsy because he's up against a fellow rookie who happened to be overall number one in the draft.

"He's referring to the last time we played them last season."

"You got hurt?"

"Yeah, but so did he." I shrug it off, though at the time, it was my worst nightmare. A fucking ankle injury. A lot like Rylee's injury. Fuck. Why am I just realizing that now? It took me four weeks to get back to normal. Ankles can be a bitch.

"That's right—you were out for a few weeks with an ankle, weren't you?"

"Never mind about that. I'm stronger than ever. I put on fifteen pounds of muscle since the end of last season."

"Shit. Still a growing boy, eh?"

"Don't you forget it."

Coach ends his spiel with his usual inspiring words. "Let's give those guys a spanking they won't forget."

THE MEDIA WANTS to talk to me after the game about my fight and two penalties, but I manage to escape the mob after ten minutes because O'Rourke was the real star of the game. As usual. I spot Dad because he's a head taller than most people—except me —and head in his direction, feeling a smile take over my face.

Someone grabs my arm and slows me down, and I turn to find the woman I should be referring to as the bad penny because she keeps turning up.

"Candice, what the hell are you doing here? They let you wander this far out of Boston?"

She laughs, and then her forehead wrinkles in concern as she touches my cheek. Or tries to, but I push her hand away.

"You got quite the shiner in that fight."

"At least I didn't get stitches like the other guy."

She laughs. "No. Somehow the black eye and swollen cheek give you a certain tough-guy *j'ne sais quoi* that only makes you look even sexier. If that's possible."

"Look, I—"

"I know. I'm holding you up. I'm actually here visiting with friends, but I wanted to let you know we set up the bachelor-about-town-date—that's what we're calling it for our feature. It's a go after Saturday's game."

"That's three days from now." In my head, I'm counting down. That will leave me five days until Rylee's expiration. Fuck. "My family is waiting, Candice. Text me the details."

I pull away from her and head for the warm embrace of my family. For a split second, I expect to see Bill here with me because he was always around us like he was part of the family, but he never made it this far. He gave up on us, on himself.

Don't do that. Don't give up. In my head, it makes no sense, but in my heart, it's all about Rylee and me, and the sheer difficulty of getting past her defenses squeezes my chest so that my super comfortable suit feels like it's a band of steel suffocating me.

"Zak, sweetheart." Mom reaches out for me first, capturing me in a hug, and even though she squeezes me, it eases the tightness, and I shove Rylee aside, determined to stay in the present and give my family my best.

After they fawn over me and my black eye and go from scolding to applauding to laughing at me for my performance in the game and the fight, we reach the restaurant, which is Dad's favorite and the one our family traditionally saves for important occasions.

Jett is here to greet me as soon as I walk in.

"What brings you to Minnesota? Don't tell me you have some bad news?" I hold onto my smile and hope to hell he has an offer from the team because I am more worried than is reasonable about bad news.

"Nothing bad. Would I do that to you?" He gives me a bro-hug and embraces my mom and sisters like he's part of the family and not intruding at all. In truth, he's always been welcome by my family since I first signed with him five years ago. He shakes my dad's hand, and we follow the hostess to a big round table in the corner.

"To what do we owe the pleasure of your company?" Dad asks as soon as the server leaves.

"We got an offer from the Brawlers that I think would be tough to refuse." He grins at Dad, who speaks his language —money.

"Spill it," I say though I don't need to hear it to know I'm going to accept it. I can't stand another minute of being in contract limbo. He tells us, and my father whistles, my sisters give each other high fives, and my mom tears up.

"You're so amazing," she says to Jett.

He points to me. "There's the amazing guy. He makes my job easy with his performance on the ice. Plus, that doesn't even count the new promotional deals I've been lining up. Did he tell you about them?"

Shit. "No, let's not talk—"

"No. Let's hear about it," Mom says. She always gets a kick out of my promotions, and my sisters look too eager because this is where they get the most out of giving me shit—for my lack of acting ability or the lame products or whatever else they can pick on every single time.

Jett winks at me. "He's teaming up with Rylee Flynn, the Olympic snowboarder, to do some commercials for a line of sunglasses."

"First I heard of it." I can't help smiling as I picture Rylee on the slopes in one of those skintight outfits they wear, sporting sunglasses with her hair blowing wild—

"That sounds like a good one," Mom says.

"I bet it pays well," Dad says.

My sisters eye me, and the loudmouth pipsqueak among them

opens up. "Why Rylee Flynn? No one's ever heard of her unless they're a snowboarding nerd like me."

"It turns out she and your brother are—"

"Acquaintances." I glare at Jett, and he has the good grace to nod.

"Really?" The pipsqueak has the devil in her eyes as she stares at me. "You sure that's all there is to it? Because she's quite attractive, and I can't imagine Boston's Bachelor of the Year being acquainted with a gorgeous woman without—"

"Shut it, pipsqueak."

My other two sisters and mom laugh, but Dad looks at me like he expects a further explanation.

"What?" I shrug. "We may be seeing each other, but it's no big deal."

Jett shakes his head, and drinks are served, thank God, putting an end to the Rylee discussion—permanently, if I have anything to say about it.

The meal goes fine after that because I turn the topic to news from home and make the girls tell me what's going on in their lives —which is probably more than I want to hear, especially from the pipsqueak.

"You can't date yet. You're too young," I insist and look at Dad.

"I agree, but your mother says otherwise." He shrugs. "Tell us more about the promotional deal, Jett. How does the money work with two celebrities? Is it an even split or what?"

Jett dives in despite my glare and attempted kick under the table.

"In this case, Zak is the main draw for the brand and would normally get the lion's share of the fee given Rylee's relatively unknown status, but Zak insisted on an even split."

The pipsqueak blows out a loud whistle attracting attention, and Dad sits back in his chair and examines me like I've turned into an elephant wearing a tutu.

"Are you crazy, son?"

"He's right. You are crazy," Jett agrees.

"Crazy in love." The pipsqueak grins at me.

I look at her, and the retort dies on my lips. Lowering my head, I stare at my empty plate.

"Is it true, Zak?" Mom's words force me to face her, and I shrug. "I'm worried about you," she says.

"Me, too. I won't lie. I'm scared shitless. But I had to help her. She needs the money."

"That's nice of you, Zak," Dad says. "But watch out for yourself."

"I will." I plan to hang on for dear life.

Jett and I have to leave, so we all stand.

"I'm so proud of you, honey," Mom says as she hugs me goodbye.

My sisters wish me good luck, and when it's the pipsqueak's turn to hug me, she holds on for an extra beat and squeezes me tight.

"Don't let her take advantage of you, Zakky. I know you're a big teddy bear underneath all your muscle."

I smile and squeeze her back. "Don't worry about me, pipsqueak." I step back and look at what a young beauty she's becoming, and a spike of worry about guys going for her makes me shudder.

"I'm serious." Her expression is fierce. "I swear I'll beat her up if she makes a wrong move."

I smirk, and my worry eases somewhat. "You and what army?"

She punches my arm, and we leave. I exit with an odd mixture of warmth from my family, satisfaction about my contract, and trepidation about Rylee because I'm unsure how I feel about her. I should be wary and cautious and keep her at arm's length.

But I can't get that reasonable approach to stick. I can't not feel the connection, and I can't not care.

Back at my hotel room, I have the bright idea to text Rylee, but she doesn't respond, doesn't even read my text as far as I can tell. I don't know if that's because it's past midnight or general principle.

Either way, the puck is on her ice. Now, she owes me a call, and I need to stay disciplined enough to wait it out.

WAITING IS OVERRATED and time wasted. That's what I think after waiting two days to hear back from Rylee. I texted her again, and she finally responded to tell me to have fun tonight. Shit.

Tonight, I need to deal with this Bachelor of the Year business and waste more time on the Rylee clock.

"This place looks fancy," Sheila says. I help her from my SUV and hand the keys to the valet as we head inside Buttermilk & Bourbon while the snow falls. No one's outside in the weather wielding phones or other cameras, which suits me fine.

The reprieve is short-lived. Inside the place, no less than three cameras wait for us—and those are the official ones. I don't know how many diners have their cell phones raised to record the commotion, but Candice and Delaney scored a hat trick of publicity with media presence, a big crowd, and glamour as Sheila takes off her coat to show her shine. Her dress may be short, but it's covered in sparkly sequins, and her spike heels make her legs over-the-top long and more than sexy. I let out an appreciative low whistle. Loud enough to make her smile, discrete enough not to make a spectacle. My usual M.O.

"You both look wonderful," Candice says. She's standing next to the blue-haired chef-owner, and we're introduced and then shown to our table.

"This place is spectacular," Sheila says as we sit.

"It's not the place; it's the people in it who make it special," I say, meaning it.

She gets giddy on me.

"I hear the food is good, too," I say, lifting my menu. From the corner of my eye, I see the cameras move in and Candice, sitting with PR at a nearby table, urging me to get close to Sheila if I'm reading her hand signals correctly.

"I think they want us to kiss," I say under my breath.

Sheila looks up from her menu. "Who?"

"Didn't you notice all the cameras aimed at us?"

She puts her menu down and glances around the room, her eyes getting wider and wider. "Shit. Maybe I ought to rethink my meal choice. I was going for the fried chicken, but no way I can eat with my hands with all the attention."

I laugh. "Whatever you do is fine with me, Sheila. You're a good sport for going along with this fiasco."

"You know me. I was never one to turn down a good meal."

"Yeah. I have noticed you enjoy your food. Beat Finn in a burger eating contest that time last year at the Tea Party."

"In his defense, he'd had too much to drink."

"You sure that's a defense?"

She laughs, and I could almost put aside the fiasco and chalk it up to part of the job when I see a woman walk through the door, and the feeling of déjà vu assaults me and knocks me over—metaphorically speaking.

Rylee walks in, wearing the same outfit she did the first night I saw her—which seems longer ago than ten days. I watch her negotiate with the hostess and realize she's not wearing her ball cap. She knew there'd be press here tonight, and I wonder why the hell she's taking such a risk. If they recognize her, they'll wonder what she's doing here instead of Park City.

The hostess nods and takes her to a table near ours, close enough so I can hear them talk. Close enough so she's noticed and turning heads. But, of course she is because she's fucking gorgeous.

She's not on her crutches, and she's not limping.

The crowd settles down, and the cameras filming us from three different angles blend into the background. I have half an eye and ear on Rylee, and Sheila keeps looking in her direction.

"It feels weird not to say hello to Rylee. You sure it would be a problem?"

"Yes. The cameras are following your every move. They followed you all the way to the ladies' room a minute ago."

"Damn." She grins. But over her head, I spot a familiar face walking past us, and I'm not happy to see him.

"Jonesy, what are you doing here?" I stop him.

"Same as everyone else. Spying on the Bachelor of the Year on his dinner date. I'd ask you for a brief interview, but Candice said she has an exclusive."

I nod.

"But she doesn't have an exclusive with Rylee Flynn," he says and sits down at Rylee's table opposite her without asking. Fuck.

I eavesdrop shamelessly as I sip my drink.

"Have a seat and join me." Her usual sarcasm brands her words.

"I remember where I saw you before," Jonesy says.

"Is that right?"

Sheila says something, but I have no idea what it is because I'm straining to hear Jonesy's response.

"At the snowboard World Cup event in Calgary last winter. You won first place in the halfpipe and second in big air. I was impressed. So was everyone else. I should've remembered you sooner since you're a member of the U.S. Olympic team, but I'm covering Boston sports this winter while my colleague gets to travel to Park City and Milan for the games."

The whole time he's talking, he alternates between looking her in the eye and eying her ankle. That's when I notice she's still wearing the compression brace.

What was she thinking coming out tonight—crutches or no crutches? I wish to fuck she'd stayed home.

"Problem with your ankle? That why you're here in Boston and not in Park City?" He finally gets to his point, and I let out a big breath.

I want to jump from my seat and tell the reporter to fuck off, but that would make things worse. I'll talk to him later and make it clear where I stand. I might have to bribe him somehow, but I'll convince him to leave her alone.

"I'm here for my mother's surgery next week," she says.

Candice chooses that moment to come over to my table.

"How are you enjoying the evening? We got some good shots so far."

"We were just leaving," I say, sliding a glance at Sheila. She nods.

"You can't leave yet. It's barely ten o'clock. You need to stay at least until eleven."

"Not tonight. Early skate." I stand, and Sheila follows. I take a detour in the direction of Rylee as she gets up from her seat. We're both headed toward the back exit.

I catch up with her outside after grabbing my keys from the valet.

"I'll wait in the car while you have a chat," Sheila says.

We both stay quiet until she's gone out of hearing.

Then Rylee clears her throat. "It was stupid for me to be here, but I figured you needed moral support."

"Liar." I pull her aside and duck into the alley on the side of the building. "You came because you're jealous."

She laughs, but her heart isn't in it. "I'm leaving now."

"Come home with me."

"What about Sheila?"

"We can drop her off."

"What about your early skate?"

"Eavesdropping?"

"No more than you were."

"You're right. I heard Jonesy. I'll talk to him and convince him he doesn't need to write anything about you and your ankle."

She rolls her eyes. "Don't do me anymore favors. I don't like owing you. Besides, something tells me he won't write about it. He has nothing but speculation. Unless I give him a reason, like showing up in public with crutches."

"No more hockey games?"

"No." She stares at me, and I stare back. A feeling sweeps over me, like when you're half asleep and you feel like you're falling, and then you startle awake and realize you're okay. Except I'm not okay. I'm left with a woozy feeling, like I'm dizzy or drunk, but different. Whatever this buzz is, I can't say I don't like it.

I wrap my arms around her and whisper close to her ear, her hair tickling my face, electrifying me, and not to mention making my dick stand up. "Stay with me. We don't have many more nights."

"You make a good case, but—"

I cut her off with a kiss, the kind with meaning and feeling and tenderness as I taste her and my tongue toys with hers, sweeping across her teeth and her lips. I want more, and I don't want to stop.

She pushes away, breathless, and I gaze down at her eyes, bright and heart-stopping in the semi-darkness. I want to get lost in her eyes and stay—

"I don't know why we should bother spending any more nights together. Our fling has run its course. It's too much trouble to keep it going with everything going on—you have your Bachelor of the Year image, and I have my ankle and—"

"Shut up, Rylee. None of that adds up to shit. We have something worth whatever trouble we have to go through to make it happen."

She scoffs. "Do we?" She pauses. "All we really have in the end is a business deal, and I don't think I'd even hold you to that if you—"

"That deal sticks no matter what."

My phone pings, and Rylee pulls from my hold. "Check your phone. It's probably Sheila or Candice or maybe some other woman who wants your attention and doesn't have rules and problems and trouble."

She tries to walk away, but I grab her and hold on tight. "You're coming with me."

She laughs. "Now, you're resorting to kidnapping? Maybe you like drama?"

"You're the one who claims you don't like drama," I say as I drag her through the alley to the back parking lot where the valet parked my SUV. Sheila's waiting in the back seat on her phone.

"Get in."

Rylee stares at me for a few beats. "Don't say I didn't warn you."

I help her into the car, shut the door, and go around, half wondering if she's going to jump out before I have a chance to drive away.

She stays put. I slam the door behind me and start up the car.

"You're trending on social media in Boston," Sheila says.

"Fuck."

"It's not so bad. People think you're with me."

I laugh. "You're a real good sport, Sheila."

"I'll put that on my dating profile and see what it gets me."

Rylee turns to her. "You won't need any dating app, honey. I predict you'll be very popular in the next few days the way you look tonight. You're gorgeous. You ought to cash in and have a ball."

Sheila laughs. "You're probably right." She smacks me on the shoulder. "Thanks, Zak."

"Sure, any time. Call if you need a reference."

It doesn't take long to get to Sheila's place in Revere on the north shore of Boston, and once I'm alone in the car with Rylee, tension overwhelms the intimate space.

She stares at me long and hard as I drive across the Tobin Bridge back into Boston. I flick her a glance in question.

"Last chance for you to take me home, or I can't be responsible for your broken heart."

My heart clatters, and my breath catches. I manage to avoid driving off the side of the bridge as I force a smile and try to get my cool back. "Why would you say a thing like that?"

She shrugs. "Seemed appropriate. You're falling, and we have an expiration date."

"Fuck." I can't lie to myself or her because it's true, isn't it? "You let me worry about me."

"Fine. But remember my rule—"

"Fuck your rules." Anger makes me grip the steering wheel tight as I pull off the highway and head to my condo. She stays blessedly silent.

Candice sends me another text, and I ignore it.

Five minutes later as I pull into my condo garage, my phone pings again. Candice sent two texts, but I don't bother reading them now.

"Let's go." My voice is tight with anger simmering on the edge of my control.

"How can I refuse your charming offer." She doesn't wait for me to come around and help her out, and we ride up the elevator in heavily charged silence. Her eyes spark with almost as much anger as I feel, and that pisses me off more. What does she have to be angry at?

She's the one callously disregarding how I feel with her self-righteous rules. Besides, I'm angry enough at myself, so there's no place for her anger. I have her covered.

She steps inside my condo ahead of me, and as soon as I close the door, I pin her back against it, trapping her, pressing my hard dick against her, and letting her feel the full wrath of my frustration.

"Fuck. Your. Rules," I goad her. Her eyes fire up, and my nerves nearly explode with the need to have her, to taste her, to be inside her.

"Never mind fucking my rules. Fuck me." She fists my shirt and slams her mouth onto mine, biting down on my lip and grinding her hips against mine.

"Jeezus, Buttercup," I groan into her mouth, tasting blood. "This is going to be angry sex, is it?" I don't wait for her to confirm, and clamping my hands under her ass, I lift her. She wraps her legs around me, and I carry her down the hallway to my bedroom, kicking the door closed behind me with a bang.

SWEATY AND SPENT, her head rests on my shoulder with her hair spread out around me as my eyes drift closed.

The blaring sound of my phone ringing jars me, and I pop up reflexively. Glancing at the phone, I swear under my breath. It's Delaney.

I can't ignore her call, or she'll call Coach—or the Brawlers' general manager if she's really pissed.

"Who is it?" Rylee asks.

"Brawlers PR."

"You're in trouble, aren't you?"

"Not as much as you are if Jonesy doesn't keep his mouth shut."

Exhausted, I ignore the phone call. Despite however much trouble is brewing around us, I have no trouble sleeping with Rylee in my arms, on my mind, and in my dreams.

Chapter 19

RYLEE

When I wake up in Zak's bed, I'm alone, and a zap of fear races through me. Bolting upright, I see him across the room, packing for another road trip, his bare back to me. I watch his muscles ripple, and when he turns, he smiles when he sees me watching him.

I try to ignore the pang in my gut that feels too much like I'm being left behind like I don't want to be left behind. So what if he's leaving? He's no one to me. I can't miss someone unless I care about them, and I refuse to care about Zak fucking Tomas.

I refuse to want him, and I especially refuse to need him.

"Get dressed, Buttercup. I'll give you a ride home. Unless you have somewhere else to be."

"I do. But not 'til later. I'll be sitting in a whirlpool at the Garden's training facilities later this morning while you're on a plane flying somewhere, courtesy of my sister getting permission for me." I watch his mouth open in surprise.

"Why didn't you tell me that you—"

"You've been busy, and like I said before, you've done enough good deeds. I don't want to owe you any more than I already do."

I watch him pull a sweatshirt over his head, the way it slides down his abdomen, hiding each indent until his skin disappears.

"Quit saying that. There's no scorecard between us." He closes in on me, and my heart palpitates in confusion. Excitement rises as his arms come around me, enveloping me completely with their raw strength the way they always do. At the same time, fear that this fling is getting out of control gives rise to panic in equal measure.

He drops me off at my house at seven a.m., and the place is asleep. He leans in for a kiss, but I stop him. "No. Kissing goodbye is a couple's thing. Not us."

The trouble that clouds his eyes nearly unravels my resolve, but I tighten my grip on the precarious hold I have on my emotions and push the door open. I run to the house, and my ankle tweaks once on the steps, but it holds up. When I get inside, I allow myself to breathe again.

I'm on my second cup of coffee, waiting for Mama and Suzie to get up when my phone pings. It's Tanya. My agent. Shit. I forgot to fire her. I've been so preoccupied with Mama and the stupid nice jerk I'm having *only* a fling with.

Taking one more sip of coffee to clear my sex-clouded head, I pick up my phone.

"Tanya."

"Hey, Rylee, sorry to call you so early, but I have bad news."

Of course, she does. Maybe Jett's already let her know about my switch. Maybe he sent her some paperwork or something to sign?

"Give it to me."

"GNU wants to cancel the promotion. They found out about how serious your injury is—"

"What? How did they find out?"

"Chuck told them. They don't want to air it since it's obvious you're injured now, and they want to distance themselves."

I take a few breaths to calm my pounding heart. This is okay. I have Jett. *Thanks to Zak.*

Do not think about Zak right now. Or ever.

"That's fine. No worries, Tanya." I manage to keep my voice normal, not a spec of sarcasm.

"I'm glad you're taking the news so well."

"I hope you take my news well."

"What news is that?"

"You're fired, Tanya."

As I end the call, I hear a screech. I need to call Jett to make sure everything is official and have him send whatever paperwork needs to be sent. I dial him up, and he answers on the second ring even though it's only seven-thirty in the morning.

I explain about firing Tanya just now and the problem with GNU promotion.

"I'm worried about GNU telling some Olympic team officials besides my coach, Chuck. If they find out about the ankle, they could insist on more rigorous requirements for me to stay on the team. I don't really know how it works, but I do know there's a whole line of snowboarders behind me, waiting for their shot, and if there's even a whiff that I'm not a hundred percent, I could be replaced."

"We need to solve the Olympic team problem," Jett says with finality. "And we can't solve it by hiding it."

"What do you mean?" I'm curious and wary.

"I have an idea."

Now, I'm scared because I'd bet my left ankle that his idea involves the big sexy jerk, Zak.

Chapter 20

ZAK

We're filing off the team charter plane in Detroit, and most of the guys, the married ones, have their phones to their ears. A shot of wistfulness jars me. Since when do I envy the married guys? Haven't I always been happy to be a bachelor?

The answer is that it was before my Bachelor of the Year status. And before Rylee, if I'm a hundred percent honest. Nowicki catches up to me as we get on the bus taking us to our hotel.

"I just heard from Suzie," he says.

"Not you too? I didn't think you'd turn into one of the pussy-whipped guys."

He laughs and then shoves my shoulder as he takes a seat next to me near the back where the single guys sit. It's funny, now that I realize it, how the team sits divided along the lines of bachelorhood versus married. Most of the bachelors are rookies, and we've always claimed to be the happily unmarried side of the divide. Now, I'm not so sure.

"You should talk. You're as smitten as I've ever seen a man."

I'm about to argue with him, which amounts to arguing with myself, when my phone vibrates in my pocket. I check it, and it's Jett.

"I need to take this call." He smirks. I smirk back. "Don't get all self-righteous. It's my agent." I face the window, keeping my voice low, and answer the call.

"I need you to do me a favor."

"Anything." My answer doesn't get more automatic.

"It's more a favor for Rylee." He pauses as if he thinks I might change my mind. If anything, I dig into my position with enthusiasm.

"What's up?" My tell-tale heart rate starts to pick up as I try to stay in the moment and not project disaster.

"Her former agent called and told her the deal with GNU for the promo she shot a couple of weeks ago has been canceled, and they're not paying the fee beyond the small advance she got."

"Why?" I know I'm not going to like the answer, and I can't help my mind spinning out of control and attributing all the bad news onto her fucking coach, Chuck Banner.

"They're concerned about her place on the Olympic team based on something Mr. Banner told them."

"That son of a—" My voice rises, and a couple of heads turn my way before I calm down. "What do you need from me?"

Jett explains his plan and my role in it, and as I nod, I don't even flinch when he mentions Candice's name.

When we get to the hotel, I'm on a mission, and it's not hockey. Skipping the team meal, I head for my room and make my call to Candice to ask for a favor. It should be difficult and uncomfortable to do, but I'm zoned in on my purpose.

"Sure, I can do that. I have a friend at the show. Let me get back to you. But if I come through, you need to come through for me."

"You're on." I end the call, and I should feel like I just made a deal with the devil, but satisfaction is what runs through me. I pace around the room while my stomach grumbles, and I ignore it. I'll eat later, after I get the confirmation from Candice.

She's agreed to ask her friend to get Rylee an interview spot on her local magazine show. In return, I've promised Candice I'll do an on-camera interview for her online magazine. In her interview, Rylee will talk about the Olympics and reveal that she's home for her Mama, who is sick and having surgery.

Once that happens, Jett is confident that he can convince the people at GNU to run the commercial and pay Rylee as promised. In the meantime, I'm fronting Rylee the rest of her fee, although I swore Jett to secrecy. He's agreed to tell her it's from GNU, so she won't balk.

All the arrangements are made and confirmed while the rest of my team is napping—while I'm supposed to be napping—before we leave for the game. In fact, I'm cutting it close as I button my shirt and hear the solid knock on my door.

"Let's go, Zak. We missed you at dinner. You okay?" It's O'Rourke.

I open the door as I finish buttoning my shirt cuffs, my tie undone around my neck. He looks me over, partly annoyed and partly concerned.

"I'm fine. I had some business to take care of."

"You get any sleep?"

I shake my head.

"Shit. Get your act together and focus. Forget about whatever your business was, and concentrate on hockey. Be on the bus in ten minutes, and when we get to the rink, make sure your head is in the game."

I take the lecture because I deserve it, and I wonder how he knows that. But he's been around the league and the team for a lot of years, so he knows things. This could be his last year which would explain his intensity. As captain, he's made it clear he expects a legit run at the Stanley Cup this year.

Sitting on the bus, I tap my leg until Nowicki smacks my hand to stop me.

"What has you so wound up?"

"Nothing," I lie my ass off.

The one flaw in my plan is that I haven't talked to Rylee about it and have no idea if she'll go along with revealing her Mama's illness in an interview. Jett said he'd take care of convincing her to do it, but that doesn't sit well with me.

That should be my role. I'm her... What? What am I? Her lover, for sure. That gives me standing, doesn't it? Friend? Maybe. On my end, she's a friend, but I wouldn't bet my balls that she feels the same way.

In the visitor locker room, my concentration is shit. I've done zero mental prep and feel disconnected from hockey as I take the ice for warm-ups. Finn comes up behind me and taps my pads with his stick as he skates.

"You're slow tonight."

"I must be if you're catching me." I try a grin and force my legs to push me. Shaking my head, I don't remember this ever happening.

Then as the cold air whisks by me and I suck in the icy air, I remember. It has happened once before. The last time I felt disconnected from hockey was right after Bill's suicide.

The whistle blows, and I head for the gate, stepping off the ice and heading down the chute to the locker room, shaky as hell.

I sit next to Finn, and Nowicki sits on my other side.

"I'm shit tonight."

"What's up?" Finn asks, examining my face as if he might get a clue.

I'm about to tell him nothing, to shrug it off because nausea swirls in my gut, and confusion reigns in my head. Do I truly know what my problem is?

Fuck yes. "It's her. Rylee. She's in my head, under my skin, and things aren't good." The words stumble from my mouth like sharp-edged rocks, bruising me and making me bleed.

Finn's eyes widen, and he blows out a breath.

"Shit. I was right," Nowicki says. "Sorry, man."

"What are you going to do about it? Does she know?" Finn asks.

I shake my head, unwilling to admit to the worst part, to spell out what I'm sure they suspect is the real problem—that she's not into me. Fuck.

Coach comes in for pre-game, and I try to concentrate.

"That didn't go well," Dad says after the game on the phone. I'd smile, but my stitches prevent it, tugging the skin of my cheek near my right eye. "What happened to you tonight?"

I pace around my hotel room while Nowicki lounges on the bed, watching me like a worried old lady.

"My game was off."

Dad snort-laughs into the phone. "You're fighting was off, too. I bet your team isn't happy with you, either. You get a penalty, Detroit scores, and you don't come back in the game, didn't even win the damn fight."

"Thanks for the summary of my miserable night, Dad." I stop and glance at Nowicki. He's not grinning, not even smirking.

"Sorry. What's wrong, Zak—and don't give me any bullshit."

"What if I tell you it's about the girl, Rylee?" There's silence on the other end of the line, and I turn away from Nowicki, lowering my voice. "I think I'm falling for her."

"I'd say you've already fallen and stumbled, hitting your noggin good and hard." He takes a deep breath. "Here's your mother." There's some commotion in the background, and then Mom comes onto the phone.

"We're on the next plane down to Boston. Don't make a move without me. I need to meet this woman." Mom's not joking. Shit.

"You can't. She's not... into me." Four words I never thought I'd be saying.

"Wait a minute," Dad says, apparently sharing the phone. "You're telling me you've fallen for a girl, and she's—" Something cuts him off, and I'm glad because I don't want to hear the words. They cut too deep and sting like a motherfucker.

"Don't tease him, dear. This is serious."

Chapter 21

RYLEE

As I park my rental car in the Mass General parking garage, I get a call, and it feels like the equivalent of an electric shock. My phone has become the harbinger of bad news and unpleasant or dreaded calls. Still, my heart races with the possibility that it's Zak calling until I check it.

Relief and disappointment knock around in my gut as I try to pull myself together. It's my new super-agent, and I need to talk to him no matter how inconvenient his timing is.

"I have some good news about the GNU deal."

"Thank you, God. I could use good news."

"I'm not God and don't thank me yet. There are strings attached, but I think you can handle it."

"I'll handle whatever I have to handle for an infusion of much-needed cash."

"Good. Here's what you'll need to do as a condition for airing the commercial and full payment of your fee—up front."

"Up front? The whole thing?"

"Yes." He clears his throat. "You'll need to do a TV interview on a local magazine show. They've scheduled you for three days from now. When they ask you why you're in Boston instead of

Park City, you tell them about your mother's surgery. There will be no mention of your ankle and certainly no hint of anything wrong with you. No limp."

"I can't do it. I'm leaving for Park City after Mama's surgery. I need to." I'm certain she'll be fine.

"What about your ankle? You have your appointment today?"

"Yes. I'll be cleared to compete. I won't be around to do an interview."

"We'll arrange a remote interview. The beauty of modern technology. How about it?"

"It's not that I don't appreciate all the trouble you're going to for me, but I don't feel right about talking about Mama's illness. Especially not on TV."

"How about if you let her decide that?"

"You play dirty, don't you?"

"I'm an expert negotiator."

"I won't lie. I need the money and Mama would kill me if I didn't take advantage of the opportunity, even if it's at the expense of her privacy." Whatever control I thought I had of my life seems to be slipping away rapidly. I have that sense of being a puppet with too many people pulling my strings. "Zak has something to do with this, doesn't he?" It has his signature all over it.

"Not exactly."

"You're lying. Never mind, I won't make you betray a confidence. No need. I know he's behind it somewhere, somehow."

"I'll let you work that question out with him."

I don't bother telling Jett that I have no intention of discussing this with Zak. The less involvement I have with him from now on, the better. We end the call and my chest feels like a field of butterflies fluttering around in chaos. Plus, I want to throw up right now because I have to get going to my appointment with Dr. Yancey.

I TRY to avoid looking at the enormous Mass General Hospital entrance down the street to my left. It's a stark reminder about Mama's surgery tomorrow because that's where she'll be. But I have to make this appointment with Dr. Yancey at his office in a nearby building. It isn't easy to keep my mind in the present, but I put one foot in front of the other because I need to.

Today, the doctor will tell me if I'm good enough to go back to Park City and provide the damn report to Chuck to make it happen officially. I hate being under Chuck's thumb. It was a big mistake to start something with him because now he thinks he owns me.

No way am I going to make the same mistake with Zak. I can't let him in any further than he already is. How did our lives get so entangled in such a short time? We're tied by a contract, for pity's sake. Plus, whatever his involvement is with the TV magazine show and the GNU promo deal. Fuck—there's no way GNU would pay me the entire fee upfront. That's Zak's doing. He's fronting me the money—that son of a hockey puck.

God, I am so stupid. But not stupid enough to become emotionally entangled. No matter how generous and thoughtful and selfless he is. I won't let that happen. Can't let that happen.

When I get to reception in Yancey's office, I'm shown to an examining room right away.

"He'll be in to see you in just a minute."

I nod and take off the compression brace, my boot, and my sock. I hope to hell this quick service means he'll rubber-stamp me and send the report without a problem. Think positive.

Better yet, stop thinking. My phone pings. It's another text from Zak.

> Good luck today with Yancey. I'd say break a
> leg, but I'm afraid you would.

I laugh involuntarily. My body always reacts to him, betraying me, thumbing its nose at good sense, and it pisses me off.

After a light knock on the door, Dr. Yancey enters and sits on the rolling stool in front of me.

"Let's see what we have here. How does it feel when you put pressure on it? Do you feel any pain or instability?"

"No." A fat lie. "It feels much better than before." Honest to God truth.

He manipulates my ankle, then presses and prods it while I maintain a stoic smile. Even when I feel a surprisingly sharp pain with one of his twists. I refuse to give in to the wince that screams through my body.

"There's a very slight swelling, but if you've been walking around on it, even with the compression brace, that's to be expected." He let's go of my ankle, rolls on his stool over to the computer on the counter, and looks through his electronic file.

After a minute, I can't stand waiting. "How is it? It feels great. Am I good to go?"

He looks up and barely changes his expression. "Mr. Banner has sent some stringent requirements from the Olympic team physician that you need to meet, but looking it over..." He returns his gaze to the computer while my heart nearly stops at the mention of Olympic team physician involvement. Fucking Chuck. If he's sold me out, I'll ... I don't know what I'll do. Besides start over. The wrench in my gut almost makes me cry.

"Yes, it appears you'll meet the requirements. I'll write the report and have it sent to Mr. Banner today. I understand your urgency to rejoin the Olympic team." He stands and finally smiles as he reaches out a hand to shake mine. "Good luck, Ms. Flynn. I hope you win a medal."

AFTER THE APPOINTMENT, I may as well be walking on air. I don't remember the last time I felt this good, and I treasure the moment despite the other things weighing on me. Mama and, I finally admit to myself, Zak. Because the idea of never seeing him again stings every time it enters my consciousness.

As soon as I get home, my upbeat humor dampens and Suzie, Mama and Mr. Argyle spend a quiet evening eating dinner like it's our last meal. After I'd texted Chuck the good news, I had to ignore a string of texts and calls from him, turning my phone off.

It's not until I go to bed at night and set the alarm on my phone that I turn it back on and notice I have several missed calls from Zak. A few minutes later, I'm under the covers and my phone rings. It's Zak again. I hesitate to take the call, but in the end, my racing heart and traitorous body win out.

I owe him the courtesy, don't I? That's my rationalization as I press the green call icon.

"Rylee. I'm glad you answered. Sorry I'm calling so late, but I waited to hear from you about your appointment with Dr. Yancey. I'm about dead from curiosity. How'd it go?"

"He gave me the all-clear. He's reporting that I'm fit to compete."

"That's fantastic, Buttercup. I'm happy for you."

I can hear the smile in his voice and my chest tightens so hard I swear I can feel it crack.

"Thank you," I whisper the words.

"Mama's surgery is tomorrow?"

The way he refers to her as Mama, so familiar, should put me off, but it doesn't. On the contrary, it nearly chokes the life out of my will to resist him. But not quite. Either way, emotion clogs my throat and I can't speak even if I did have something I to say. Everything that runs through my head is all wrong. *I miss you. Come to the hospital with me tomorrow. Let me go and never call me again.*

I can't say any of those things and after a few seconds of

silence, where it feels like he hears the things I can't say, he finally clears his throat.

"Tell her I said good luck with the surgery. I'll be thinking of you all."

"I... thank you. I have to go." I end the call and viciously swipe the damn tears that drip down my cheeks. What's wrong with me? He's a fling, a man I barely know and so not good for me the way he makes me depend on him, doing all those favors, helping me as if I want or need his help.

From the first night I met him, he's been insinuating his kindness, starting with the ice pack.

How can I resist that? How can I stand up to relentless thoughtfulness?

But I need to because no matter how relentless it seems, I know it will end someday, probably sooner than later.

MAMA'S quiet on the way to the hospital and refuses to be fussed over. Suzie squeezes my arm and my hand alternatively the whole time until they roll Mama away to surgery. We're sent to a windowless waiting room with lots of empty chairs and a coffee vending machine. No other people are waiting.

"Looks like we're first in line for surgery today." I walk into the middle of the room and don't bother sitting on the couch with the table littered with magazines.

"You're not going to pace, are you?" Suzie flops down. "That's good we're first. The surgeon will be fresh."

I pace and give Suzie the finger when she tries to stop me on my fourth lap. She laughs, but it's a strangled version of her usual bright and bubbly laugh. My fifth lap is interrupted by the vibrating phone in my pocket. I contemplate not checking it, but the monotony of pacing is already getting to me, so I do.

It's a text from Zak. Shit. I feel my emotions rush to the surface as I read his words, unable to stop myself.

> Give Mama a hug from me and tell her to break a leg. At least she'll know I'm joking.

MY SMILE FORMS reflexively before I know it. I dart a glance at Suzie to see if she's watching, but she's thumbing through a magazine. I slip my phone back into my pocket and resume pacing, even though it's probably not the best thing for my ankle. Maybe. I know it's not a hundred percent, but if I keep wearing the compression brace until the games, it should be fine. That gives me another ten days, maybe.

Suzie tosses the magazine onto the table with some violence as if it offended her, and she stands. "I'm going to call Nowicki. They're in Chicago for a game tonight. He should be up, right? I don't care." She doesn't wait for a response and walks down the hallway for a private conversation.

I give up my pacing, and when Suzie returns, she sits next to me, handing me a cup of vending machine coffee.

"Thanks."

"Don't thank me until you taste it."

I take a sip and screw up my nose as if it's awful. She laughs.

"It's actually not that bad. How's Nowicki doing?"

"They're at the hotel in Chicago. Getting ready to leave for the rink. Guess they test the ice out early. He said Zak needs to redeem himself tonight after his fight and major penalty in Detroit. You should call him. I bet he'll make you feel better. I saw the smile on your face when you read his text. You could cheer each other up."

A blush of embarrassment that she saw my smile rushes to my face and I turn away. The little devil is getting sneaky.

"Let sleeping dogs lie, Suzie. I'm not going to call him. We don't have much to talk about besides business and I'm not in the mood." It's true that I'm not in the mood, but I know the look she's giving me and it's an uncomfortable combination of disapproval and knowing sympathy.

I want to shout at her not to feel sorry for me because I'm fine, but I'm not a good enough actor to pull it off.

Eventually a doctor emerges from surgery, still in scrubs, to put us out of our waiting room misery.

"The procedure went well. She'll be in post-op for a little while and then you can visit her in her room. The nurse will show you there when she's ready. I'll be in later to check on her."

When we finally get escorted to Mama's room, she's still a little groggy, but it's good to see her alive and well, her rhinestone glasses perched on her face and her big eyes magnified behind them.

"Is Mr. Argyle here?" she asks after we hug her.

"That's what you have to say?" I'm surprised and maybe mildly offended, but I'm smiling.

"No, Mama. It's family only," Suzie says in a gentle voice.

"I'm surprised they let you two in then."

"Don't say that. We're family. Of course we're family."

"I know that. It's not official is all. I should have made it official." She takes a deep rattling breath and I listen for a hitch, but there is none. "Maybe it's not too late—"

"Don't worry about it," I say. "We're as official as we need to be."

"I want to make sure you inherit my estate when I'm gone." She has her tongue in her cheek, literally.

I smile and Suzie laughs.

The doctor comes in a minute later, checks Mama's breathing and lungs with the stethoscope, and looks at her charts. He does all this without saying a word and it's unnerving. I want to shake him and yell at him to tell us how she's doing, but I keep my increasingly elusive cool.

"How are you feeling?" He smiles at Mama.

"Like I just had something shoved in my ribs. Feels tight."

"That's normal." He turns to me and Suzie. "The procedure went well and she'll be good to go home tomorrow. We'll give her a couple of prescriptions and have her in for a post-op checkup in a week."

Relief sends a surge of joy through me. "Thank you, doc. That's exactly what we needed to hear."

"You can visit for a little while, but then your mother needs her rest." He aims a kind smile at each of us and then leaves.

I tell Mama and Suzie I need to leave for Park City today.

"What about Zak?" Suzie asks.

"What about him?"

"If you leave today, you won't have a chance to say goodbye to him."

I shrug, pretending it doesn't matter. Mama glares at me from bed and coughs. Panic rises and I rush to her side.

"You okay, Mama? Should I call a nurse?"

"I'm fine. But I'm worried about you. Blowing off a perfectly fine young man like that."

"I'm executing my plan. I told him I was leaving after your surgery."

"Chicken shit." Mama continues to glare at me, looking no less intimidating propped on pillows in a hospital bed. The rhinestones rimming her glasses flash like sparks.

"I agree with Mama," Suzie says.

"At least I'm a whole chicken shit," I say.

"You think you're going to fall apart if you care about a man?"

"You're the one who taught me to be independent." Anger and panic rise and I bat them down.

"That was my loneliness talking."

I glare at her. "Whatever. It was, and is, sound advice. I'm leaving because I don't need him. He can't make promises and has no business making promises he can't keep."

Leaning in, I hug Mama, taking it easy because she feels frail. I bite my lip to hold in a whimper. "Take care of yourself, Mama. I'll be back as soon as I can."

"Go win a medal for me, Rylee girl, preferably a gold one, but I'm not too fussy."

I smile and choke back a laugh-sob. "I'll call you when I land. Chuck arranged the flight and it leaves soon. I have an Uber waiting out front."

"Chuck?" Suzie questions.

"He's my fucking coach. That's all he is."

"Too bad he doesn't know that," she mutters under her breath as she gives me a quick hug. "Knock 'em dead, Rylee."

Squeezing Suzie's arm without looking her in the eye, I leave.

When the elevator doors open, I fly through the lobby and out the hospital's front door, and run to the waiting car, testing my not-quite-healed ankle. If it doesn't hold up—never mind. That's what cortisone injections were invented for. I don't care how short-term a solution it might be.

Fuck tomorrow.

As soon as the plane lands in Utah, I text Chuck. Not that I'm anxious to see him, but I want to make sure he saw the report from Dr. Yancey. Almost immediately after I hit send, as I walk through the airport to the exit, he calls.

"I got your email. Checked out the report. I've seen sketchier results." He pauses. "We can talk when you get here. For now, you still have a seat on the plane to Milan, Italy, if you want to risk it."

"Of course, I'll risk it. No strings attached?"

He sucks in a breath. "There were never any strings. Not unless you count my heartstrings."

I laugh. "What heart?"

"I'll show you if you'll let me."

I'm too tired to argue. "I'll be there in half an hour."

"I'll be there in fifteen to pick you up at the airport. Wait for me."

I don't argue. I'm not proud of taking advantage of the ride he's offering, but my energy gave out halfway through the flight when I couldn't stop the tears. Fucking tears.

I broke my own number one fucking rule over Zak Tomas, a professional hockey player. No crying.

It doesn't take long before we arrive at the USANA Center for Excellence in Park City, or it feels that way because I fell asleep. Chuck insists on carrying my bag inside and I follow, still groggy as he walks down a hallway and opens the door to a two-room suite. I walk inside and collapse on one of the two beds.

Then I pop up again and level an accusing look at him as he sits on the edge of the bed, smiling. "Whose room is this? Mine or yours?"

"What difference does it make?"

"Plenty. I'm not staying with you." I push him away and get off the bed.

"It's my room, but you were so tired, I figured it would be easiest to let you rest here instead of going through the hassle of checking in."

He sounds reasonable. He always sounds so reasonable, but I know what he wants because he makes no attempt to hide it. Like right now as he stands and slides his arms around me.

That's when someone knocks on the door and Chuck calls out to come in because he's Coach and has a literal open-door policy.

Only it's not a member of the women's Olympic snowboarding team who walks in the room.

It's Zak.

Chuck immediately tightens his hold on me. But I'm too preoccupied watching the stormy expression on Zak's face like I've never seen before, like he's about to go supernova and break heads. Chuck's head.

"You're with him?" His voice is fierce and quiet and sends a chill of fear and excitement down my spine and straight to my pussy. When will I stop reacting to him this way?

"No," I say and pull away from Chuck.

Chuck moves in front of me, closer to Zak, apparently unaware of the danger, unimpressed with the man twice his size and packed with hockey muscle, looking for a place to unwind. "What if she is? It's no business of yours."

Zak ignores Chuck and turns to me. "I called Mama Cass to see how she was doing." His voice shakes and I push Chuck out of my way and go to him.

"I..." I have no idea what to say to make this better. My heart thunders and my head hurts with the emotions whirling inside me like I'm caught in an avalanche about to tumble out of control.

"She told me you left, that you came here and gave me your contact information, or I wouldn't have... I thought it would be all right."

I nod.

"It's not all right," Chuck growls and tries putting an arm around me, but I pull away from him again. He stares at Zak. "This is my room and you're not welcome here."

Zak sucks in a breath and looks back and forth between us once, then he turns and slams the door on his way out.

I run after him going on instinct, without thought, my flight or fight instincts telling me to do both as I run. Until I run into a group of photographers outside the main lodge. Literally. The world slows down as I hear a scream and shouts and I see Zak a few yards ahead of me.

I stop and turn, and slip on the snow and can't stop the momentum, my heart drumming as I fall on the pavement near the step where my ankle catches, and I can't hide the flash of pain.

Zak gets to me first as the photographers flash their cameras, and I wonder how the universe managed to concoct the worst possible storm of nightmares to test me at my most vulnerable moment.

"Back away. Give her space," Zak says and bends over me, blocking most of the cameras. But he can't stop their questions, and I hear them shout at me as if I'm deaf.

"You're Rylee Flynn. What would an injury do to your status on the Olympic team?"

"Why were you running in slippery conditions?"

"Are you hurt?" I look up at the last question shouted in a familiar voice. It's Chuck.

Zak helps me to my feet, holding an arm around me to take my weight. He asks under his breath, "How's the ankle?" I shake my head and turn to the lodge.

Zak addresses the small crowd. "She's fine. We're going inside. Everything is cool."

"Who are you?"

He doesn't bother to answer them, but someone in the crowd of sports reporters says, "That's Zak Tomas, a hockey player for the Brawlers. What are you doing here, Zak? You going to play for the Olympic team, or are you just visiting?" There are snickers in the crowd, but Zak ignores everyone as he helps me up the stairs to the door.

Before we go inside, Chuck comes after us.

"I didn't finish our discussion about your team status, Rylee." His voice is loud, and he's red-faced and angry, none of this a good sign.

"Back off, Chuck." Zak throws him a menacing stare.

Chuck takes a step back with his hands up and smiles, but it's an ugly smile. "Fine. Have it your way." He looks at me with an intense regretful look, then turns to the dwindling crowd of photographers and reporters as they're dispersing.

"Before you go," he says, projecting like he's holding a mega-phone. Most of the people stop and turn back to listen to him and he comes down the steps until he's standing in the middle of the group. No doubt they know exactly who he is—coach of the U.S. women's snowboarding team.

"This is as good a time as any to let you know that Rylee Flynn, member of the women's snowboarding team, has an ankle injury and may be put on the IR list pending an exam. She may not make the trip to Italy for the Olympics in two weeks. As of now, her status is day-to-day."

He turns back to me and storms up the steps, sweeping me from Zak's arms.

"We have official Olympic business to take care of." He gives Zak a murderous look and takes me away. I watch like this is a movie because I detached from the moment, from the here and now of my life, the minute he said I might be put on injured reserve. Numbness doesn't cover my current state. My mind flashes back to the car crash where I blocked everything out for weeks, for too long.

I glance at Zak, and his face is grim and confused.

"Rylee, what are you doing?"

What *am* I doing? I tug my arm from Chuck's grip yet again. Zak's question wakes me from my zombie state, or maybe it was shock, the kind that blocks pain like it did after the crash. I know this because the pain comes rushing in now, flooding me and killing me and making me stand up, infusing me with life and the will to do what I need to do.

"I'm going to compete in the Olympics, Zak. Nothing is going to stop me from doing that. Not Chuck, not the doctors, and...*not you*."

I walk away through the crowd of reporters and photographers who took notice of the scene Chuck created and who shout questions at me that I ignore because they're mostly about Zak. I turn around to look back once. Chuck is following me.

And Zak is standing there, with people surrounding him taking photos, shooting questions at him as he watches me leave, and it's the most heartbroken face I've ever seen.

The pain that rips through me now makes the pain in my ankle feel like the kiss of a snowflake on my cheek.

It melts away like a dream, like it was never there. Like whatever wisp of childish fantasy I thought Zak might be. Here one day, gone the next. It's best to stay in the moment.

I walk on my own and shiver, suddenly feeling the cold, until Chuck catches up to me and suggests we take the ATV that's just pulled up beside us.

"No, I'm not riding with you. I'm fine. My ankle is fine, and I will compete in the Olympics, and you can't stop me."

Chapter 22

ZAK

Spending my Allstar-Break in Boston by myself was not the plan, but as I get off the plane from Utah, I pull my ball cap down and head for the exit. It's bad enough I didn't make the all-star team this year, but I thought I was making lemonade from lemons by going to Park City to sweep Rylee off her feet. Now? I'm dejected and pissed and heading for a taxi cab like I plan to hijack it.

Maybe my pipsqueak sister is right about my ego. Too big and, it turns out, unjustified. I get in a cab, and when the driver asks, "Where to?" I hesitate because I don't know where I want to go. The last thing I want to do is spend time at my condo with Nowicki and Suzie. And if they're not there, I don't like the idea of being alone because I'm not good company for myself right now. This is an occasion to inflict my misery on someone else if ever there was one.

"The Tea Party. Canal Street in Boston." The cabbie nods at me in the rearview and we take off.

When I get there, I jog around the building and come in the rear exit. I know my teammates and the groupies will be sitting in the back and that's where I find them. I slide into the end of one of

193

the two adjoining booths with a small crowd and give a nod to Finn at the other end.

Sheila, her friends, and a few other non-all-star team members are pounding beers and playing table hockey with wadded up napkins and their thumbs.

"Look who's here," Sheila says to no one in particular. Then her smile fades and she lowers her voice. "You don't look happy. You definitely should've made the second all-star—"

"Fuck the all-star team." I almost snarl at her, but I immediately regret it. "Sorry, don't mind me."

"I'd ask if your puppy died, but I know you don't have one. Not unless you count Nowicki as a puppy."

I snort a laugh at that. "Where is Nowicki?"

"He went home with Suzie a few minutes ago. She's a real cutie. I like her."

I nod and congratulate myself on making the right choice to come here. The only right choice I've made recently.

"What's wrong, Zak." She leans in and whispers, "Is this about Rylee? I hear she left to go back to Park City."

My head snaps up. "You knew? Am I the only fucking person she didn't bother telling?"

"Oh." Sheila's face goes soft, and her eyes droop in sad companionship. "I'm sorry, honey." She pushes one of the two bottles of beer in front of her over to me. "You need this more than I do."

Picking up the bottle of beer, I take a swig. I'd rather have a bottle of whisky right now, but beggars can't be choosers, and I'm not gone enough to start making choices that will demolish my hockey career. It's the only thing I have going for me right now, right?

Plus, my family. While I'm uselessly trying to drown my problems in beer, Sheila is busy talking to her friends in whispers. They glance at me and nod. Great. She's telling everyone I'm a pathetic loser.

One of the ladies comes around to give me a hug. "Don't be sad, Zak. We still love you." It's really a sweet gesture, so I can't complain, but I don't hug her back or invite her to sit on my lap like I would have a few weeks ago. Sheila takes some photos.

"What are you up to?"

"I'm posting these on social media. We'll have you fixed up with a new girl in no time."

"Shit. That's the last thing I need, Sheila. I appreciate the effort, but—"

"No worries, Zak honey. I'm sending the pic to Candice—"

"Why?"

"Because she likes you and—"

"And I'm not into her. At all."

She sighs. "I know. Right now you're only into Rylee. But that won't last. You'll get over her. I promise." She rubs my back and tries really hard to make a dent in the dark nasty feeling I have in the pit of my stomach that I won't get over Rylee any time soon because maybe I don't want to get over her. I want to fucking win her over. I know she's hurting right now and that deep down, way deep down, she's really into me. I think she might be falling for me and it scares the shit out of her.

I know the feeling well and can't blame her for being scared. It's terrifying to feel so vulnerable and so out of control, like your life has been taken over by someone else. Getting up from my seat, I go down to the other end of the table to talk to a few of the guys.

Candice Montgomery shows up, and she and Sheila come over and surround me.

"Can I buy you a drink, big guy?" Candice asks, putting a hand on my back. "I hear you need consoling."

"Hello, Candice. I'm fine. I'm going to take off after I finish this beer."

"Nowicki is at your place with Suzie because he thought you were out of town," Finn says.

Normally in a situation like this, I'd find someone to hook up with and go to their place. Forcing myself to look around, I don't see a single woman who interests me. Not even a little. Not even the sweet server who has a crush on me and would take me home without batting her fake eyelashes.

Candice nudges me, "You know you can always stay at my place. I mean, no strings. We can play it by ear."

She sounds sincere, but there's too much hope in her eyes, and I wouldn't do that to a woman, not any woman, not even Candice Montgomery, the recent bane of my existence who's now, heaven forbid, growing on me. Strictly as a friend. *Shit.*

"I can't go home with you, Candice. I'm in love with someone else."

"Really?" She sounds more excited than disappointed, and I laugh an ironic laugh.

Finn gives a hoot. "You're shitting us?"

"Really. I've been struck by Cupid's bow to put it in the ridiculous language of the Bachelor of the Year article."

"That's spectacular," Candice says. "Is it Rylee? Please, let it be Rylee—nothing personal, Sheila."

I zip my mouth because it was stupid to admit I'm in love in a bar to this group when I've barely admitted it to myself. But all it took was a few beers and the threat of spending a night with Candice to make me talk like a fool. I can't mention Rylee's name. I still feel protective of her, and Candice isn't exactly discrete.

But who knew I should have clamped a hand over Sheila's overly talkative mouth? Me. I should have known.

"No problem, Candice," Sheila says. "You're right. It is Rylee... She'd be perfect material for a follow-up article. I'll bet she wins a medal in the halfpipe at the Olympics. You know she's a snow-boarder, right?"

I take a healthy gulp to finish my beer, only half listening to their conversation because the whole point of coming out tonight was to forget about Rylee, not talk about her.

"Yes, I heard." Candice eyes me because I'm the one who told her all about Rylee and the Olympics when I asked her to score the magazine show interview. "But there is one wrinkle…" She taps her chin with a perfectly manicured finger. She has my attention, and I don't like the look on her face or the ominous sound of her voice. She stares back at me, not talking, waiting for something.

I put my empty bottle down, trying not to lose my patience. "What's the wrinkle, Candice?"

"I saw some social media recently, and it looked like she was dating the Olympic coach, Chuck Banner?"

The words hit me like a puck to the groin without a cup. "She's not dating that fucking loser."

"Tell me how you really feel." She pauses and levels her calculating look at me.

"What?"

"Does Rylee know how you feel?" Candice smiles, but it's an understanding smile as if she really gets this shit. Sheila levels the same look at me. It's like everyone else in the world knows about relationships but me.

"Sure," I say though I'm anything but sure. "She must know. It's obvious." Shit.

"Bingo. You never told her, did you?" Candice says.

I shake my head in confirmation.

"Then she has no idea."

"I…have no idea if she has any idea. You think it matters?" I can't believe I'm asking Candice, the Bachelor of the Year lady for relationship advice.

"Shit. Are you asking Candice for relationship advice?" Finn asks, leaning over in time to catch the worst part of the conversation.

"Fuck you." Candice and I both say at the same time. Finn laughs. I laugh. It's a small laugh, but the first since I got to Utah and laid eyes on Rylee when she was being held in the asshole coach's arms. But I know better. She's not with him.

"You need to tell her," Candice says in a gentle voice with more sympathy than calculation, and she reminds me of my mom, only younger, and ugh... totally different.

"She's right," Finn says. "You need to lay it all on the line. Spell it all out and spill your guts. It's like in a game when you leave everything on the ice and give it the best game you have. Then if you lose at least you have no regrets."

Leave it to Finn to put it in language I understand. A shiver of terror runs through my body at the prospect of leaving my emotions bare-ass naked for Rylee to trample all over.

But what's my alternative? They all look at me expectantly, like I'm going to leave now and run back to Park City.

"What? You don't expect me to fly back to Park City now, do you?"

"No," Sheila says, chewing her lip. "And this isn't something you can do over the phone, so don't you dare try."

"It needs to be a romantic grand gesture and something she can't ignore, somehow making her feel loved and feel the sincerity of your words when you tell her." Candice sounds convincing and Finn and Sheila nod in agreement.

"Thanks, guys." I push myself from the stool and turn to leave.

"Where are you going?" Candice asks.

I give her a wink and keep going. I have no idea where I'm going or what I'm doing tonight, but a plan forms in my head. My first and only grand romantic gesture to win Rylee over, to convince her I'm the one guy who's not going to disappear because I keep turning up everywhere she goes, because she can't get rid of me—because deep down she doesn't want to get rid of me.

IN TWO DAYS, we're back in the locker room with the team mostly rejuvenated from the short break. I feel like the most rejuvenated guy of all as I hum *Don't You Worry* by Black Eyed Peas, Shakira, and David Guetta while I lace up my skates.

Finn walks in and sits next to me. "You're unexpectedly chipper. What's up?"

"Glad you asked. I have a plan, and I'm going to need your help."

He furrows his brows. "My help? Why don't I like the sound of this?"

I slap him on the back and give him a grin, which probably does nothing to reassure him, but since I've embraced the spirit of the tune stuck in my head, I'm for real not worried.

"I'm flying to Italy next week when the Olympic team is there, and I'll need your help to cover for me because I'll miss two days of practice."

"What the fuck?"

I whisper, "Keep your voice down. I've worked it out so I won't miss any games or anything crucial. I just need you to back up Nowicki when I tell coach I'm going home for an emergency. Because once I'm in flight, I won't be in touch. You have more creds with coach than Nowicki, and I don't want him calling home."

"What happens if he does call home?"

"If you think he will, then you'll have to call home for me and warn my parents."

"Shit. What are you going to do?" He eyes me for a split second and then he says, "Never mind."

"Can I count on you?"

"You have to ask?"

One week later, I board an Alitalia flight for Marco Polo Airport in Venice with determination churning in my gut, a smile on my face and that song still playing in my head.

Chapter 23

ZAK

F lying to Italy was the easy part of pulling this off. Calling Coach to tell them I had emergency personal business to take care of, implying I was going home, proved hard on my conscience because he trusted me, and he let me go so easily. A part of me wishes I'd told him the truth, but he would never have agreed to it, and my contract hasn't been finalized yet.

I checked.

Calling mom and dad was easier because I told them the truth, but it was harder to convince them to cover for me with coach. Dad got it, but mom was reluctant. In the end, she said she would do whatever I asked, but her last words stayed with me the whole flight here and echo in my head now as I walk through the airport hearing the voices in Italian bouncing around me.

Mom said, "You know Coach and the Brawlers management are eventually going to find out the truth. And then what will you have to say?"

I make my way to the SIXT rental car kiosk to pick up the Range Rover sport Sheila arranged for me, a vehicle equipped with navigation. She helped me out a lot. I gave her my credit card, and she took care of the travel, car, hotel, and the tickets to the

Olympic resort at Cortina d'Ampezzo and women's snowboarding events. I didn't ask how much it cost. I only know she was relieved that I didn't care. I promised to buy her something, and glancing around the airport as I wait for my rental paperwork and keys, I note there are some nice shops. I'll pick her up something on my way home.

A rush of adrenaline bubbles in my gut. There's a lot I need to get through before I go home.

Once in the car, I set the navigation to Cortina d'Ampezzo and Valtellina, the mountain center where the snowboarding events will be held. I'm hoping I'll see her at her event, and those are the two places to look. The snowboarders are being housed in Flame, a small town outside of the village of Cortina, but I doubt I'll have access there. I'm told it's a one-hundred-forty-eight km drive from the airport. I'm cutting it close, but I make it there in under two hours.

When I get into the village, I find a place to park and stay and take a bus to the mountain where the women's halfpipe qualifying round starts in an hour. I know Rylee will be there, and it's my best chance to find her and talk.

My biggest trepidation is trying to communicate, but the bus driver speaks English and so do most of the workers at the Olympics who all wear badges. Still, alone and with a lot of unknowns surrounding me, I fight like hell not to feel like a kid lost in a crowded mall.

The bus driver tells me which direction the women's halfpipe event is being held, and I slip him a twenty-dollar bill.

"Sorry, I didn't convert my money."

He laughs. "No worries, *signore*. This is good. Good luck with finding your signora." I almost stop to ask how he knows I'm looking for a signora, but he tips his hat and smiles, and the crowd moves me along.

The snow-covered landscape makes me feel at home, and the festive atmosphere buoys my spirits as I trek to find the slope where the U.S. women snowboarders should be. In the distance, I see the halfpipe and a lift with a line of boarders. There's a fence of netting around them and stands off to the sides where most of the crowd is heading.

When I spot the official U.S. Olympics gear on a few of the women, my heart picks up its pace and I jog over. Everyone's competing in the qualifying round today, so there are dozens of women on the other side of the fencing, some of them with their faces obscured by goggles, but I move as close as I can and study every one of them as they wait for the official start of the event.

An announcement is made in Italian, and then in English, that the event officially beginning. The lift jerks into motion and boarders begin loading equipment. My heart beats faster, fighting away the doubt and defeat that seeps in at the edges.

That's when I see her. Her goggles are up and she's staring at the halfpipe as if she's studying it, standing still and beautiful as a statue. I push the rope to the side at the edge of the fencing to catch her before she takes the lift up to the top of the halfpipe run.

Standing on the edge of a group of media types, I call out, "Rylee."

She turns. When her eyes meet mine, she's stunned. But so am I because, in truth, the sight of her always stuns me. She hurries over to me.

"What the hell, Zak?" She's breathless and she's not smiling, but she's not frowning either.

"I had to talk to you. It's important."

"You couldn't call?"

"No." I pull her aside, a few steps away from the curious glances of some of the media.

"Seriously, what are you doing here? Is something wrong?"

"No. Everything's right. We're right, you and I."

Now, she frowns.

"Before you give me your nothing is permanent speech, let me have my say, okay?" She nods. I lower my voice and step closer.

"I'm falling for you, Rylee. Madly, head-over-heels, crazy in love." I hold her arm and lean close. It takes every ounce of my willpower not to pull her into my arms and kiss her until she begs me for more.

Her face opens up, the silent shock showing in her brilliant blue eyes, and I don't blink. Instead, I stare back, stalwart and unshaken, because I know what she's thinking. She thinks I'm full of crap, and I'll disappear, that I'm not dependable, that no one is dependable, that nothing is forever.

"I believe you are crazy."

I smile. "Is that all? Do I get some creds for flying to Italy in the middle of hockey season to tell you how I feel, to put every ounce of my soul out there, to bare myself, naked and vulnerable, to you?"

Her face softens, her mouth taking a Mona Lisa pose. "Zak... you can't make promises."

"I know what you're thinking. I can't promise forever. Maybe you're right. But I can promise you my whole heart, everything I have for as long as I can, as long as I can see, as long as you can stand me." I pause, and she looks around and blinks her eyes. I touch her cheek and turn her head back to face me.

"I'm worth a chance. We're worth a chance. Nothing is guaranteed. We both know that. Not a gold medal, not a Stanley Cup, but we work for them anyway. Maybe we can work on something more between us besides a fling."

She lets out a breath and shakes her head.

"If you're honest with yourself, you'll admit we've already passed the fling stage anyway. We have a relationship, Rylee. You and I are a couple. Admit it. Go for it. Give us a shot."

The lift rumbles forward, and we both turn to see the boarders start lining up, the first few jump on to ride up the slope to the top of the chute for the halfpipe.

"You're crazy," she says. "I have to go. You didn't expect me to run off with you now, did you?"

"No." I hold onto her arm and lean in for a quick kiss, my heart pummeling my chest because my time is up. The clock has ticked down to zero. "Good luck today. Win a medal. I hope to see you when you get home, but whatever happens between us, know I love you, Rylee, and I hope that all your dreams come true." I brush my hand over her cheek. "You're gold no matter what happens on the pipe."

"I have to go."

I squeeze her hand. She squeezes back, and it feels like she's squeezing my heart.

"So do I, or Coach will kick my ass off the team for being AWOL for tomorrow night's game."

She shakes her head. "You really are crazy, you know that?"

"Crazy in love." That shuts her up. Her brow creases, and confusion flies across her face before she clears it for her polished camera-ready smile, the one I've seen flashed on the screen every time ads for the Olympics air in between hockey games. The one she'll wear when they drape the gold medal around her neck.

Someone pushes past me roughly, and when I turn, I see red because who else would it be but the infamous asshole Chuck Banner, shoving me out of the way.

I push back.

"What the fuck are you doing here?" he says way too loudly.

"Back off, Chuck," I say, keeping my voice low and controlled. "You know why I'm here." I look at Rylee.

She stares back at me with those eyes that tell me everything she's not saying, begging for understanding. I see the need, the fear and the spark of what I hope is more than lust.

"I came for Rylee because I've fallen for her, because she's the one for me. For real." People are watching us now and listening.

"She wants no part of you." He screams the words and more people stop and stare. A crowd gathers, backed up from the lift because we're blocking the line, but if he doesn't give a fuck about causing a scene, neither do I.

"Stop it, Chuck." Rylee's voice is firm and anxious.

"Stay out of this Rylee." He pushes her aside.

I step close to him and speak in a low growl. "Lay a hand on her again and I'll flatten you out."

While I stare him down, I hear Rylee suck in a breath, but I don't look at her. He doesn't back down.

"I can touch her if I want, I have every right—" He reaches out a hand to touch her hair and she flinches. I see red and time for talking is done because I'm not capable of talking right now.

Instead, I fist up and throw an uppercut that hits him squarely in the jaw.

I hope I knocked some of the fucker's teeth out as I feel the sting in my knuckles. He teeters backwards, falls into a couple of boarders, and they catch him as he bellows, holding his mouth. Blood seeps through his hands.

Rylee looks at me in disbelief. She doesn't run to his side or defend him, but she doesn't rush into my arms either. She pushes her way around the astonished murmuring crowd, all with their phones out taking videos, pushes through the line of snowboarders to the gondola and disappears in the crowd of athletes and equipment. I watch as she jumps on the next lift up the mountain and away from the fiasco I just created.

People in the crowd are talking to me, some in Italian, some in English, some night be reporters, and in the distance, I see security headed our way.

Congratulations, Zak. You're now perfect gossip fodder for TMZ sports. Fuck.

I DID what I came to do, laid my heart on the line, and emptied myself at her feet.

Now it's up to her to decide. Underneath the edge of stark

terror that I might lose her, I find a measure of peace and hope that I won't.

This is what's chief on my mind as I sit in a windowless room guarded by security, waiting for Italian law enforcement and Olympic security officials to determine my fate.

Lucky for me, Italians are a romantic lot. When I explain I was trying to protect Rylee from Chuck because he touched her when she didn't want him to, thinking he was going to hurt her, and a couple of witnesses backed me up, the officials decide not to press charges. I don't see Chuck again, thank God. But then I also don't see Rylee again because it's suggested by an Olympics security official that I leave on the next plane out of the country.

On the flight back to Boston, I drink several shots of whiskey to welcome me back to reality, and then fall asleep in my first-class seat.

When I arrive on the red-eye in the morning with a game tonight against the Devils, our main rivals, I don't feel fit enough to play against an all-girl pee-wee team. No surprise there.

Walking into the locker room early, I pace around to stave off the urge to puke. I don't know if it's the whiskey, lack of sleep, or the knowledge that Rylee is halfway around the world, holding my heart in her fist while I wait for her to decide what to do with it, with me.

"You look like shit," Finn says as he walks in.

"There you are," Nowicki says, following Finn. "You came straight to the rink without stopping home?"

I glance at my luggage stuffed in my cubby. "What was your first clue?"

"Things didn't go well?"

I shrug. "Game's not over yet." Not until the beautiful snow-boarder sings. "Either way, I'm turning my focus to hockey."

Nowicki slaps my back with a grin. "Good luck with that. You look like shit."

It's true. I'm in rough shape to play, but I buck up to take the ice because no way am I letting hockey go down the drain. I can handle this. I'm an adult, a man. Billy's face floats through my head, and I hear his laugh, feel the joy he always had playing hockey. I'm not going to quit on life because I lost a battle. I can handle loss. I can handle hurt. I won't let it bring me down. *Not like poor Billy.*

Marching with the team through the tunnel, I step onto the ice and the freeing effect takes hold. I look up into the stands because my mom is here, and she's always reminded me that every day of life is a gift. *Don't leave anything on the table.*

"No regrets." I say the words aloud as I look up to her and raise my stick.

I start the game hyperaware of my surroundings, the rough feel of my gloves on my hands, the pressure of clamping down on my stick, the stretch of my jersey across my back as I lean forward to anticipate the puck drop, and the noise of the crowd. As soon as the puck is dropped and O'Rourke wins the faceoff, the puck pops back in my direction, and beating the Devil's winger, I grab it and back away, giving the guys a chance to set up outside the blue line.

Circling around, I hold off the winger who's attacking aggressively, and with laser sharpness, I pass the puck up to O'Rourke as he's breaking over the blue line into the Devil's end of the ice. The game feels like a million games I've played before, and at the same time, crisp and new.

The puck gets passed around and as soon as it hits my stick on the left side just inside the blue line, two things happen simultaneously. It feels like slow motion, but I know it all went down lightning quick.

First, I stare down a straight line to the goal and grip my stick tight as I let a wrist shot rip down that clean line.

Second thing that happens, but at the same time, is that Devil's wingman charges at me, coming hard, and I see the blur of motion from the corner of my eye, timing it so I get rid of the puck before impact.

As soon as he hits me, time speeds up again, and I'm on the ice, teeth rattled and disoriented for a blink, but I'm not out. My teammates crowd me, and the horn signaling a goal blares.

"Helluva way to start a game," O'Rourke says. He reaches out a hand to help me to my feet, and we skate to the bench as the crowd's deafening cheers fill me with euphoria. Coach gives me a nod and maybe a hint of a smile.

"I don't want to know the details of your emergency absence," he says, "but if you play like this when you get back, you have my permission to leave if you ever have another emergency. But don't. Just keep playing."

I nod and climb over the boards to sit, silently thanking the heavens, but mostly thanking Rylee for being in my life and hoping for her to demolish the halfpipe and big air competitions. The rest of the game is tight, but we play tough on defense whenever the Devils' work the puck into our end. We win in a three-zip shutout, and I end up contributing the goal and two assists.

At the final buzzer, Finn comes out of the net instead of waiting for the team to come to him, and he meets me at the blue line with a shove. The rest of the team piles on, and for a few seconds, I'm lifted in the air, which is no small feat.

When we file off the ice, I become aware of the soreness in my shoulder where I hit the ice and the aching of tired muscles, but it's the best feeling in the world.

"You were awesome, big Zak." Finn hits me on the head with his big goalie glove on the way through the tunnel to the locker room. "You were an absolute beast. What got into you? I want some of that."

"I second that," O'Rourke says, his grin unreserved.

A swell of pride settles in because O'Rourke is stingy with his praise. It has to be earned. We file into the locker room, and the team buzzes with that special victory vibe that happens after some games. All wins feel good, but some carry a bit of extra with them.

This is one of them, and I couldn't tell you why. Maybe it's all in my head.

"So, what happened to set you off?" Nowicki says, knowing the answer and teasing me. "Does it have anything to do with punching out the Olympic snowboarding coach?"

I dart a sharp glance at him and my chest tightens. Fuck. "How do you know about that?" Last I heard, the Olympic security team was busy squashing that story back in Italy.

"It was on the Boston Magazine social media account. Candice is showing a killer video. Dude, great uppercut." He snickers and more than a few guys in the room take out their phones to check their social media.

Fucking Candice. "Just when I thought she was a friend," I mutter.

"Look at what it says," Finn holds up his phone as if I'm going to read it. "Says you declared your love for a certain snowboarder."

But I don't care if I'm on the record about Rylee and my unrequited love. "Now you know what got into me." I shrug as if it doesn't mean everything in the world to me, as if it isn't the most important thing that's ever rocked my world. More important even than Billy's death. "Nothing like a little tragedy or a broken heart to make you feel every bit alive, to make you appreciate the value of leaving no effort untried, no energy unspent." It's the other side of the blade edge of life, but I keep that to myself because the guys are staring at me without a clue what to say.

Coach comes in long enough to confirm my feeling about the game. "Men, congratulations on playing your best game this season. Keep it up."

I hit the showers, and my mind wanders under the steamy stream of water as my body relaxes, and I wonder if I'll ever see Rylee again.

Or if the stabbing pain between my shoulder blades, having nothing to do with hockey, will ever stop.

Chapter 24

RYLEE

After the qualifying round, I'm in fourth place, and one of my teammates is in second. We have a third woman in eighth place who made it into the final round—Betsy, a young lady who came out of Vermont. I remember her from the regional competitions when she was a kid and I was still in high school.

Chuck called a meeting for us in the evening with the final round in the morning, presumably to give us a pep-talk. The three of us sit at a table in the makeshift community space that doubles as the dining room during the day in the temporary accommodations in the village of Flame. We're silent, but I feel the questions in their surreptitious glances because they've seen the social media clips showing the debacle of the punch. No one's talked about it. An Olympic official I never saw before forbade anyone from saying a word about it, and my teammates haven't broken that promise. At least not in my company.

Then again, they've not said much else to me either, besides congratulations when I made it to the final round. The wind swirls and howls outside, and I feel the breeze come through the windows and walls of the structure, but I'm well-dressed to deal with the cold. The U.S. Olympic team has been outfitted with plenty of gear from sponsors and donors.

"I'm so nervous," Betsy says. She looks like the proverbial deer in the headlights. "Nothing prepared me for the media attention. You'd think I was the first sixteen-year-old to ever compete in the Olympics."

"You're hiding your nerves well. Just keep flashing that smile, and keep your mind on performing," I say, the advice just as relevant for me because I've never been such a bundle of nerves in my life. Only it's not all about the Olympic medal being on the line.

I can't lie to myself and pretend the heightened skittishness isn't due to Zak and everything he said, because I believe him, and because no matter how I try to suppress them, I have the same feelings about him, the same need to be with him, to have that relationship. And it scares me more than wiping out on the final run with the gold medal on the line.

Chuck finally barrels through the door with his parka zipped up to his nose and sheds his coat on his way to join us, but he doesn't sit when he reaches us.

"Ladies, I won't keep you long because a good night's sleep is most important tonight." He pulls a thermos from a bag he's been carrying and three cups. "I brought some warm milk, juiced with some key nutrients and melanin to help you sleep." He pours it out for each of us. None of us says a word, but he's right to assume we'll need help sleeping.

"You feeling the nerves? The pressure?" You all did a great job today, both on and off the slope. Just give us more of the same tomorrow. Only, notch it up. You're all here because you've been able to perform in the big moment when you've had to at one time or another. Hell, just making it onto the Olympic team took some doing." He pauses and looks around at us, but I don't meet his eyes.

Separating Chuck the jerk from Chuck the coach suddenly feels impossible when I see the shadow of bruising on his face. It's as if the impact of Zak's punch hits me, right in the heart every time I see Chuck.

He runs over each of our routines, giving reminders of what we need to do to overcome each of our tendencies, and then he runs down the likely conditions, the weather report, and what to look out for on the pipe.

"That's it, ladies. Any questions?" He looks at each of us, and when his gaze reaches mine, I take a sip of the warm milk and look away.

Betsy asks a couple of things, and I stand because I've reached the limit of my ability to be in Chuck's company.

"I'm going to bed." I turn away, and Chuck says nothing. He wouldn't dare say a word in the others' company because we're all doing our best to pretend the punch never happened.

Except I can't. That punch looms larger and larger in my head, but instead of distracting me from my goal, I use it to give me motivation. Because I want to win, and I want him. I want both.

And it's as if I can't have him unless I can prove to myself that I have what it takes to be on my own first, to win a medal and achieve my personal goal before I can allow the compromise of my independence with a relationship.

THE MORNING IS COLD, but the wind has died down and the crowd of boarders is smaller, but the size of our audience is ten times bigger with the media dominating the line around the fence where we line up to start our ascent to the top of the halfpipe.

I scan the crowd, half expecting to see Zak pop out again, but I know that's not possible. The security officials notified me by text this morning that he was sent home without charges being made, and that news buoyed my spirits more than the bright sunshine and perfect layer of snow covering the pipe.

Waiting at the top of the halfpipe is the hardest part of the competition. I don't watch the others compete before me. In the second run, I'm still in fourth place, but I have a chance to pull ahead to second or third if I nail this one—if I nail the frontside 1080 and follow it with a cab 540, frontside 900, and finish with a McTwist and Haakon flip, aka cab 720.

My turn comes, and I slide to the edge of the pipe, heave a big gulp of icy air, letting it spread through me to make every cell in me come to life, then I jump into the pipe. The air speeds past, and I rise up over the wall of the opposite side and know I'm going to do this.

When I land after the final cab 900, I glide to the bottom where the others on my team stand cheering, and the crowd roars. *I've moved into second place.* A fucking silver medal in the Olympics is within my reach. Possibly gold. I let the roaring fill my ears and my head and feel like my entire body lifts from the sounds, the vibration of victory in the air.

Except there's one more crucial run that could mix up the standings because the point totals are close. We all head for the top of the pipe again. A couple of women could pull ahead of me, including my teammate, Betsy. She moved into fourth place from eight with a monster first run.

As we wait our turns, I see Chuck consulting with her, and I have no doubt she's going to go for broke because she's young, and that's what I would do if I were her, what I did when I was seventeen at my last Olympics. I came in fourth place then and was too young to be discouraged. Too disciplined and competitive not to get here again.

I don't feel my ankle. It's like nothing ever happened to it. As each of the boarders takes their turns, I concentrate on keeping warmed up and limber until it's Betsy's turn. I watch as she jumps into the pipe separating myself from the competitor and hoping for the best for her because I once was her.

She starts with a back side 1080, and my mouth hangs open as her performance unfolds and she flawlessly pulls off a second 1080

—a cab 1080—followed by an Alley-oop 540, a backside 540, and finishing with a frontside cork 720.

I don't even need to see the scoreboard as the crowd erupts to know that she's moved into a medal spot. When I steel myself for a glance, it's confirmed. She's moved ahead of me into second place. I'm still in the bronze spot, but the burning need to do better doesn't quit.

Chuck approaches me, and I know what he's going to say, but I listen when he says it. "You need to include a second 1080 in your run to move up. Are you going to do it?"

"You have to ask?"

He smiles and, in that moment, I let go of my anger, and he's nothing but my coach, a long-time mentor, and maybe, even a friend. But I'm up now, so I snap my focus to the halfpipe as I slide into place.

Staring down at the steep incline, I see the culmination of all my dreams, knowing that if I nail this run, I have a shot at the gold. So, gathering every ounce of my determination and strength, and feeling all the positive karma from the people I love—Suzie, Mama, and especially Zak—I jump in. I nail the first backside 1080 and feel invincible.

But the thing about invincibility is that it doesn't exist. My board catches the top of the pipe, an extra chunk of ice, a nick from a previous run, an extra bump of slush from the sun, I don't know. Whatever it is, it knocks me off my rotation, and my second 1080 goes off course. I lose my orientation and land heavy on my heels.

I don't know if it's the pain that's worse or the knowledge that the run is ruined, and with it, my chance to advance. But when I try to stand, unclipping my board, I get my answer, because I immediately fall in a heap, the sharp pain in my ankle shouting at me that this is the real thing.

This is a level three sprain, a tear, and I'm not competing again for a while. No big air event.

❄

STANDING on the podium for my bronze medal in the halfpipe, even on crutches, feels amazing enough to wipe out the disappointment of my fall. As soon as the music stops and I step from the podium, what dominates my mind and has me feeling that same bundle of nerves as I did before the final round, is Zak and the need to see him and make things right.

Since I won't be competing in the Big Air event, I'm given the option to stay and watch as a cheerleader for my team or to go home early. I opt to take the next flight home.

During the flight, the constant mantra plays in my head that I need to see Zak. I need to erase that picture of his heartbroken face from my mind and replace it with his natural joyful expression, the giant happy smile and the lighthearted air that he exudes because I need it.

On the way home, I catch up with emails from Mama and Suzie. They're worried about my injury, and I let them know the doc in Italy told me it was a level three sprain, a complete tear, and I need to keep off it and be strict about helping it heal. Everyone around me expects that I'll be a professional about it and do everything I'm supposed to do, heal and come back to the circuit as the badass U.S. woman snowboarder they expect. Of course I will, if that's what I decide. But right now, I can't even think about that.

I google hockey news to find out about Zak, ignoring the reports about his altercation. I find out he had a killer game and has been playing well and that makes me smile, but it also unsettles me. Trepidation that maybe he's moved on, that I'm too late and I pushed him too far, has me more on edge than I've been since I lived in the group home with Suzie and I pushed Mama to take us both.

I took a chance then, and it worked out to be the best thing I ever did. I'm not going to let the fear that's threatening now keep me from taking this chance I have with Zak. Because I think it could be another one of those best things I ever do.

That Mama and Suzie might disown me if I don't throw myself at Zak's feet has nothing to do with my decision, but it doesn't hurt in giving me much-needed confidence to overcome the snowball-size glob of emotion lodged in my throat as I take the taxi ride to his condo.

Suzie sends me a text, and I read it before I pull myself from the cab, backpack in place and crutches in hand.

Since when doesn't Rylee fucking Flynn go for the fucking brass ring?

SINCE NEVER.

AFTER A BRIEF CHAT with security in the lobby, I ride the elevator up to his floor and find myself standing at his door on crutches. A wave of dizziness hits me, and I stiffen my spine.

Fear isn't going to stop me now, not even the fear of rejection by a man who has gotten so far under my skin now I don't want to know what I'd do without him.

Balancing on one crutch, my heart pounding dangerously, skittering up into my throat, I raise my fist and pound on his door.

Chapter 25

ZAK

I open my door and see Rylee standing there on crutches as if my most impossible wish has been suddenly granted by some force of the universe. Before my heart beats again, I sweep her inside.

Crushing her to me, embracing her, crutches and all, I kiss her hair, her temples, her face, and finally her lips, tasting salty tears, and I don't know if they are hers or mine, but it doesn't matter. Emotions of every kind overwhelm me.

"Rylee. You're here. I wanted to see you so much, to touch you, to be with you after that fall—" I push back from her and glance down at her ankle. "How is it?" I hold my breath for her answer because it has to be a crushing disappointment.

"Don't stop kissing me, and I'll be fine. I won a medal, Zak. Aren't you going to congratulate me?"

I laugh and lift her, letting her backpack and crutches clatter to the floor.

On the way to the bedroom, I stop in the kitchen and grab an icepack from the freezer as I carry her in my arms. She laughs and cries, and I don't have to ask what the tears are all about. I feel the emotion coming from her, and it mirrors my own.

I lay her down on my bed, and after I slide her pants off, taking time to kiss each inch of exposed skin on the way down as she sighs and giggles, her tears stop, and I place the icepack over her ace-bandaged ankle.

"What now, big boy? That icepack is pretty cold. You going to keep me warm?"

I stand at the side of the bed gazing down at her. Her arms are open in invitation, and my knees almost collapse with the sheer disbelief, joy, and the rush of blood heading from everywhere in my body to my starving cock.

"Don't you think we should talk first?" I know we need to talk, but she can talk me out of that being what we do first, and I watch her eyes, losing myself in the breathtaking depths. They still have the same effect on me they've had since the first time I saw her.

"Make love to me, Zak." Her voice is an intense whisper and sends a rush through me, my heart welling and pumping madly. "Let's make love like it's the first time."

I don't have to ask what she means because it'll be the first time we acknowledge fully to ourselves and each other that it's love-making and so much more than fucking for fun. Not that it won't be fucking fun.

A smile splits my face automatically. "Whatever you want, Buttercup." I strip off my clothes before I climb in bed with her and proceed to take off the rest of her clothes.

"Should I be worried about all your bruises?" she whispers, feathering her hand over my shoulder. I feel nothing but a shiver of excitement and shake my head.

Her panties are last, and I eye them. "My bruises are fine. You're the miracle cure for whatever was bothering me." I put my tongue in my cheek and nuzzle her neck, nibbling on her earlobe like it's my appetizer. "Only thing is I'm starving, and there's only one meal that will cure that."

She draws in a big breath. "You're a greedy and needy s.o.b., aren't you?"

"You have only yourself to blame," I say as I kiss her face, lingering on her soft warm mouth and then moving on down the column of her neck before I get distracted. Because I could spend hours, days, kissing her succulent mouth, getting lost in the intimacy of it, the connection those kisses create absorbing me.

Instead, I move onto her inviting breasts, sucking each nipple into my mouth by turns, flicking my tongue, tasting the rosy flesh, and nibbling at the irresistible pebble as she becomes aroused, her moans driving me deeper and wilder.

"You created the monster," I say, lifting my head to glance again at her because I can never get enough of the sight of her, especially when she's aroused and panting, her amazing eyes glazed with need.

She slips her hand down over my abdomen as I suck in, and she grips my raging hard cock, forcing me to let out a groan.

"You're right. It is a monster." She squeezes, and I see stars.

"Fuck that feels good. Too good." I bite out the words, barely gathering my control so I don't lose it in the next five seconds.

"Then how about if I cure you of your problem?" she asks breathlessly. Without waiting for an answer, she lifts herself with one knee, the icepack falling away, and rolls on top of me, centering her hot wet pussy on top of my twitching dick.

"Buttercup, you're driving me crazy. What about my meal—"

"You can eat later. Right now, I need you inside me." She lifts herself, and I help, clamping my hands on her hips as she takes hold of my cock and teases her opening with my head. I don't know whose groan of pleasure is louder as I bite down on my control, clamping my jaws tight as I slide inside her.

"Fuck, you're so damn ready. Were you thinking about me on the plane ride here?"

She sits up, her hands pressed on my shoulders and her lush dark hair draped around us, creating an intimate cocoon as she slides slowly up and down, her breathing hard but regular.

"I've been thinking a lot about you... Oh, my fucking God,"

she cries out when I press my thumb between us and find her clit. It's swollen and hard like a slick marble. The feel of it sends a rush of desire shuddering through me.

She drives her hips down, sending my cock slamming into her back wall, and I grind my teeth to hold on. She doesn't let up, panting for release.

"Don't stop touching me, please..."

I circle my thumb and flick her nub before she slams down on me again, and I feel her pussy clench around my cock in a hard spasm as she shouts.

"Oh, my God... Zak... You..." She stops breathing, but I don't stop pumping and flicking her clit as it explodes under my touch.

"I love you." I barely hear her words as she shudders around me.

But they reverberate through my head and through my entire body, setting off every nerve ending into a massive blinding burst as I thrust my hips deep inside her, pumping wave after wave of everything I have in me to her.

Pulling her down on top of me, I ride out the aftershock of spasms holding her, kissing her face, her eyes, her mouth, and feeling her heart thud against mine as they slow and beat together in rhythm and our breathing returns to normal.

I don't know how long we lie there in silence, but I hear the door and people walking around and talking outside the bedroom.

"Fucking Nowicki."

She laughs—no giggles—and the sound is surprising and refreshing and makes me swell with affection.

"We need to talk," I say because I can't hold it in.

"I'll go first," she says, sitting up on one elbow, staring at me, her lashes thick and dark and her eyes vivid, stunning me into silence. "I'm smitten with you."

"Smitten? Is that anything like in love?"

She blushes, and I wrap her up in my arms.

"You already admitted it once. Say it again."

She burrows her head in my shoulder, and I wince.

"Sorry." She pops up and sighs, the blush of embarrassed vulnerability gone. "Okay, you win. I love you."

"Louder."

She yells it again and again. My heart goes into overdrive, and my dick shoots back to life.

Then Nowicki bangs on my bedroom. "Keep it down in there, will ya? Some of us need to sleep." I hear the grin in his voice and laugh.

We both laugh and hold each other, not bothering with an answer, and not bothering to keep it down—the noise or my dick.

I lick the salty tears from her cheeks and kiss her eyes and then her mouth, my new ritual, and one I hope to repeat every day and night for the foreseeable future. Finally, she settles into my arms.

"Sorry about the tears. It must be the exhaustion." She closes her eyes.

"Is that it?"

She smiles but doesn't open her eyes. "That's me. One and done."

I laugh. "Me, too."

"What do you mean?" She opens one eye to look at me.

"One and done has taken on a new meaning for me. You're the one for me, and I'm done with other women."

Epilogue

RYLEE

It turns out all my exhaustion wasn't from the competition and traveling, and having an IUD isn't one hundred percent protection from getting pregnant.

Of all the risks I've taken in my life, including agreeing to live with Zak while my ankle heals and then part-time when I'm back on the world tour, having bare-cock sex with Zak Tomas was the biggest risk ever.

And the worst-*best* possible outcome—the scariest and most thrilling ever—a baby. Or soon to be baby according to the ultrasound movie I'm watching now as tears run down my cheeks out of terror and joy and anger—the kind of anger that elevates our lovemaking to the next level because it's the flipside of crazy, head-over-heels, stark-raving-mad, silly-in-love love. Which is needless to say, the way I feel about Zak. The big jerk.

"Look at that baby. She's ours." The screen has Zak mesmerized.

"She? I thought we agreed—"

"I don't need the doctor to tell me it's a girl."

"I didn't say a word," said doctor says. "He's guessing."

"Not a guess. I guarantee we're having a baby girl."

I smile because really, either way, I can't lose. The tiny baby starring in the movie inside my womb is perfect according to our doc, and gazing at her because I can't keep my eyes off her, even with Zak's hand caressing me low on my belly near the edge of my panties when he thinks the doc isn't paying attention, our baby mesmerizes me, too, with his or her perfection. Boy or girl or whatever doesn't matter because our baby is healthy, and I've never worked so hard to keep her—I mean them—that way. Shit. Is he winning me over with his confident pick for our baby's sex?

What else is new? He has a habit of winning me over with his confidence and enthusiasm and everything else about him—especially the massages.

NOWICKI MOVED OUT, but the good news is Suzie moved in with him into their own place. I've convinced Jett to have her included in a promotional with me and Zak, and now she's part of the story in our ads for a certain brand of sunglasses.

We were worried about Mama Cass living alone until we went over to surprise her with donuts one morning and found Mr. Argyle, the apparently *former* grump next door, in her kitchen. He was wearing pajamas and a robe. I barely held in an outrageously joyous laugh out of respect for Mama.

He's taking care of her now—way better than we could have. There are no ashtrays in sight, and the air is fresh without a filter anywhere.

"Is that baby finally popping? Let's see that tummy of yours," Mama says without a smidge of embarrassment or explanation about Mr. Argyle being in her kitchen in a robe at this hour.

"So, Mr. Argyle, did you take a detour on your way to the bathroom this morning and end up over here in Mama's kitchen? Should we be worried about you?"

He chuckles and has the good grace to look chagrinned,

turning slightly pink and clearing his throat. But Mama? She smacks me on the arm and then does the shaky finger point like I'm a fresh-mouthed ten-year old. I suppose I'm worse. A fresh-mouthed twenty-two-year-old.

"That's no way to treat a guest in my house, a man who's been very helpful to us both."

"Helpful. That what you're calling it?" I say because my sarcasm knows no bounds. This time, Suzie, who'd been snickering behind me, thuds me on the back.

"Quit it, Rylee. Can't you see they're a happy couple?"

Mama coughs at that, and all lightness leaves me, replaced by panic. But Mr. Argyle doesn't panic. He comes to Mama's side with her inhaler, and she takes a breath, returning to normal within two—or maybe three—of my very fast heartbeats.

"You okay, Mama?" I whisper while all sorts of horrible scenarios spin out of control in my mind, chief among them the idea that she might not live to see her first grandchild.

"I'm fine. I haven't felt better in a very long time." She leans into her Mr. Argyle as she says this, and she's convincing and very calm and peaceful.

I shake my head. "I guess we shouldn't have brought these wicked unhealthy donuts then—"

"Don't you go anywhere with those donuts. You know they're my favorites. Besides, the doc didn't say anything about my diet. She said to keep active."

And this is where she winks at Mr. Argyle, and I'm the one who is embarrassed enough to want to shrink between the floorboards. I laugh. Suzie laughs, and Mr. Argyle gives Mama a big hug.

Tears spring to my over-emotional eyes, always tearing up these days, and I have a strong longing to be in Zak's arms right this minute. Not for any reason except to have him hold me, for his reassurance, his strength, the solid wall of strength to handle any trouble that we have when we team up together. God, I love him.

My phone pings, and my heart stutters because I know it's him. I pull the phone out and grin.

Suzie rolls her eyes as I walk to the door. "I gotta go. Zak's home."

Second Epilogue

Zak

"Come home," I say to her, knowing she will, knowing I don't have to ask, feeling the impossible jolt of joy that we have a home and I have her. The truly most impossible part of this arrangement, is that she wants me—and our baby.

It doesn't take her long to get home, all sweaty and out of breath from carrying the extra twenty pounds of baby bump. I meet her at the door and my hand goes automatically to her belly.

"Any kicking?" I ask as I kiss her to soften the blow that I've asked about the baby before asking about her.

"You have a one-track mind these days and I'm not at all sure I like the fact that it's not *my* track."

I pull her in and nuzzle her ear because I know she can't resist it. That fact that I know about all those little things that get to her —and the ones that don't—satisfies me to no end.

"Come on, Buttercup. You know it's impossible to separate you from our baby. She's part of you." I caress her belly and slip my hand lower. She swats at me, but it's a half-hearted attempt to deter me, a signal she wants more, that I need to work harder.

And so I do. I work very hard to satisfy my Buttercup. If *work hard* actually means I make fucking mind-blowing love to her until she's melted butter all over my hands, my tongue and my cock.

Me? I end up a deliriously happy, if useless wasted fool-in-love without a care in the world beyond my precious universe of three. Rylee, my baby and me. Period. End of story.

Rylee

SIX MONTHS LATER

IT DOESN'T TAKE me long to get back into snowboarding shape. Maybe it's all the working out I did during pregnancy—using the term *working out* very loosely and crazy-with-giddy-girlish joy—that's kept me fit. But the truth is, snowboarding and competing —and even all the promotional dollar-signs—will forever take a back seat to my new baby—we named her Cassie after Mama—and Zak, my baby-daddy and our new life.

The new life? It involves lots of visits to Grandmama's house which now looks like the palace she always deserved. Mama's trying to teach me to cook so poor Zak, as she refers to him, won't starve. As if. But I don't tell her he has all the food he could ever want every day at the practice facility or nearby in the north end at one of the dozens of world-class restaurants, because I'm getting into the challenge of learning something new that doesn't require me to leave my baby behind.

The only thing that bugs me these days is that Zak was right about our baby being a girl. I don't mind that she's a girl—hell no! —I only mind that *he was right about it* and never lets me forget it. *The big jerk.*

He's the biggest hunky, soft-hearted, generous, gorgeous,

funny jerk I ever met and I can't even help admitting this to him sometimes—he knows what I mean when I call him a jerk, without adding all the other adjectives.

A girl can't get too mushy all at once overnight, can she?

No—except when he has me in his arms, naked and breathing heavy, heart hammering, and he's staring in my eyes and I see all the way down to his amazing beautiful soul and then I see how I feel in the reflection in his eyes.

Completely and utterly owned, taken without a look back at my past or a question about why or how it all happened, only grateful that it did. Forever and always. The end.

The End

Thank you for reading my book. 💙 *Stephanie Queen*

Get the next book in the
Some Girls Likek It Cold Series
THE DO-OVER GIRL
a second chance hockey rom-com

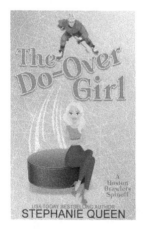

TEASER:

Kali

Nikki knows I haven't seen Nash since high school, since my spectacular humiliation at the senior dance. I step closer until I'm practically on top of her dented metal desk and lower my voice. "Can we talk privately?"

Archie grunts. "I'm outta here. See you at the arena, Nash."

"I'll come with you," Nash says.

His voice sounds edible, but I refuse to turn my head and look at him again. I sense him moving to the door behind me, a waft of his unforgettable male scent almost blowing me over on his way by..

He stops and says, "See you around, *Lollipop.*"

I whirl around so fast my yoga instructor would shriek with warning if she saw me.

"Don't call me that. You can't call me that. Never again."

"Never's a long time."

That's all he says. Not even a tiny hint of apology in his tone. The one memorable dimple pops in his lopsided smile and it's all I have in me not to slap him—*or throw myself at his still overpoweringly gorgeous self.*

Then he walks out the door with that same swagger all the girls in high school used to obsess over. *But that was seventeen years ago. Stop it.* I'm a successful grown woman now and I don't need the kind of man who was the kind of boy who broke a young girl's heart.

Lollipop? He would have to call me that now. It proves how heartless he still is. The name drags up a well of sensual memories I thought were long forgotten. The kind that make me want to unpack my *magic O wand* first thing.

Lollipop is what he called me back when we were so madly in love we wore each other's souls, learned how to make each other die and come back to life with endless blinding orgasms. I drove him crazy sucking his dick like a lollipop and he gave me that name. We managed to keep the origin of my pet name our secret even though he used it all the time. I still remember the way it made me feel when he said it, the name rolling off his velvety tongue like a caress, as if he were between my legs and I—*shit-- never mind*. Suffice it to say, everyone assumed I loved lollipops.

And I did—if you count his hot, hard dick the size of the Empire State Building as a lollipop...

Pre-Order *THE DO-OVER GIRL* now!

SNEAK PEEK HERE!

Why do I get the sensation that I'm back in high school all over again—as a thirty-four year old woman? The once-imposing front doors of Andrews Point Academy stand a few yards in front of me, waiting.

It shouldn't be so hard returning to the scene of all my high school crimes. I did all the things, class President, head cheerleader, Valedictorian. I had a ball for four years. All the way up to the very last night.

It was only one night and I should have forgotten about it by now, seventeen years later, but I haven't.

That night? It was the night of our graduation dance, the devastating night when all my girlhood hopes and dreams were exploded to dust by one boy, the one reason I haven't been back until now, Nash Lewis.

The familiar scent of the autumn air and the rustle of leaves carry me back in time as much as the sight of the old school. Retrieving my poise, I walk up the broad path leading to the front door of Andrews Point Academy. A young girl, very cute but unsure, walks towards me, wearing the same uniform I used to wear--plaid skirt and knee socks. I smile at her because she's so fresh and innocent, the way I was. Hopefully her experience will end better than mine—not that I let it hold me back, did I?

The girl smiles back, and then before I can say something—because I feel compelled to talk to her--she trips on a crack in the cement and drops her books and papers.

"Let me help you with those." I immediately bend and retrieve the folder with papers while she gets her books. I hand them back to her.

"I'm glad no one else was around to see my clumsiness," she says. "That's all I need."

"You're fine. No one would hold that against you. We've all had our moments. You're here a day early. Are you new?"

She nods. "You're a teacher here?"

"Yes, I'm new too. As a teacher at least. Once upon a time I was a student at APA."

"Cool. Must be strange coming back. I mean as an adult." Her gaze takes in my white linen Versace suit, pink leather Kate Spade pumps and matching bag and she looks impressed.

"Honestly?" I lower my voice. "I'm scared out of my wits." Her eyes widen in disbelief. "How about if we make a pact to have each other's back as newbies this year?" I grin, forgetting that I'm more than a decade older than this young girl. "I'm Kali Austin. I suppose you'll have to call me Miss Austin—once school starts tomorrow."

"It's a deal... Kali. I'm Mia. Volara." I put out my hand and she shakes it. "It'll be cool having you there for me—even if you are a teacher."

"I'm sure you'll make lots of new friends in no time. Do you have any interests?"

"I was a cheerleader at my old school."

"Perfect. We hope to see you at the tryouts coming up soon."

She nods and departs with a big grin while I walk to the doors and go inside the school.

Andrews Point Academy has hardly changed after all these

years—except for the worn floors and the flaking paint on the trim. And the gigantic display in the lobby, a tribute which includes a nearly life-sized sculpture dressed in full hockey gear including his stick, the school's all-time star athlete, none other than NHL star Nash Lewis. My chest tightens and I head straight to the principal's office.

The name on the door says Nikki Beauchamp, my best friend from high school and bestie to this day, the person who talked me off a recent ledge and talked me into this job. But the voice booming from the other side of the door belongs to our old classmate, Archie Rinkowski——a hockey team alum turned Athletic Director for the school.

"We'll get all the best recruits." He sounds confident. "We'll draw attention—and donors—from all over. We'll be able to keep the school open for the kids in town at least a few more years until the town's economy improves."

I grip the handle and push the door open until I see him standing next to the desk where my bestie sits.

She stands and smiles.

"Glad you made it, Kali. I was going to send out the dogs—namely Rink—to find you."

Archie grins at me. "How the hell are you? Looking gorgeous as ever." He comes forward and gives me a hug. I hug him back swallowing my emotions.

"It's been a while, Rink. You look like a happy family man."

"I am," he admits. "Glad you're here to help Kali. We need you. My family needs you," he laughs. "If we make our goal, the Board of Trustees promised me a big fat bonus.so I can finally repair our roof."

My brows knit, mildly concerned about Archie's joking about poverty—the school's and his—but I smooth them out as Nikki spreads her arm in the direction of the corner of the room, towards someone hidden behind the door.

"We'll make our goal because we'll win the state hockey championship with our new super-coach."

I push the door all the way open to meet the new coach, more than a little curious and maybe even a little nervous. With the door open, I glance at the man standing there.

And my heart nearly stops, then stutters to a rapid fluttering beat.

He leans against the windowsill, hands in his pockets, messy wet hair looking like he came directly from the locker room, his dark stubbled unshaven chin looking like it was meant to give a girl whisker burn—between her legs...

My knees collapse from shock and the weight of too many emotions piling on me all at once as I grasp onto the door handle hard to hold myself up. I stumble anyway but manage to catch myself before I fall all the way to my knees, literally at his feet.

He looks down at me as I hastily straighten up.

"Hello Kali." His voice is the same, made of sinful velvet decadence and hard raw sex.

I gulp. "What are you doing here?"

"Like the lady said. I'm the new coach.."

I tear my stare from him and look back to Nikki in panic. Her brows wedge together in worry. "I know you haven't seen Nash, er, Coach Lewis for a while, but—"

"A while?" I concentrate on Nikki because if I look in Nash's direction again my churning tummy may forfeit those banana muffins I ate this morning. Nikki knows I haven't seen Nash since high school, since my spectacular humiliation at the graduation dance. I step closer until I'm practically on top of her dented metal desk and lower my voice. "Can we talk privately?"

Archie grunts. "I'm outta here. See you at the arena, Nash."

"I'll come with you," Nash says.

His voice sounds edible, but I refuse to turn my head and look at him again. I sense him moving to the door behind me, a waft of

STEPHANIE QUEEN

his unforgettable male scent almost blowing me over on his way by..

He stops and says, "See you around, *Lollipop*."

I whirl around so fast my yoga instructor would shriek with warning if she saw me.

"Don't call me that. You can't call me that. Never ever again."

He studies me while the pulse in my neck jumps around and tension all but stops me from breathing. He looks me up and down, hiding whatever he thinks behind his game face. Then he unleashes the weapon of his oversexed voice on me for another shot.

"Never's a long, long time, Kali."

That's all he says. Not even a hint of apology. The one dimple shows up in his memorable lopsided smile and it's all I have in me not to slap him—*or throw myself at his still overpoweringly gorgeous self.*

Then he walks out the door with that same swagger all the girls in high school used to obsess over.

But that was seventeen years ago. Stop it. I'm a successful grown woman now and I don't need the kind of man who was the kind of boy who broke a young girl's heart.

Also by Stephanie Queen

If you love sports romance, then you're in luck!

Try these exceptional *HOT* sports romance novels by

USA Today Bestselling & International Digital Award-Winning Author Stephanie Queen

Portsmouth Whalers Series

Steamy Hockey Rom-Coms

The Big Puck

The One Timer

Two Pucks

Boston Brawlers Series

Steamy Hockey Romance

First and 2nd 3 Book Sets

Boston Brawlers Spin-off Books!

The Puck Bunny & The Do-Over Girl

Delicious Hockey Rom-Coms!

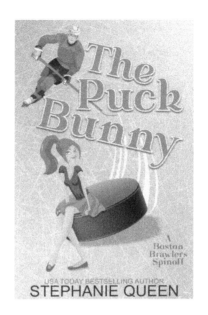

Steamy College Sports Romance

Big Men on Campus Series

Big Men on Campus

Best Man on Campus

About the Author

***USA Today* Bestselling Author Stephanie Queen**

The compulsion to write stories has been

with me always. I've written for fun since I was in second grade. In college, I started to work seriously at writing, and have been writing ever since (a wicked long time!) (I'm from the Boston area).

Improving my craft remains a constant goal, but I finally couldn't wait to share my stories, ready or not. And here I am now, 50+ books later, sharing all over the place and loving it!

Writing romance is me sharing my heart and my deeply held view of the world. An enthusiastic optimist, needing to envision the best in humanity, I bring this view to life in my stories, where the good guys always win and two people fall in love and live happily ever after.

What else besides writing? Ready for chocolate, morning,

noon and night, I also adore kittens even though I'm allergic, love dancing like a maniac, bright sunny winter days that make you go snow-blind, and UConn Women's Basketball (go Huskies!).

Every December I take the month off from writing to enjoy my all-time favorite holiday. I'm one of those people who goes crazy at Christmas, decorating, cooking, connecting with family and friends, and soaking up every minute of the fun, giving, loving spirit of the season.

Socializing may be distracting for some writers, and downright scary for others, but I *thrive* on it. So, write me any time at Stephanie@StephanieQueen.com and I will reply. Can't wait to hear from you!

Join my Newsletter HERE!

Join the Stephanie Queen Team HERE!

Find Me Everywhere

Printed in the USA
CPSIA information can be obtained
at www.ICGtesting.com
LVHW041006050923
757271LV00024B/141

9 798395 670953